Boxwood

Camilo José Cela

Boxwood

Translated by Patricia Haugaard

A New Directions Book

Book design by Semadar Megged
Manufactured in the United States of America
New Directions Books are printed on acid-free paper.
First published clothbound by New Directions in 2002
Published simultaneously in Canada by Penguin Books Canada, Ltd.

Library of Congress Cataloging-in-Publication Data

Cela, Camilo José
    [Madera de Boj. English]
    Boxwood / Camilo José Cela; translated by Patricia Haugaard
        p. cm.
    ISBN 0-8112-1497-4 (alk. paper)
Haugaard, Patricia. II. Title

PQ6605.E44 M2313 2002
863'.64—dc21

                                                                    2001051202

New Directions Books are published for James Laughlin
By New Directions Publishing Corporation
80 Eighth Avenue, New York 10011

Boxwood

The skies they were ashen and sober:
The leaves they were crisped and sere.
The leaves they were withering and sere.

Then my heart it grew ashen and sober
As the leaves that were crisped and sere,
As the leaves that were withering and sere.

Edgar A. Poe, Ulalume

I

MARCO POLO SHEEP

(WHEN WE GIVE UP RUGBY FOR GOOD)

CELSO TEMBURA, the sacristan, whose friends call him Barnacle while others have dubbed him Winkle and he doesn't take it amiss, guts scad and broils little birds better than anyone: sparrows, goldfinches and greenfinches, he also stuffs toads and owls, all for a bit of a lark, but he doesn't bother with weasels for they cast their coats, he has flat feet, bushy eyebrows and a fitful mind, well, he stutters you see, Celso also sings Portuguese *fados* and Oporto tangos tunefully and will cook a slap-up feast to order, the harder the wind blows over the sea the better for everyone, though he doesn't provide the prostitutes since his position would more or less preclude him, but he needs for nothing, folks who earn their crust indoors sometimes turn to bad thoughts, bad feelings, but Celso is spared this for he is serious-minded and well-meaning, you can tell folks who are fearful of God by their solemnity, and at the end of the day they save their souls, his brother Telmo was helmsman of the Finisterre fishing smack *Unxía* but was lamed by a tremor which tossed him over the cliff at Raboeira point, or Demon's rock they call it, and now he's a gravedigger in the parish cemetery of San Xurxo of the Seven Dead Foxes, not far from the San Xiao of Moraime monastery where the Swabian kings were crowned amidst oak trees, laurels and golden gorse, Hilario Ascasubi, the Gaucho poet, was born in Posta de Fraile Muerto and small wonder, the Moors who fish for gold-flecked sea bream south of the Gibraltar straits say that the wind passes but the sea remains, the sound of the sea does not come and go as Floro Cedeira, the cowherd, thinks, but has always come, whoosh, whoosh, whoosh, from the beginning until the end of the world and all its misery, the city of Dugium

Duio, the Nerian capital, was swept away by the wind and buried
beneath the sea, they say it lies between the Mañoto rock and the
Centulo, those rocks that have stood there for one thousand, two
thousand, three thousand years now, a breeding ground for scallops
and goose barnacles, but the sound of the sea does not come and go
as Floro Cedeira, herald of the wholesome goodness of raw octopus,
believes, octopus is just the thing for curing rheumatism and wry
neck, but the wind has always come, whoosh, whoosh, whoosh, from
the beginning until the end of the world and maybe even before, others say that Dugium perished in an earthquake in the channel which
used to separate the island of Finisterre from the mainland and
linked the beaches of the Outer Sea and Langosteira, and when the
earth grew back the city was buried forever, the sea lows like a disgruntled ox, like a whole squadron of hoarse, disgruntled oxen, or
maybe the sea bellows like a chorus of a hundred calving cows, or
more, and in San Mereguildo de Gandarela, the city which was
engulfed beneath the waters at the time of that Johnny Jorick business, the Dubliner who was castrated for a bet at a *romería*,* the bells
peal forth in three four time so that we Catholics may sing the prais-
es of the virgin Locaia a Balagota, the wench whose virginity the heathens tormented with fetid brine, painting the nine hollows of her
body purple, she was a sight for sore eyes.

"We should kill all the heathens."

"Maybe."

"Shoot them or hang them?"

"Makes no difference."

The sea has never ceased since God invented time all those years
ago, God invented the world at the same time as time, the world did
not exist before time, the sea never wearies, time never wearies, nor
does the world, it ages every day though never wearies, the sea swallows up one boat or one hundred boats, it sweeps away one seafarer
or one hundred seafarers and keeps on grumbling in its hoarse voice,
that peevish, querulous voice of a disgruntled, quarrelsome drunk.

* *romería*: a festival at a local shrine.

"Does it frighten you?"

"No, not me for I'm used to it."

Cirís from Fadibón mounted the devil on Cabernalde hill, clutching him by the legs and pinioning him so that he could not escape, they say that Fiz o Alorceiro, the half-wit from Coyiños, saw him and took leave of his senses at that very moment from sheer fright, but with his black arts the devil distilled the sticky pitch which he carried within his belly and, as a result of this magical, perilous cunning, Cirís from Fadibón stayed spliced on to him until he died of hunger and thirst, what a hoot to see the devil rolling and cavorting in the gorse with Cirís from Fadibón glued to his backside like a leech! the priest in San Xurxo of the Seven Dead Foxes performs miracles with one single hand so skilful is he, he's called Father Xerardiño Aldemunde and has been dead for many a year now, you can tell by the stench from him, from that reek of rotting fish, but he uses magic arts to feign life and goes about his business without a care: he hears confession, plays cards with all and sundry, polishes the spigot on his still, sings free of charge at the funerals of dead goose barnacle fishermen and cooks up clams with onion, parsley and a dash of white wine.

"Isn't this getting a little jumbled?"

"Just a shade jumbled."

"Like life itself?"

"Yes, though I try not to say so."

The gods began to speak through the mouth of Chubby Manteiga, the Prouso Louro half-wit, the Reburdiños oracle, who is not a person of flesh and blood but a mere flight of fancy, shortly before his fifteenth birthday, one morning before sunrise he began to howl like a wolf and folks—sailors, peasants, woodcutters, shepherds, craftsmen and peddlers—said he was howling for his mother who abandoned him as a newborn babe on Seiside beach to be devoured by rats, but he was rescued by a mermaid who gazed at him tenderly, he looked just like a mountain pine marten, it's not true that on Nemiña beach there is always a dead beached whale, gnawed by horseflies, crabs and gulls, folks tell tall tales, you can't believe a word that some folks

say, it has been some years now since wolves ventured down to the
seashore, they are easily scared off, they scent the wind and flee far
from the villages, skirting the ponds, the trace of blood which gives
the wolf away is retreating eastward, the point of the compass rose
tamed by tradition, inertia even, when you do things against your
will you wind up burning like phosphorus in Old Nick's cauldron, for
against physics or chemistry you cannot go, Minguiños the Poltroon,
the Xures half-wit, sold the alarm clock which he inherited from his
father and now he's afraid that his father will return from the dead to
reclaim it, James E. Allen, the overseer, has ginger hair and a freckled face, he's English but looks like an Irishman, James plays the
accordion well—waltzes, polkas and mazurkas—and recites the
poems of Poe aloud, to hear them at night is mighty eerie, how far do
the notes of the accordion reach? can the whales hear them?

> It was night in the lonesome October,
> Our memories were treacherous and sere
> For we knew not the month was October.

James E. Allen had been a winger for the Hunslet Boys rugby
team in Leeds but gave it up for good at the age of twenty-five
because he felt he was getting past it, world-famous locomotives are
built in Leeds, on Nemiña beach there is only a beached whale on the
occasional full moon, not on every one, on some full moons there is
while on others there isn't, sometimes the whale isn't dead but dying
though the horseflies, crabs and gulls devour it just the same, then
Dosindiña—since she turned thirty she has been known as Doña
Dosinda—is overcome with lust and carries on with the males of
three species, how indecent and nonsensical! "Savor the gluttony of
feasting on the fat of the land!" the Reburdiños oracle tells her,
"Then hit the hay with your insatiable males," Doña Dosinda sins
unsmilingly.
  "And mocks the laws of nature, too?"
  "She does. But God forgives her."
  Maria Flora, housekeeper to Father Socorro, the priest in
Morquintiáns, brews herself a cup of chamomile tea—chamomile

from Romelle is highly sought after—sits down in her rocking chair, pulls her Manila shawl over her head and weeps patiently though without distress.

"Don't you think that with every day that passes folks have less shame?"

"Well, yes, maybe, I don't know where all this will lead."

Dogs are not much use because their hobbles are a nuisance after the pleasure is gone, truth to tell there is no point in trying what you already know.

"Is the devil hobbled?"

"I don't believe so, if he were we would know."

"What about billy goats?"

"I don't think so."

"And the Portuguese?"

"I don't think so, the Portuguese are like the Spaniards."

"Donkeys?"

"No."

Perched upon the wall of the Caneliñas whaling station, swinging his legs to and fro and gazing out over the sea, you must always look out over the sea, never forget that you cannot turn your back on the sea, my uncle Knut Skien, who has one pale blue and one bottle-green eye, sings the verses of Poe to the accompaniment of the accordion.

The skies they were ashen and sober;
The leaves they were crisped and sere,
The leaves they were withering and sere.

Some folks call Cusiñadoiro point Cape Vela, this was where the merchant vessel the *Arada* foundered, they say that people from Camelle pilfered even the binnacle and drank the captain's gin, my cousin Vitiño Leis Agulleiro, and hereabouts we're all more or less related, he's the eldest son of my Aunt Milagros, keeps a tryst with Dosindiña, or Doña Dosinda, rather, in the Lires estuary with its tiny creek and bay to match, in the cabin on Calboa point they make love amid obscure philosophies.

"I don't get it."
"Neither do I."
"What about them?"
"I wouldn't know."

Neith and Bandin, the gods of war, the bards of war, descend from the heavens to say which soldiers should die in battle and who should be spared, when the sun sets Chubby Manteiga rolls upon the sand weeping disconsolately, perhaps he is awash with sorrowful memories and cannot bear to be looked at, Get away from me, you gruesome flies from corpses! It disgusts me to watch you binge on the liquor of my suffering! Don't you know that vultures hatch their eggs within my heart? Time passes gently and uncertainly, like the trees which grow without anyone realizing, this growth business has more to do with the throb of intuition than with the sense of sight, man is such a crude animal that he doesn't even see the grass growing, my cousin Vitiño Leis is brave and very strong, only one fellow was ever able to beat him at arm wrestling, a fellow from Baxantes by the name of Feliberto Urdilde and he went and died, he was struck by a bottle of gin which split his head in two and killed him, the ghost of Feliberto Urdilde amuses himself now by pissing on the nests of albatrosses and sowing rancorous dregs of remorse in the hearts of widows, once he appears to them they never sleep peacefully ever after and suffer from the cold, it is improper for widows to drink too much coffee, some elderly seafarers say that mermaids were the first lacemakers in Camariñas, that they copied the patterns from seaweed and starfish and the transparency of waters where cormorants have just dived, there are scarcely any mermaids left these days and Camariñas folk have lost their fondness for wooing them, nowadays they no longer take little crocks of cream to the seashore, nor, on moonlit nights while the sea surges, gratify them by playing old anthems on the bagpipes, certain historians also claim that the first recorded person from Finisterre was the fruit of love between a seal from the Lobeira islands and a mermaid who stretched out to sun herself one sunny day on the South Camouco, on the Lesser Lobeira island, the one closest to the mainland, off the Cabra coast and the

village of Curra, though this may not be true since it goes against
common sense, when my father made his first communion there was
a madman from Orense by the name of Farruco Roque, also known
as Don Paco, a cheerful soul who hailed from Celanova, Don Paco
had never seen the sea nor had he any wish to do so.

"All that water in one place cannot be good, it can be beneficial
neither for the health of the body nor for the tranquility of the soul."

Winkle, the sacristan Celso Tembura, has a loophole in his feelings, I've already told you that he has a fitful mind, and catches her-
ring-gulls with a fishing-hook, later on he frees them since they are
no good to eat, their flesh is too tough, he uses sardine guts as bait,
Winkle or Barnacle, I mean Celso Tembura the sacristan, is orderly
in his ways and strides across the flagstones on the quay without
treading on the cracks so as not to slight the holy cross, the lads
Noah Rebouta, Chelipiño Pérez, Doado Orbellido and his brother
Froitoso, Lucas Abuín, Martiño Villartide and Renato Fabeiro—one
for each of the seven dead foxes of the San Xurxo parish—were a sort
of revolutionary, republican bunch and didn't give a toss about the
sermon, they challenged everything, upset the whole applecart and,
of course, wound up with their souls in damnation, the ringleaders to
burn forever in hell, and the others—the followers—to roast for a
while in purgatory, at times you can watch them loafing about with
the Holy Company of souls along the banks of the river Maroñas,
which are shady and overgrown, eerie and lonesome, when James E.
Allen gave up rugby because he was getting on in years, his
Norwegian uncle Knut Skien, who was also my uncle, took him off
to hunt Marco Polo sheep in the Pamir mountains, they shot only
one so it cost my uncle Knut a pretty penny, now he has its dessi-
cated head hanging over his fireplace, but they managed to play
buzkashi, which is a type of rugby on horseback played with a head-
less calf instead of a ball, buzkashi is a tough sport and the contest-
ants lash one another with whips, some players have an eye gouged
out but they take it all in good part for it could happen to anybody,
Allen's freckles sparkle when he speaks of it, after that he started
work at the whaling station, the wealthy one in my family was not

my great-grandfather but his brother Dick, who hunted whales off
the Azores, around here rich men hunt whales, while the poor fish
for hake and the poorest of the poor pry goose barnacles from the
rocks, hereabouts everyone gets their fair share, and in the shadow of
Dick, my maternal great-grandfather's brother, we all prospered,
some more so and others less as is only natural, but that is a matter
of character and predisposition.

"Don't you think that Dick's wife, Dorothy, was a bit of an
oddity?"

"You mean she liked women?"

"No, not that."

Dorothy was always prim and proper, Dorothy feared her emo-
tions and never undressed in front of any man, Dorothy never listened to music, undertook no charitable works nor did she believe in
God, Dorothy sat through mass with her eyes tight shut and her
mind blank—not easy though it can be done—lest she sense the presence of God, Dorothy did not read the verses of poets or attend exe-
cutions, her friends loved to see hanged men wriggle and writhe,
blacks are the ones who die best and most rhythmically, it's a delight
to see fear transformed into harmony, directly afterwards they turn a
greenish hue, Dorothy always endeavoured not to know herself too
well, to think otherwise is but an impertinence, neither did her husband believe in God although he tried to conceal this, and only on his
deathbed did he confess to his brother.

"Listen, Cam, stop waffling and take what you like out of what
I'm about to say, you know, it's all very simple: I worked so hard
throughout my life that I had no time to fall in love, be superstitious,
or believe in God, the only license I was able to take was getting
drunk every Saturday without fail. You see, Cam, I wanted to build a
house with boxwood beams and now I'm on the road to hell without
ever achieving it, I garnered all the money I needed but time was
what I lacked."

"One day you told me that roots were what you lacked."

"Indeed, that's true, I also lacked roots, in our family we have all
moved around more than we ought and at the heel of the hunt we are

always buried on foreign soil, it grieves me not to have realized this earlier."

On Traba beach some time ago a beaked sperm whale was stranded, some people fall ill once removed from the routine of life and death, the worst thing is not knowing how to forgive, people possessed need help to spew forth the devil from their bodies, they brought the body of St. Campio in military dress to the parish of San Ourente of Entins in Outes, the two saints get on like a house on fire, St. Campio was a soldier, and served the King loyally, now he is a body unconsumed upon the altar of San Ourente, the close friendship between the two saints is also spoken of, St. Ourente was a bishop and St. Campio a soldier, now that they're getting on in years they're together on the altar, the ceremony to flush out the devil you know already: wash your face and hands in water from the fountain of Our Lady of Rial, touch your head nine times upon the holy stone then do nine rounds of the stone cross, six in one direction and three in the other, proceed as far as you can with the exorcism of the devil, you succour persons fortified by the flight of Satan by serving them pig's head stewed with turnip tops and chickpeas or chopped pork served with fried eggs and potatoes in their jackets, as dessert you should also offer them chestnuts in syrup laced with plenty of *aguardiente**, liquor scares the devil away, people believe the contrary but they are mistaken, the devil is like a viper and what he likes is mother's milk, also white pumpkin pancakes dredged with cinnamon, little Ribadavia cakes and Allariz honey fritters, warlike St. Campio is the patron saint of conscripts and travellers, he protects young lasses and makes them fall in love, on San Guillén mountain, on the Finisterre promontory, there was a hermitage to which the Hungarian gentleman Grissapaham retired in order to seek God's forgiveness for the carnage he committed in the war of Naples, other folks say that the hermit was William of Aquitaine, Count of Toulouse and Poitiers, while some folks confuse him with William of Orange, Charlemagne's paladin who trounced the Saracens, defended the

---

* *aguardiente*: colorless liquor distilled from wine

antipope and, upon return to the path of righteousness for reasons set
forth by Bernard of Clairvaux, became a hermit in expiation of his
erroneous ways, some say it was Don Gaiferos de Mormaltán, the fellow from the ballad, and that he remained at the top of the Cape until
the late XVIII century when he was ordered down by the lord Bishop,
St. William's or San Guillermo's bed was a great slab of stone upon
which barren couples would lie, on Pindo mountain there is another
stone with similar properties and leaping over nine waves on
Lanzada beach also helps favor that elusive child, Telmo Tembura,
the trawler skipper who tumbled over Demon's rock cliff and is now
gravedigger in San Xurxo, knows many a tale of Pindo mountain,
though he's not always willing to recount them and you have to ply
him with pancakes laced with *aguardiente* in order to loosen his
tongue, he knows the story of the earthquake which changed the
course of the river Xallas better than anyone, even though the event
took place in the times when Marco Polo was journeying to Cathay,
he must have been in Kunduz, Faizabad or thereabouts at the time
eating rice with herbs, houses should not be swept at night lest you
scare off souls seeking to warm themselves at the hearth, souls suffer from the cold when they come out of purgatory for the procession
of the Host, or the Holy Company as it is also called, souls always
wish to return to the houses in which they lived and nobody should
bar their path, it is not right to be cruel to anybody, much less to
souls, you should pray and have masses said in order to shorten their
torment, Father Xerardiño performs miracles with one single hand,
he scares off the devil, restores speech to the dumb, heals the pus
oozing from ulcers, Father Xerardiño smokes like a chimney, he
keeps a bundle of fag ends in the sanctuary and at times even smokes
while saying mass, the parishioners in San Xurxo of the Seven Dead
Foxes are fond of Father Xerardiño for he is a generous soul and lets
the Xures half-wit sleep by his hearth when the nights turn wild and
windy, souls in purgatory appear whenever they can, always once
midnight has struck, souls come to entreat intercession or forewarn
of death, disguising themselves as bumblebees, bats, or agnus Dei qui
tollis peccata mundi, now that's a hell of a cheek, you could lose your

composure and decency for less, they whinge listlessly, like ancient God-forsaken crows and clank the fetters which shackle them to the other life, they turn into quartz pebbles which cry out when trodden upon or into the jawbone of an ass in order to be able to kill their brother, it's a well-known fact that both the glory and the death of a brother are hard to bear, souls appear in dreams and traipse forth in the Holy Company with their torches ablaze wafting the scent of candlewax and cowdung, in front trudges a living though sickly being who tolls the bell, walking with his hand outstretched and his fingers bleached white, whoever encounters the Host has to guide them until they meet another person to take his place, in the case of a woman her period stops for nine moons and then she gives birth to a huge black spider that looks like a crab and bears the seven stars of the Ursa Minor upon its back, if you say an Our Father for them the Holy Company will serve as an alarm clock, when a corpse turns in its coffin it is a sign that death is close at hand and you should then say the Credo with your eyes tight shut, holding your breath so as not to lose your wits, Chubby Manteiga said to Barabbas one morning: "I know why you are always lurking about, you take your bearings from the stench of carrion and are forever on the lookout for corpses," Liduvino Villadavil, the traveling laborer, did not hold his breath and even farted while he was praying and as a punishment he was struck blind forever, nowadays he wanders about at *romerías* singing ballads, my uncle Knut Skien hunts rorqual and sperm whales in the old style with his bare hands and a harpoon and even chortles.

"I drink the blood of the animal because I respect it, I kill not for killing's sake but in order to live."

At times you come across finbacks, and even blue whales, too, in these seas they all swim against the Gulf Stream, which flows down from the North Pole, the finback is not a rorqual but a humpback whale, seafarers from Finisterre, where this world ends and the land of the dead begins, know each and every whale and address them by name as though they were people or horses: Elsinda, Maruxiña, Quintián, Sabela, etc., rarely confusing them, only when there's a whole pod bobbing around together.

"On top of one other?"

"Not really, but almost."

"Do you believe that Almighty God can play cachalots as though they were codling?"

"Why, yes I do, Almighty God can always do anything he pleases."

In Finisterre, before motorized fishing vessels came into use, also in Laxe and in Camelle though not in Muxía nor in Camariñas, they used the *traíña*, *rapetón* and *recú* * to fish under sail for sardine and cod, the *rapetón* is longer and more graceful than the *traíña* and carries two sails, while the *recú* has a shorter waterline length.

"I will not bury you, with your thousand horses, whinnying as your corpse passes by! I will not bury you, with your thousand hounds with which you used to hunt, baying as your corpse passes by! I will not bury you, with your thousand women with whom you used to lie, only to teach them a lesson with your wrath, weeping as your corpse passes by! I would leave you stranded upon a rock where the sea surges with clement wrath, however I acquiesce and am resigned."

The youngest of seven brothers is a werewolf, or lycanthrope, in certain circumstances he turns into a wolf but is spared if his eldest brother stands as godfather to him, then he does not feel himself to be a wild beast nor is he inhabited by melancholy, the youngest of seven sisters is a witch and can do much good with her gift and bring healing to the sick and consolation to the heartsore, it is not true that Camariñas lacemakers turn consumptive, nor do mermaids, this business of making bobbin lace is wholesome for you don't swallow much spittle, young ladies turn consumptive from reading too much poetry and playing the piano, some lacemakers smoke cheroots like fishwives but that does them no harm for smoke drives out germs and strengthens the bones, Fideliño the Pig, whose face was red and pockmarked, looked like a boiled crab, his feet were black as soot and hard as flint for he always ran about barefoot and his feet would knock sparks from the rocks when he bumped against them, he was

---

* *traíña*, *rapetón* and *recú*: traditional gear for sardine fishing

not from Morpeguite, but lived in the village because he was married to Marta the Scad, a local woman, weary of grinding poverty, Fideliño the Pig went off to shoot himself in the mouth at the Five-fingered Woman crag on Pindo mountain, this little piggy went to market, this little piggy stayed at home, this little piggy had roast beef, this little piggy had none, he had to trudge quite a distance and scale a fair height and when he came hurtling down he bashed his face against the rocks and wound up looking like a squashed tomato, Fideliño the Pig would trot like a fox, in short, wary hops, and almost every night he ventured as far as Nemiña beach to see if the sea had cast up anything, some hardwood boards, mahogany, ebony, lignum vitae, a couple of bales of virgin rubber, a barrel of gin, maybe even a dead man with a gold tooth.

"Are there any left nowadays?"

"Indeed there are, though fewer and farther between, a dead man with a gold tooth is a blessing from God!"

One night Fideliño the Pig chanced upon another fellow who was knocking around at the same enterprise and Fideliño took offense, he tried to keep a cool head but lost his temper, small wonder in that, now, the other fellow was Xan from Labaña the Chainsmoker, a starveling burdened down with a string of children and pangs of conscience, he had also run up debts, suffered prostate problems and was forever pissing himself, but everything in its proper place and preparing for the birth of a country child is not the same as preparing for the murder of a prince, Fideliño and Xan nodded to one another and continued on their way without a word, distrust soon puts a brake on conversation, a few days later, in order to scare off Xan and keep the shades of night strictly for himself, Fideliño decided to dress only in shirt and underpants like almost all dead bodies washed ashore, then he lay down on the shore just above the waterline, as though drowned, Xan soon approached this fake corpse and, once he came within earshot, Fideliño leaped to his feet with arms outstretched and bellowed in a voice like one from beyond the tomb:

"Bury me on hallowed ground, Xanciño, oh, bury me on hallowed ground!"

Xan from Labaña the Chainsmoker took to his heels and didn't stop until he reached his house, it isn't true that on Nemiña beach there is always a stranded whale, a dead mermaid or sailor, or a dead pig with a bloated belly, Xan from Labaña the Chainsmoker had plenty of strength to flee, Johnny Jorick the Dubliner was castrated at the Caneiros *romería* far from here, Moncho Méndez—who had been a civil guard in Betanzos but was booted out for drunk and disorderly conduct—squared up to Johnny Jorick and told him:

"I bet you a flitch of bacon that if you as much as step on my shadow I'll cut the balls off you."

Then Johnny Jorick trod on his shadow and Moncho Méndez castrated him with three slashes of his knife but, since he was neither a skinflint nor spiteful, Moncho excused Johnny Jorick the flitch of bacon, after marrying Roquiño Lousame, a male nurse in the Fuentes Clinic in Corcubión, Rosa Bugairido was carrying on with Xeliño Méndez, Moncho's younger brother, there were fourteen boys in that family: three priests, three civil guards, three postmen, three commercial travelers, Moncho and Xeliño, Rosa Bugairido committed suicide some three years back by throwing herself off the cliffs at Cape Vilán into the sea, her eye and part of her brains splattered over the barnacles at the low-tide mark, her body was washed ashore on Traba beach, where some years ago a rare beaked cachalot whale was stranded, north of Laxe point.

"Tomorrow is the anniversary of your mother's death, Lord rest her, perhaps we should take some flowers to the cemetery."

"Maybe!"

There are fewer and fewer corpses upon which to sleep off sickness or a drinking spree, there are days when the whales swim so close together that the tuna fishermen have no room to fish with pole-and-line, the whales foul the lines with their backs, Don Sadurniño Losada, an elderly freight skipper, now retired, knew this coast like the back of his hand, he knew it by heart and sketched it in great detail in his notebooks, from Malpica to Carreiro point, where the Muros estuary switches inland, Don Sadurniño also jotted down in his notebooks wise sayings and strange happenings, the names of magic herbs and their local variants, some very rare and others well nigh embarrassing, for these jottings Don Sadurniño would write in green ink, nobody prays to the virgin Locaia a Balagota nowadays, devotion to her is on the decline, this business of the radio giving out news and soap powder commercials all day long is what leads to it, heathens have neither conscience nor manners, they taint the waters and spill crude oil and blood in them, they bury the earth beneath dead bodies, they line up rows of dead bodies on top of the earth and quench the embers so that souls catch cold and spit in the wind to disorient the gulls and make them crash into the rocks, in the Pedrullo stand the dilapidated ruins of San Xurxo castle, country folks say that Queen Lupa's treasure is hidden there, but it has never been found, the oak trees on Pindo mountain burned ceaselessly for seven years, that must have been horrible, like a Great Flood of fire.

"What Dick never managed to build was a house with boxwood beams, maybe you can do it, Cam, it is difficult to cut boxwood beams, they have to be very small, Dick would have liked to make boxwood jewellery cases, lined with moiré and fitted with a little silver key, Dorothy was an odd sort of character, a character like a spot of bilberry jam."

"Currant jam?"

"No, bilberry."

Although there are those with not an ounce of respect in them who shout it from the rooftops, Dorothy was not a lesbian, but she lacked goodwill, sneezed a great deal and maybe even wound up possessed, you never know, traveling from south to north, as you know, the great bank of whales moves within the main flow of the Gulf Stream, only the weakest swim on the outside, in these waters there are magnetic rocks which disorient both whales and boats.

"Roots were what we lacked, this business of being buried abroad not a good thing."

The hex is sometimes confused with the evil eye, children turn rickety and adults start to spit blood, cannot sleep and suffer from severe headaches, there is the hex of the living and the hex of the dead, as well the hex of women and the hex of men, the hex of the maiden, the non-virgin spinster, the menstruating woman, the pregnant woman, the mother of more than three children after lying with her husband, the woman consumed with envy, the hex of the excommunicant, the person damned to eternal flames, the hanged man, the consumptive, the dead half-wit, all these may be kept at bay with clear running water, poultices made from local red wine, unsalted mutton broth, infusions of aromatic herbs, cloves of garlic, sprigs of wheat, rye straw, feathers from a bantam hen, tail feathers are the best, Carlos III copper coins, oil from a lamp which has lit the Blessed Sacrament and so on and so forth, the Apostle St. James traveled these lands preaching the Gospel which is the book wherein all truths are contained, and before that the Celts were here, if the oak and the box tree are entwined with mistletoe you must slay two white bulls because it is a sign that a beneficent spirit is hovering at hand, after that the Phoenicians came and left us the Serpent Stone in Gondamil, which was the image of the dragon Baal to whom creatures were sacrificed by beheading with a boxwood axe so that they bled slowly to death, the god Melcate was made an offering of peasants who were then cast into the sea: soldiers would hunt them down, tie their hands behind their backs with a vine shoot or a honeysuckle bine and then hand them over to sailors, who cast them into the sea some thirty or forty miles offshore to be crushed by whales passing above them, the god Melcate was more than likely a relation of St. John of the bonfires, on St. John's night in a north-facing window place a glass of water with a herring-gull's egg in it, say nine Hail Marys, request whatever it is you seek without opening your mouth or even moving your lips, only in your thoughts, and in the morning, when you crack open the egg, a figure which you should be able to decipher will appear in the water, some old women are unerring and can cure a young lad's pimples merely by glancing at him, there are three good colors: white for innocence, blue for the sky above the clouds and green for the sea and trust, and three colors which are the scourge of the soul: black for the devil incarnate, scarlet for blood flowing from the veins and yellow for envy and its evil counsel, on days with "r" it is unwise to trade or purchase cattle, Tuesdays are best for shaving your beard and trimming your hair and nails, a pig should not be slaughtered on a Wednesday, Thursdays are not advisable for milking cows, or even nanny goats, with the left hand, Friday is the day of the werewolf and you cannot eat meat nor lie with a woman unless your own or a trusted neighbor not a day under sixty, on Saturdays it is customary to wash the feet every second week at least, and you can also play dominoes and cards, while on Sunday we Catholics attend mass and pray for our dead, you have to put to sea every day in order to earn your crust, animals cannot live without food, nor can man either, without food you cannot sail, hunt whales or even fish for scad, or go to war against the French on the side of the English, some crimes first flit through the head of a criminal who then ponders them in every last detail, the criminal is quickly discovered by the Civil Guard because he often makes a blunder or is in too much haste, the perfect crime is not figured out but divined, Holy Innocents may come close to the perfect crime and confound the judge, even numbers are bad, odd ones are preferable especially 1, 3 and 9, in truth 5 and 7 are fine too, by tracing the sign of the cross in the ashes of the hearth you scare away hobgoblins and ward off misfortune, if you place an open pair of scissors and a dish of coarse salt upon a corpse you stop the belly from bloating, it's also good to say the Our Father, in certain parts of Castile they call the cantharis the Spanish fly, a green-colored insect which lives in lime and ash trees, as well as in olives and myrtles, when crushed to a powder it is used to straighten and strengthen the pecker, people who die from their carnal excesses arrive at the gates of hell writhing in pain but still joined as one, Don Sadurniño Losada sketched and recorded in one of his notebooks the rocks upon which many boats foundered, almost all the boats swallowed up by the sea in the waters hereabouts, the most notorious was the *Serpent*, an English naval training vessel which was wrecked a century ago now, on November 10, 1898, some folks say that it was September 10 but they are mistaken, she had one hundred and seventy-five men on board of whom only three sailors were saved, a fellow named Bourton, another fellow called Gould and the last fellow was Lacsne, they were washed up on Trece beach, and not a single officer or midshipman was spared death, their bodies were also washed ashore on the same beach, some several days later, and perhaps not all of them made it, the Xaviña parish came to the aid of the three survivors and recovered many bodies, prayed for their souls and gave them a Christian burial, but the Camariñas parish did nothing because the dead were not Catholics, Protestants belong in hell and there is little point in wasting time on funerals which would do them no good, besides they are not entitled to burial in hallowed ground, Protestants are worse than Mohammedans, perhaps the *Serpent* was not a training vessel but a warship with midshipmen in training, a third-class battleship 225 feet in length, 36 feet beam and 15 feet draft, 2,700 short ton displacement, which could sail at 17 knots, these are the official data, the *Serpent* struck the Bois reefs, the shoals of Bois, which have been known as the Serpent shoals ever after, only three mementos of the shipwreck remain: the English cemetery at Porto do Trigo, in the shadow of Veo mountain which ends at Cagada Point, the plaque in San Carlos park in Corunna and the Bearded Man, the figurehead from the *Serpent* purchased by Don Paco de Ramón y Ballesteros to adorn his house in Corcubión, back in the years of the Primo de Rivera dictatorship at the Jesuit college in Vigo Don Paco was a schoolmate of the famous Spanish writer Camilo José Cela, the British Admiralty sent gifts as a token of gratitude for the conduct of the Galicians: a rifle to the priest in Xaviña, a gold fob watch to the mayor of Camariñas and a top class barometer to the Town Hall, every year the English used to send a warship to pass in front of the cemetery, fire a gun salute and cast a wreath of flowers upon the sea, today this beautiful custom has fallen into disuse and the English cemetery—and this is the fault of the lazy Spaniards who had no wish to maintain it—is overgrown with brambles and buffeted by gales, the albatross crosses the Finisterre isthmus to roost in the rocks in the Outer Sea, the gulls fly over the sea to Gavoteira, the cornice where hundreds and hundreds, perhaps thousands and thousands, of birds build their nests facing westward over the sea which stretches to the horizon where the whales pass back and forth, the cormorant is darker than the gannet, some people confuse the albatross and the gannet, cormorants nest on the Centulo rock, the *Book of Proverbs* states that a brother helped by his brother is a fortress, when the *Book of Proverbs* is forgotten, Cain comes back to life, disinters the jawbone of an ass and, gazing into his evil mirror, one brother turns into the other brother's worst enemy, it's a bitter thing to see families decimated by envy and the rancorous ill will of women who were too late to clamber up onto the victor's chariot all bedecked with diadems of semiprecious Brazilian stones and festooned with garlands of brightly colored paper flowers, when a black man starts to foretell the future or heal the sick the neighbors report him to the courthouse or the local barracks lest he be in league with the devil, it is only right to be on your guard and perceive danger as soon as it rears its head, in order to foretell the future and heal the sick you have to be white, young Berdullas has powers of prophesy and healing granted by the Immaculate Conception and the Holy Trinity, Father, Son and Holy Ghost, amen, Lord Jesus! oh, Holy Trinity send not more billows against our hearts and cure us of the mange and ringworm, too, amen, Lord Jesus! oh, Holy Trinity swamp not our souls nor our memories and assuage the grief of our hearts and the throbbing of our bowels, amen, Lord Jesus! oh, Holy Trinity stop not the ears of our understanding and heal the filters of our kidneys as well as the caverns of our livers, amen, Lord Jesus! oh, Holy Trinity spit not in the eyes of the faculties of our souls and drive forth the ringing from our ears and the spots from before our eyes, amen, Lord Jesus! oh, Holy Trinity beat the living daylights out of us but let us live, amen, Lord Jesus! oh, Holy Trinity, make us breathe and float like the rorqual whale, amen, Lord Jesus! the yak is a cross between goat, horse and ox which, on high mountain passes, squeezes through gaps where it can barely fit and never loses its footing, the yak is as tough as the Khirgiz and the Pathani, who are fierce warriors indeed, when Marco Polo told of a sheep with more than six sets of horns, nobody believed a word of it but when it was discovered to be true they named the sheep after him, the first Westerner

to hunt it was George Littledale in 1888, Nematula Khorami, king of
the Kusani, died in a brothel in Lisbon feigning youth through black
arts, the veteran Nematula was a great buzkashi player and could
also box English-style, a little to the north of Gavoteira point lies
Cape la Nave connecting with the isle of Berrón where the sea roars
never stopping for an instant, seafarers hasten offshore when they
hear it, Telmo Tembura, gravedigger in the parish of San Xurxo of the
Seven Dead Foxes, was a pal of Blas de Otero's, he met him in the rectory a couple of years prior to his death and fried him up some small
sardines, Telmo likes to recall the verse of the poet in his own voice,
he doesn't do it that well although he tries hard: that fierce festival
of living and dying, never mind the rest, you can cure croup by placing a stinking, sweaty sock around the throat of the patient and asth-
ma by taking five ounces of the fluid which trickles from the dung of
a newly calved cow on a fasting stomach for nine days, it should be
collected at full moon in the month when the flowers bloom, Holy
Christ of Finisterre with his golden beard came bobbing along in a
wooden crate, he was carved by Nicodemus and cannot bear the
Moors to mock him, he converts them all to Christianity or casts a
curse to shrivel their testicles, Moors are not to be encouraged, on
both Lobeira islands the gulls wheel in cruel, fearsome flocks, a fearful sight to behold, during the November spring tides they gather
onshore above the whaling station in Caneliñas, scaring off the
mountain rabbits and foxes, the herring gull is a fierce, ferocious bird
which never wearies, the whaling station was set up in 1924 by a
Norwegian named Christophersen, it lies opposite the Bois shoals,
now that's a name you hear a great deal, and the rocks of the two
Carrumeiros, between Galera and Caneliñas points, by land it lies
between Gures and Ameixenda, which is priest country for they have
a great number of vocations there, Father Ambrosio cures carbuncles
by smearing them with lukewarm blood from the crest of a black
cockerel, when the rooster pines away and dies the carbuncle is cured
leaving a swastika-shaped scar twirling in a clockwise direction,
teeth from skulls are good for dispelling nervous headaches,
migraine, earache, toothache, sore throats etc., they also get rid of the

stench of snot from rhinitis, the Christians placed a cross on top of
the Phoenicians' Serpent rock, monuments and symbols should not
be destroyed, transforming them into something else is enough,
Winkle has only a smattering of Latin but he has the phrases off pat:
Dominus vobiscum, et cum spiritu tuo, gloria tibi Domine, confite-
or Deo omnipotenti and a few others besides, but he knows all of the
fifteen mysteries of the Holy Rosary and the litany, of course, and
believes firmly in the four latter ends of man and in the seven gifts
of the Holy Spirit, ephideries are demons with long, curling fangs
which suck blood from sleepers dreaming of herds of wild boars in
flight, the Rebudiños oracle keeps ephideries at bay with his voice,
the flesh from razor shells tastes better than the meat from mussels,
a puppeteer from Santo Antonio dos Olivais, near Coimbra, taught
Winkle to sing *fados*, he met him when he was buying cod in
Porriño, his brother Telmo rattles on about the Swabian kings and
yearns for his days as a trawler skipper.

"Misfortune strikes when God ordains it so there's no point
sticking your head in the sand nor running away, you have to ride out
the tempest, misfortune is as bad as tortuous dreams of indifference
and nobody knows how to remedy it."

Floro, the cowherd, plays well-nigh forgotten tunes upon a myrtle flute: sea shanties, *Get Movin' Irene*, *A Chinese Shawl*, and he
believes that the sound of the sea comes and goes like a heartbeat or
the pendulum of a grandfather clock, but that's not true, the sound of
the sea has always come whoosh, whoosh, whoosh, like the wheels
of an ox-cart squeaking along the mountain track to scare off the
wolf, it's a well-known fact that the squeaking of an ungreased axle
upsets wild beasts and gives them the creeps, raw octopus cures
almost every known sickness bar nervous disorders, the man who is
not cured and whose spirits are not lifted by chewing raw octopus
sprinkled with maize flour and snake's eggs has one foot in the grave
already, you should treat the dead with compassion though not condescension, condescension can prove tricky and treacherous, let us
honor our dead, certainly, but with prudent aplomb and serenity, the
dead should not disturb the lives of the living or strike fear in them,

Floro's cows are doughty and long-suffering, they feel neither heat nor cold, Floro's dun heifers are cloaked in the wind blowing from the sea, at times a word is more than a word and is worth as much as a charcoal outline or a chalk sketch.

"And you lost your eye at a *romería*?"

"No, I lost it in the war, it was snatched from me in the battle of the Ebro, and by the time I realized what had happened the water had swept it clean away," the worst thing is seeing death advance limb by limb, molecule by molecule, because all of a sudden you realize that you can no longer drag the weight of your own body around, can a soldier start to rot in life like a bunch of grapes? can someone fray at the edges of their own consciousness like a moth-eaten corduroy cape?

The puppeteer from Santo Antonio dos Olivais was called Spirito Santo Vilarelho, he spluttered, coughed and squinted shamelessly as though taking the piss, in Porriño the Portuguese also bought chocolate, two-tone typewriter ribbons and papier-mâché dolls, there were some with glass eyes but the dolls with painted eyes were cheaper, the river Xallas flows into Ezaro bay along the Covadoiro coast across from the Biogas sandspit and reaches the sea between Finsín to the north and Xemadoiro point to the south, the mouth of the river is called the falls locally, around here there are tasty sea bass, the river Xallas is also known as the Ezaro, beyond Mallón and Ponte Olveira now lies the Fervenza reservoir, in days gone by you crossed the river at the Barca dos Cregos ford between San Crimenso and Santa Uxía, entering low wastelands of gorse, bramble and birch, beside these blessed plants and fruits dog garlic grows wild, fox garlic Winkle calls it, in Santa Uxía there was born the renowned cyclist Guzmán Reboiras, known as Gumesinde, who won a stage of the Tour of Galicia shortly before the Civil War, he was killed during the Civil War, served in the Galician Legion under the command of Barja de Quiroga and was killed on the Huesca front by a shot to the throat, may he rest in peace, near Santa Uxía they began to canalize the river which cascaded in three falls and was the highest waterfall in Spain, it was a delight to see the water slicing through the air, later on they piped it, but that was akin to tempting fate and, although the tunnel was small, the day laborers died of silicosis while the military engineer in charge of operations also died, I knew his name once but it escapes me now, it was Moncho Méndez who told me, he was a municipal guard in Betanzos, but it escapes me now, it was the prostitute Melibea Magnolia the Scallop-seller who always reminded me of it, she used to nibble sultanas and had a memory like an elephant, do you recall that the marrow can weep within the bone? nobody would wish to be a harbinger of doom, best wait until God shows his hand, on the other side lies Moa with its squat stone crosses and Peñafiel castle on Pindo mountain, which is violet in color and has the most beautiful, mysterious rocks in the world, some are cursed but you should not pay that too much heed despite excommunication by bishop princes because Our Lord makes those he wishes to damn lose their bearings, a soul entering hell either has no compass or else one which is out of kilter, the Serpent shoals, where the English school ship foundered, have a core of that same magnetic rock which makes the compass waver, Telmo Tembura knows that the oars of the fishing smack cannot obey the orders of the Pole star when it is covered by cloud and the compass wavers, in order to escape death you have to put out to sea, that is the sailor's golden rule, for this reason the story that peasants along this coast used oxen with burning brands lashed to their horns in order to lure boats ashore in the throes of a northwesterly gale is most certainly untrue, for boats put out to the open sea to escape the sea surging over the rocks, seafarers steer clear of lights rather than seek them out, what peasants do is to risk their skins pillaging lost and foundered vessels, often crewed by the ghosts of dead mariners, the inhabitants of Camelle, Arou and Santa Mariña were well-known for such plundering of the dying, the very same people who rescued the three survivors and hauled from the sea the one hundred-odd bodies of English sailors from the *Serpent*, so put that in your pipe and smoke it! Telmo Tembura speaks like the Finisterre and Muxía fishermen, the way the bream and sardine fishermen of Finisterre and Muxía have of pronouncing Galician, fishermen speak a funny, sloppy slang which does not extend beyond the sound given to certain letters, inshore fishing is skilled work and is reckoned by the day, the boats don't sail beyond twelve or fifteen miles offshore, the fishermen are not paid a wage but go shares, the skipper and the boat owner are usually one and the same person, and the crew, usually four or five of them, twelve at most, are nearly always relations, offshore fishing is reckoned according to the tides and vessels spend a fortnight or three weeks at sea, the time it takes to fill the hold or use up their bait, they sail on the high seas and when under trawl they are deemed to be on the open ocean even though they may not be far offshore, these fishermen are paid by the day and usually there are no more than twelve of them, the owner stays ashore because he is the owner only, someone else acts as skipper, in fishermen's jargon the sound of the letter "a" becomes "e", while the letter "e" becomes "i": jacket, jeckit, though that's just a rule of thumb, of course inshore fishing requires both net as well as rod and line skills, fixed or drift nets may be used, Knut Skien, the Norwegian uncle of James Allen, the rugby player who aged all of a sudden, used to fish for sea bass with a rod and line baited with crushed crab, sardine guts or live capelin, that skill lingers on now only in Finisterre in the lee of the Muñía shoals, the Sambrea, below Robaleira point, and the Carraca, you can use a boulter to catch sea bass and perch as well as conger eel, while hake, cod and sea bream are fished with a hook, the trammel net has at least two layers of mesh while the dragnet is fixed on the sea bed, much like the dredge, and used to scour or rake the seabed for lobster, spider crab and ray, in drift net fishing it is the boat itself which trails the net while in ring fishing the hake nets are cast into the sea in circular fashion, there are not many hake fishermen left nowadays, a few linger on in Finisterre and Cedeira, it is a costly trade and you have the rest of the inshore fishermen agin' you, in the cabin at Calboa point, Doña Dosinda left a note written in her graceful convent school hand for my cousin Vitiño Leis, who had been sleeping off a drinking spree, which read as follows: Farewell, my love, sleep tight and when you get home have a wash with permanganate, kisses and all the hanky-panky you want, Yours, D., you will not stop dreaming until the head of the last condemned man rolls, take my word for it and don't keep trying to break with custom in your head-strong way, the priest in Carnota is a good-hearted big fellow, shy and kindly, and is known as Stumpy, his young housekeeper has blue eyes, wears her hair in a long blonde braid tied with a bright blue ribbon, her name is Margalida and she speaks only Galician, Margalida cooks Galician fish stew and clams better than anybody, Stumpy eats with his hands and then, choking with laughter, wipes them on Margalida's behind, *the sun is called Lourenzo and the moon Margalida, Margalida glows by night while Lourenzo shines by day*, her mother Doña Palmira prepares a tasty shin beef stew, one day when Stumpy was a child, the musicians in the band stood watching a stallion mounting a mare while Stumpy's father urged him: Go on! go on! you boy, you! good health to the musicians! the boat known as the Finisterre *lancha** has two small lazarets, one in the bow and one in the stern, where lines, food and *aguardiente* are stored, the *lancha* is scarcely used at all now, it all but disappeared in the 50's, before then it was a delight to behold the carpenters from the shores of Finisterre hard at work next to the women salters from Porcallón and Fonte Raposo, this boat was rowed by four pairs of oars, at times with the aid of a lugsail, all seafarers throughout the world, even though they don't always admit it, like to sail, the *lancha* handled well in all seas, even on the false sea burning with phosphorescence sent by the devil Cacheiro, a merciless rapscallion driven away only by the sign of the cross, smaller than the *lancha* is the *gamela***, at least that's what they call it up Camariñas and Muxía way, Muxía folk use it under sail, it is a flat-bottomed boat, easily handled, and used for fishing velvet swimming crabs and taking the children of summer visitors out on day-trips, in Corme this boat died slowly on dry land, and standing on the hard earth beside the harbor—though I don't believe she will withstand many more winters—is the catama-

---

* *lancha*: flat-bottomed punt used for inshore fishing, particularly in the Finisterre area

** *gamela*: small flat-bottomed punt used for inshore fishing, may be rowed, used under sail or with an outboard motor. Also called *chalana* in certain areas.

ran *Sea Falcon* dismasted while rounding the cliffs at Roncudo point
dotted with wooden crosses in memory of the goose barnacle fishermen who perished there, Father Antucho Recesinde, the priest in
Rabuceiras in the days when there was a priest in Rabuceiras, told
my brother-in-law Estanis Candíns who is now a schoolteacher, and
before that he was a basketball player, Father Antucho's chin would
start to wag after a couple of glasses of coffee liqueur:

"Beware sins of the flesh for base instinct is the driving force
behind it, in the seminary we took a course where they warned us
that the devil lies in wait to lure us into sins of the flesh by disguising himself as a widow or even an old biddy, women should be kept
out of the sacristy so that they don't get ideas above their station."

My uncle Knut Skien invited me to have a glass of gin with sweet
vermouth and spoke to me of life and death.

"Hunting whales is the only thing we know how to do, we know
nothing but killing whales and some day the whales will run out and
then the family will feel the pinch, nature is highly organized, the
whale in the sea, the gull in the sea breeze—gulls over land, fishermen damned—the ox, the mole, the wolf and man on dry land, as
well as the scorpion, the earthworm and other wretched things, but
all we know is killing whales and their revenge is what frightens me,
for whales have long memories."

At the factory gate in Caneliñas there hangs a sign which reads:
No entry, Beware of the dogs, on the rocky slopes of Touriñán which
end at Buitra point, something is gnawing out the innards of the
scrawny, lackluster cattle, a hen partridge crosses the track with her
ten or twelve chicks around her, slowly and confidently she struts,
over the rocky ground of das Negres which shelves away on the other
side and ends in Cusinadoiro point, you will see wild horses shelter-
ing in the lee of the crags, in the Lires estuary, at the mouth of the
river Castro, kelp—a seaweed which works wonders for the health—
thrives, at the narrow mouth of the Corcubión estuary lie the Lesser
Carrumeiro rocks and across from the Dead Woman's rock, where
the river Xallas enters the sea, lies the Old or Great Carrumeiro rock
above the two Lobeira islands, my brother-in-law Estanis says that

kelp contains fluorine, chlorine, bromine and iodine, this may be
true but it seems to me a tall order that these four elements should
be found together, tincture of iodine is extracted from the ash from
kelp, on Carnota beach which is four miles long medicinal seaweeds
also thrive, the Carnota priest is well up on these types of seaweed,
the weed which produces agar-agar costs an arm and a leg, big money
is paid for it, in the rectory field the Carnota priest looks after the
longest grainstore in Galicia, tourists ask permission to be pho-
tographed standing in front of the stone pillars upon which it is
perched, Celso Manselle, coachman to Don Fiz Labandeira, proprietor of the Labandeira Saltworks, murdered his wife by suffocating
her with a pillow, he was a hefty fellow so it didn't require too much
effort, Viriquiña had been unfaithful to him with the gas man and
Celso was serious-minded, intransigent and guarded, some things
just should not be allowed, the judge found at least one hundred photographs of Viriquiña with her mouth slashed, it is unwise for a dying
child to see anybody tremble, when the sun sets in the Finisterre sea
it swells to a hundred times its size or more, the mermaid at the
lighthouse moans twice every minute, Finisterre is full of Pekinese
lapdogs which look utterly out of place, they're a laugh to see, on
Rostro beach, facing the sea which drowns out shrieks and silences,
all the wild animals live: vixen, weasel, wild boar, badger, ferret, buz-
zard, falcon, owl, it is some time now since a wolf has been seen, the
Norwegian Luisiño Nannestad lived with an Andalusian woman,
Catalina, and died in her arms, why, they weren't even hitched but
were wedded *in articulo mortis*, the Avería shoals running into the
Cabezos and the Meán are shallows lurking in the Corme estuary,
the Serrón shoals run from Gralleiras point and the Oriseira and
Leixón rocks, which the sea never covers, and last winter a yellow
rorqual whale called Crispinciño was stranded there, seafarers from
Laxe named him Crispinciño and he was playful and gentle, when
they managed to refloat him he swam off happily, the Biscuteiro
shoal lies opposite the church and is marked by rocks which show at
low water, hereabouts Cósmede the deaf-mute used to fish for velvet
swimming crabs and fly his kite when he was a boy, Cósmede was

born in the village of Cospindo and was left deaf and dumb after an apparition, when his parents passed away he started to walk and did-n't stop until he reached Gures beach, the winds are named accord-ing to their quarter, that is, the compass point from whence they blow: the N. comes from the north, as you will know, the S. wind they call the wind from below, the S.W. is the big wind, the E. is the offshore and the W. is the sea wind or wind of the Holy Rocks, which stand on Facho mountain, not even a hurricane could budge them but you can shift them easily with your little finger, my friend Valentiño Cambeiro—in *Sacred History* by Father Nemesio Alibia his real name is said to be Casto Lagoa—has a taxi in which you can journey to the end of the world while he imparts his wisdom to any-one willing to lend an ear, Finisterre lies on the outer edge of this world where it borders upon the world beyond, Cósmede Pedrouzas the deaf-mute lives on Gures beach in a shack made of uralite, with an aged, sickly, decrepit wolf and a tame bear, which is also elderly and has an iron ring grown into its flesh, "grown into the felesh" Estanis drones through his nose, Cósmede found the wolf under a chestnut tree above Ponte Outes, bleeding from one ear, while the bear was given to him by a Hungarian who could no longer feed it, Cósmede and his two animals live on grass, octopus, crabs and scraps, it is no easy matter to starve to death, it takes time, octopus and crabs are fished by hand, some skill is required, but patience comes from within, some blackguards gave Cósmede a hiding just for a laugh, someone gave the bastards a few bucks, what a scream to see how deaf-mutes shout when they get a hiding, but the wolf and the bear rallied to his defense, licked his wounds and curled up beside him to keep him warm.

"Isn't this a little garbled?"

"Maybe just a little."

"Like life itself?"

"Not really, anyway, some things just shouldn't be said."

Cósmede once saw a peacock, in Muros there lived an American who kept a pet peacock, and ever since he has imagined that the bot-tom of the sea is full of peacocks in myriad colors which are not even wet, there are fish which look like peacocks, they live deep down in the dark, so they are blind and hardly ever show themselves, only when the crust of the sea bed trembles, in other words, once every hundred and fifty years.

"Is that figure correct?"

"I think so."

Winkle the sacristan spins many a yarn and frowns as he tells them, he also twists his mouth to one side as he speaks and smirks like a lizard, hereabouts there are ash colored lizards with a green stripe on their bellies, to ward off witches they say.

"Off Uña de Ferro point a dragon as big as three whales once rose from the sea, it was wearing a gold-braided dress coat with a crown of thorns and viewed from one side it looked like an admiral while from the other it looked like the Lord Jesus Christ, begging your pardon! a dazzling light shone about its head and it sang Aragonese folksongs in a Castilian accent, fishermen from the trawler *Señoriña II* wanted to capture it but the dragon melted their nets simply by breathing on them," when Winkle realized that nobody believed a word he was saying he stood up with solemn aplomb, with great gravitas and dignity, it would strike awe in you to see him:

"May I be struck down, if I tell a word of a lie! May God strike me down! When I was a slip of a boy, they put me through the mill yet I overcame sin, I have no fear of sin."

The room was tiny and the little window cramped, in order to redeem your soul by working you don't need a very large room, a cobbler requires less space than a joiner of coffins, whales don't fit anywhere but sardines can be fried in any little nook or cranny, fishermen know what fish are swimming in the sea below from the wheeling of the seabirds—herring gull, cormorant, shag and gannet—if they dive from low over the water: mackerel, if they dive from a height: sardines, Carballo folks hail from the south, exactly whence is not known, and they're not to be trusted, they are bad people, up around Terra de Bergantiños you see Carballo folk, they are said to steal the very toothbrush from Spirits and to toss children under the wheels of passing cars in order to claim the insurance.

"Compensation you mean?"

"What difference does it make?"

Intelligence, independence too, leads to loneliness, almost every-thing leads to loneliness, luck and misfortune, sickness and health, Don Victorino, bookkeeper in the Agapito Ferreiro and Sons sawmill, used to compose romantic verses and thought for himself, but there is a price to pay for this and the price may be loneliness.

"It is truly painful to see that people know that you are above them for they gang up on you, draw down the shutters against you and won't look you in the eye, that is sheer treachery, it is hard to live with treacherous people, living with treacherous people shreds your nerves, if there are others there they will go for someone else, for folks are cowardly and fearful."

When he grew weary of sailing and living, skipper Don José Eutelo Esternande set off for the notary in Sobrelo and issued his final instructions and last wishes: in this my last will and testament which I hereby date, sign and seal, I request that, when the time comes and my body starts to stink, it be incinerated upon a pyre of boxwood, *Buxus sempervivens*, the ashes of which are to be scattered at sea, from the leeward side of a trawler, not less than seven miles offshore between Finisterre and Toriñana, off Caldelaxes point more or less, where my beloved Ariadna, the woman whom I loved above all others in my life, drowned, I charge my eldest son to fulfil this wish and, if he be unwilling, or unable, so to do, I likewise charge any of my other children, including my daughters, in descending order of age, to fulfil this wish and if they should be unwilling, or unable, to fulfil this request, I hereby provide one million silver *pesos* for a sea-farer from the Upper Estuaries, for a fifty-year-old blind in one eye (empty socket), a one-armed person (amputee), or a one-legged person (amputee), in that order, to substitute for my children in carrying out this task... just now I was speaking about Moncho Méndez, the municipal guard from Betanzos who castrated Dubliner Johnny Jorick for treading upon his shadow and also excused him the flitch of bacon, no detail is too trivial to mention, Estanis has pointed out that Moncho's surname was not Méndez but Mínguez, not that it

really matters, newly castrated Johnny Jorick started collecting the
seven wild flowers from the cliff edge, the seven magical flowers
which are good for curing the lovesick and hid them where nobody
would find them in a tin box decorated with the Spanish flag behind
a buxom, smiling negress, while on the box was written: La Cubana
chest lozenges, manufactured by the Widow and Sons of Serafín
Miró, Reus (Tarragona), Spain, boxwood is hard, compact and polishes beautifully, box is also a poisonous plant which can cause death,
my maternal great-grandmother's brother, Dick, wanted to build a
house with boxwood beams but never managed to, he died before he
had the chance, boxwood does not float for it is denser than water,
nor does it burn but smoulders slowly before catching fire, my brother-in-law, Estanis, claims that three things can be made from boxwood, at least three things though not much more than that: pipes
for smoking a blend of incense, Dutch tobacco and crushed nettles,
flutes for lulling whales to sleep—children are trained in the craft by
lulling codling—and dildoes, between Roncudo and Insua points,
where the Santa Rosa hermitage is perched on top of the hill, many
boats were wrecked, this is commonplace in these waters, as you
know, the look of the water on the shoals over the Ataín rocks,
which are low-lying and located off Arnado beach, tells Camelle shell
fishermen whether it is a good or a bad day for gathering goose barnacles from the rocks, the *Ataín* was a vessel which went down
many years back, nearly two centuries ago now, Traba beach is
lashed by the open sea, halfway between the villages of Mórdomo
and Boaña lies a lagoon the waters of which cover the city of Valverde
cursed by the Apostle St. James, Slayer of Moors, for allowing abominable sin to flourish there, the lagoon is populated by useless shrimp
and jet-black fish which nobody eats, at times you can even hear the
bells of Valverde toll, offshore an English vessel, the *Kenmore*,
foundered and whether she was carrying slaves or coal was never
known, quite a number of sailors were saved although a few
drowned, some after battling against breaking seas for three full days,
the dead were buried not in the Traba cemetery but at the roadside,
and were not given a funeral service but a wake which was not quite

as splendid as wakes for dead peasants with men in black capes leaping over bonfires of herbs belching thick, aromatic smoke to ward off evil spirits, followed by a banquet where all comers drink and make merry while the keeners keen until nobody pays a blind bit of attention to them, then they grow weary, collect their dues and depart, a faggot is unfit to win the hearts of women, it is not the same to be loved by women as by men, the love of man for man and the love of woman for another woman has led to many an excommunication, such ways of going against nature were the custom in the city of Valverde, hereabouts there are places with strange names: the Cove of the Scorched Corpses, some crews burn with their boat, the Bird of Prey rock, some lads die five at a time, the Skittles of Fortune, some rocks bring good luck and attract blessings, in order to win the heart of a woman you must spruce yourself up, wash your feet, draw the heart from a virgin dove, if it is a white one so much the better, but don't kill it first, it must die over time, make a serpent swallow the heart whole while still bleeding, then suffocate it by wrapping its head in silver foil and hanging it head downwards, next sizzle the head on a hot, though not red-hot, iron plate or in a spotless hollow stone that has been placed on the fire for a long time, then pound it in a mortar with a few drops of laudanum until it forms a fine powder, smear this substance over your hands and touch the beloved, if you can do so beneath her clothing so much the better, Charlemagne laid siege to Valverde for a year and a half then, seeing that he could not conquer the city, he joined forces with the Apostle who helped him to storm the city walls, there was great and barbarous bloodshed and when the city fell he found nobody willing to acknowledge the one true God, or to be baptized, so he ordered the beheading of all save innocent babes in arms who were taken where they might be christened, then he cursed the heathen stones of the city which tumbled down with a tumultuous crash and were subsumed beneath the waters, so much blood was shed that it flowed down Traba beach and stained the sea red, in order for a woman to win the heart of a man a different procedure is required: take as big a male toad as you can find, clasp it tightly in your right hand and pass it five times between your legs while you repeat: Toad, oh, toadie, thus I pass you under my belly, thus may Josie (or whoever) have no respite until he yields to me body and soul, off Camelle head two colliers foundered, one English the other Spanish, the *Chamois* and the *Clara Campos*, without loss of life, then take a fine needle and stitch up the eyes of the toad with a green silken thread, but cause it no injury otherwise the beloved will go blind, and repeat the following: Josie (or whoever), now you are my prisoner bound like this toad, unable to see sun or moon, I will not release you until your love is mine, on Porto rock the sea swallowed up the English freighter *Yeoman*, four men were lost, as well as the Spanish freighter *Natalia* and the Russian oil tanker *Boris Screboldaef*, without loss of life, there are also more urbane ways of carrying this out: buy a length of ribbon, look up at the heavens and think, in the heavens I spy three stars and the star of Jesus four, now I tie this ribbon about my leg until Josie (or whoever) falls in love and marries me, on the *Antón* shoals the coastal cutter *Antón* went down laden with pig iron, all hands were saved, hereabouts there are more sunken ships, at Percebeira point the English colliers *Huelva* and *Saint Weller*, all hands saved, take three or four sprigs of mallow, place them under your mattress and upon waking you think: Josie (or whoever), these sprigs of mallow were plucked by me and have lain beneath me, thus by the power of Lucifer you are my captive and will leave me only when the clergy witness the mallow growing through force of grace, repeat these words every morning for nine days followed by a Hail Mary, on Curro beach in Arou, the Spanish collier *Castillo Monteagudo* foundered without loss of life and they managed to refloat her, on Arou beach the Italian collier *S. Mazzini* and the freighters *Nil*, which was French, and the *Santa María*, Portuguese, without loss of life, many boats founder without loss of life, thank God! though fewer than would be wished, on the Black Rocks of Arou there foundered the English colliers *Wolfstrong*, with the loss of twenty-eight lives, the *City of Agra*, with twenty-nine lives lost, the *Revanchil* and the French vessel *Perranchins*, without loss of life as well as the Norwegian vessel *Standard*, with the loss of three lives, on Friday at the hour of the dog star gather a few sprigs of verbena, before picking them you pass your left hand over them and say: *quasi factum dictum Dei*, the word of God is almost fact, flowering plant serve my ends, then wait until the plant dries, wrap it in parchment and white linen scented with incense and make a scapular which you wear over your heart for nine days, during that time you should make no sinful utterances nor frequent discotheques, limping Telmo Tembura says that drinking coca-cola is for lily-livered softies, for mice that fear their own shadows, the same goes for eating ice cream and waffles, drinking linden-blossom tea, strawberry cordial and sparkling mineral water, and playing snakes and ladders and whist, there are cowards who cover up by blinking endlessly, who don't know that they are cowards, nor even have an inkling of it, cowards who are slow in their ways and cowards as haughty as fighting cocks, Telmo Tembura is an electrician as well as a grave-digger, he also carts manure from cowsheds, sweeps chimneys and chops firewood, Telmo is a hard-working jack-of-all-trades and can turn his hand to anything, Telmo Tembura has no wish to starve, he may be lame but is still alive and kicking, Floro Cedeira, the cowherd, is deeply worried for he looked in the mirror—Concha the gypsy's mirror—but could not see his own reflection, some of the dead do not know that they are deceased, for not all the dead have heard the bells toll their death, there are the dead who may have been smitten by the hex from another dead man hanged by the justice of men, the justice of God does not resort to the gallows, you answer for your sins in purgatory in the fire of slothfulness and indifference, Father Xerardiño Aldemunde, the priest in San Xurxo of the Seven Dead Foxes, has been dead for many a year now, you can tell from that stench of bromide off him, from the fact that neither his armpits nor his forehead sweat, that his nose shines abjectly and that he may be overcome with a fit of spluttering and coughing all of a sudden when you would least expect it, maybe he has made a pact with the devil, best not even think about it, the devil who tempted St. Antonio Abad was turned into a swine by Our Lord, the basilisk can kill with its very glance and there are moons when it disguises itself as a black cat with golden eyes, the fishing vessel

Naldamar I was wrecked without loss of life on Roncudo point, a little farther north lie the Abrulliñas rocks where the Italian steamer
Padova foundered laden with bales of burning burlap, the flames
were her undoing, again without loss of life, box has upright branch-
ing stems and glossy, evergreen leaves, coffee and drinks at wakes are
served after midnight, at wakes for deceased little children sweet
anisette liqueur is served with quince jelly as a reminder of the
virtues of the souls of the dead who did not reach the age of reason
because God called them home early, some dead bodies sit bolt
upright in their coffins and greet the living, while some even fart and
guffaw, the dead fart a great deal, a picture falling from the wall fore-
warns that death is at hand and that you should be wary, some graves
open of their own accord so that the dead may feel more at ease and
skulls can appear without warning, emerge all of a sudden unan-
nounced, why, some still have a full set of teeth, near the Montelouro
convent there slumbers a stone with a cross on top which some
moonlit nights turns into a sailor perished at sea who appears to his
relations while the seashells echo to ensure that everyone—even
those who are not related—takes heed, the family is a weapon to win
the fight against the devil, otherwise it turns into an encumbrance
which prevents you from moving with aplomb and sidestepping danger, the face, hands and feet of those guilty of heinous sins sweat,
they cannot look you in the eye but tremble in a peculiar fashion
which does not escape the serene eye of the man above, they could
be bumped off and no need to go wasting time with pretence, the
German ship *Salier* laden with accordions foundered off Corrubedo
point where it curves towards Ladeira beach, her entire crew were
swept away by the sea playing accordions which can still be heard on
certain nights, on the rocky ground at Caldelaxes opposite the
Curtiseiras rocks you can see piebald colts which have a turbot as
one grandparent and a soul from purgatory as the other, they are
tricky to mount since their wild nature—a worthy, special sentiment—protects them, at Puntela point near the Almirante rock and
in the shadow of the Holy Rocks a Panamanian-flagged ship with a
Chinese crew on board recently broke up, Telmo Tembura says it was

the *Good Lion* but that isn't true, the *Good Lion*, also Panamanian-flagged with a motley, mutinous crew of Greeks, Cypriots and Lebanese aboard, ran aground on the coast of Finisterre on the inner side of the peninsula, all hands were saved, no, this Chinese ship was a different vessel altogether the name of which neither Telmo Tembura nor I can recall, sure anybody would know the name of that vessel for she was wrecked only recently, her skipper was saved but her Chinese seamen all perished, sixteen or seventeen of them, not drowned but strangled by their non-regulation-issue life jackets, cheap substandard jackets which did not work properly, not a single one of them worked, well, the thing was that they worked the wrong way round, it was quite a paradox, the corpses were laid out neatly in the fish auction hall, looking like bluefin tuna, people went to gawp from idle curiosity.

"What did they say?"

"Nothing, they said nothing, some were suffering pangs of conscience, it's true, it also filled them with shame to look at the seafarers so solemn, neatly laid out with their Chinese eyes open two by two, the staff tried to cover them up for their consciences were troubling them, as I say, also because it made them feel ashamed to look them in the eye."

Madalena das Preseiras was burned at the stake, Madalena das Preseiras restored the flow of milk to the withered breasts of mothers and semen to the shriveled testicles of fathers, you may as well feed an open mouth, shortly before he was castrated, Dubliner Johnny Jorick took a posy of wildflowers to the virgin Locaia a Balagota, violets and oxeye daisies, the gorse bears yellow blossoms, as well as white and blue flowers, all of which are used to show love, the Austrian cargo vessel *Oscar* transporting maize, the Spanish fishing vessels *Gladiator* and *Pazoco*, the coastal cutter Mary and the Greek collier *Anastassis*, were wrecked on the Roncudo, all without loss of life, there were six coastal cutters at least, the one already mentioned and the others: the *Sisargas*, the *Everilda*, the *Corme*, the *Young Consuelo*, the *Felicity* and the *Franch*, that makes seven, the Portuguese woman Maria Rodríguez was burned at the stake because she confessed to being the wife of Satan and lover of Lucifer, the Carnota grainstore is the longest not only in Galicia but in the whole world, in not one of the five continents is there a longer one, Ana Rodríguez was burned at the stake because in order to combat paralysis caused by the love hex she used to prepare miraculous brews with herbs from twenty-one cemeteries and pebbles from bridges over which seven bishop princes had crossed, each mounted upon a white mule, the living swallowed up by the sea and those the sea gives up with seaweed in their eye sockets and gums are all hewn from the same block, Bernardiña Catoira was burned at the stake for turning newlyweds into rats or snakes, depending on what day of the week it was, Marta Fernández was burned at the stake because she cured contagious patches of mange on cows with the magical luck summoned from three droplets of wax, when somebody sneezes you must say Bless you! so that the devil cannot enter through their breath, sight, hearing or smell, Elva Martinez was burned at the stake for lying with the devil in the dungeon of those damned to burn at the stake, in order to cure females with the staggers, makes no odds whether ewes or women, tie the still bleeding head of a bat about their necks and they cannot sleep until it is removed, then rinse their feet with rosewater and say three Hail Marys, Fiz o Alorceiro, the Coyiños half-wit, took leave of his senses from the fright he sustained on Cabernalde hill, Fiz Labandeira is someone else altogether, he is the proprietor of the saltworks, there's no need to go on about things, clearing them up is enough, the figurehead from the *Serpent* was purchased by Don Paco de Ramón y Ballesteros, as I've already said, when I was hereabouts in the 80's we used to have coffee together every morning in Cee in the Hotel Galicia, run by Concha and José González, the *aguardiente* which flows from Father Xerardiño's still is second to none, Feliberto Urdilde beat my cousin Vitiño at arm wrestling but was killed by a blow to the head from a bottle, now he appears by night to widows to set them on edge.

"Do you know, my good man, how the film *Butch Cassidy and the Sundance Kid* ends?"

"No, ma'am, I didn't get to see it, for when I went to buy the tickets it was already sold out."

"And *Diamonds Are Forever*?"

"Nope."

"Same thing happened?"

"It did."

The city of San Mereguildo de Gandarela lives on beneath the waters and is thronged with the dead.

"Do they never appear to Christians?"

"No, ma'am, never ever."

In the Pedrullo, which lies above Pindo mountain, and in Moa, there are rocks which resemble dreaming, bewildered men and beasts, on the slopes of Os Aguillóns stands a naked woman, also made of stone upon which the moss drew flowers and limned patterns, the wind took charge of sculpting her and the damp of painting her, one night she said to the ghost of the San Xurxo priest:

"Look here, Father Xerardiño, Yours Truly is not naked, and may the blessed St. Roque call me to account if I tell a word of a lie, Yours Truly is swathed in the scent of dead whales which gives great shelter, it revives herring gulls perished with cold and octopus battered by northwesterly gales, you know, octopus are resentful creatures and suffer greatly when overlooked."

Cirís from Fadibón's capers caused Fiz o Alorceiro to lose his wits, Knut Skien took his nephew Hans E. Allen—Knut was also an uncle of mine—off to hunt Marco Polo sheep, which are reddish brown in summer and reddish grey in winter, Dick, who was the rich man in the family, wanted to build a house with boxwood beams, whims are not beyond the provisions of Divine Providence, but he died before he had the chance to, women whose periods are late should be given two ounces of apricot wine with a pinch of ash from the dung of a male wood pigeon mixed with fifteen stamens of saffron to drink for five days in a row, this works a treat, the coastal cutter *Franch* sank just south of the Roncudo off Estrela island, it was Don José Baña, the man who knows more than most about such skirmishes with the sea, who told me about it, he tells the story well, the priest in Morquintiáns is called Father Socorro, María Flora, his housekeeper, rules the roost from her cane rocking chair.

"Don't you think we're going from bad to worse?"

"Well, indeed, maybe so, a body wouldn't know how all this will turn out, as far as I'm concerned it's all to do with the Masons, a body wouldn't know why they won't leave well enough alone."

My uncle Knut Skien has one blue eye and one green eye, this happens in certain cats and mountain goats when they are about to go blind, when he grows lonesome my uncle Knut Skien sings verses from Poe and plays the accordion, whenever she can Doña Dosinda runs off to the cabin on Calboa point, she knows what she's up to, Doña Dosinda also does her sinning in the Dodge belonging to Micaela's Carliños, Feliberto Urdilde's soul flits forth from purgatory to sow remorse in the hearts of widows who drink too much coffee, some widows puff English cigarettes on the q.t., the Lady of Pindo is a woman of stone with a hairdresser's coiffure standing on the rocky road to Coloso, above Carnota beach, it was Marfany who gave her that name, in the parish of San Ourente of Entíns St. Campio the soldier divines the doubts of Finisterre man Luciano de Andrea who can make neither head nor tail of the behavior of women, oh, what a laugh, Auntie Louise, she let a fart beneath her chemise! the Xures half-wit runs errands for Father Xerardiño as a token of his gratitude and meekness, it's always a fine thing to see meek and humble souls, when the diaphoretic antimony is reverberating well veritable miracles can be wrought with the brains of a dolt, it's all a matter of putting your faith in God and praying an Our Father to the Holy Company so that the cherubim and seraphim may sound their trumpets and St. Rita may apply it to her own pious intentions, Xan from Labaña the Chainsmoker couldn't get a wink of sleep at night until Fideliño the Pig shot himself in the mouth up at the Five-fingered Woman crag, some frights end only with death, while others may remain with a man even after death, hunger makes women prattle without rhyme or reason, men fare better for they know that staring into a dazzling light is not the same as blind eyes devoured by sparks, eyes which will never look at you with compassion however entreatingly you gaze at them, vengeance grows modestly, routinely in the soul of the innocent, vengeance is slow to ripen, it's not enough to save money because you will never have enough to buy the bellowing of those condemned to death, those ignominious harbingers, waking the sleeper who is to be murdered is a proper thing for real men to do, remember that any old axe may serve to decapitate and also to sever the hangman's rope, God has magical scissors which may sever the hangman's rope, the noble squire wished to drown in gold, a vile wretch married to a very beautiful woman, but on seeing that he did not have enough he gave Niceto the hired assassin a few copper coins to tie him naked to Vela rock on the Great Lobeira island where the gulls devoured him alive, there's no point in not feeding an open mouth, the Cabalgada rock surveys the Finisterre sea from the top of Pindo mountain, it would strike the fear of God in you to pass beneath it, at Eira da Pedra those spirits which cause the hex can be scared off, the best is for an elderly widow woman who has mothered at least seven children—makes no difference whether they lived or died—for three nights in a row to light upon a newly fired tile a handful of bay twigs and aromatic herbs, and make the person bewitched leap over the flames nine times, four the first night, three the second and two the third night while she chants: all you dead who lie buried within these sacred temples, from without and within, from land and sea, from mountain and fountain from seven leagues around, angels all of you, give breath to the living and bring comfort to the dead, etc., the river Xallas is called Ezaro or Lézaro, the Celts lived between the Tambre or Támara, the river which flows into the sea in Noya, and the river Xallas, while the Nerians lived to the north of this, in the Tower of Moa there lies a gold hoard buried by the Romans, the thing is it never shows up, the sea requires its own knowledge, navigation would be even trickier if you were not careful and accurate, the sea requires great responsibility, the town of Malpica lies to the north on the road to Corunna southeast of Cape St. Hadrian and the Sisarga islands, some people claim that the Coast of Death stretches from Malpica to Carreiro point, at the entrance to the Muros estuary, some make it longer and some shorter, some make it bigger and others smaller, all depending

on their tastes and individual requirements, the town and port of
Malpica nestle at the foot of Atalaya mountain, they constructed a
floodgate at the harbor mouth so that the fishing fleet can shelter
there, although larger vessels cannot fit in, to the northwest lie the
coves of A Barrosa and O Boi together with the beaches of Area Maior
and Seaia, Cape St. Hadrian runs from A Pedra das Areas to Boleiros
point with its Seadog rock jutting from the waters in the lee of
Mount St. Hadrian, the hermitage stands halfway up the hillside
painted white and clearly visible from the sea, providing a useful
point of reference, the mountain is also known as Bao and del Castro,
the Sisarga islands lie off it, at low tide the Sisargas form one single
island while at high water they are three separate islands, herring
gulls, cormorants, bracken and eerie legends abound on the Sisarga
islands, on the Great Sisarga mermaids can still be seen bewitching
seafarers with their charms, Rostro and Chanceira points are their
favourite dallying places, on the island of A Malante or O Atalaieiro,
the second biggest, on certain stormy nights there appears the soul in
torment of Lieutenant Jack Essex, navigation officer on board the
Captain, the English monitor which went down on the Centulo,
many miles hence, over a hundred and twenty years ago now, thirty
other crewmen perished with him, the soul of Lieutenant Essex sings
sentimental ballads in a tuneful voice, everybody can hear them
either directly or with the aid of a solid-state radio, it's best to look
at one-eyed persons in profile, panic makes the hearts of those who
have seen many one-eyed persons pound fitfully or miss a beat, this
is an idea which comes and goes, the spilling of blood makes those
who have seen a great many one-eyed people drowsy, King Joseph
Bonaparte once appeared on the Lesser Sisarga island at the outbreak
of the Civil War in '36, there are somewhat garbled accounts of this
event which we have been unable to verify, caution should be exer-
cised when dealing with these oral traditions, Don Eudaldo
Vilarvello, Land Registrar, told me that the king had been a close
friend of General Cabanellas, Joseph Bonaparte was short in stature
although, indeed, fairly cultured and kindly, and he could distinguish
the passage of time and its significance from the incessant drumming

of the rain and its meaning, not everything means the same thing, King Joseph Bonaparte scoffed at superstition, love is a naive and beneficial frailty, King Joseph Bonaparte always knew that the gods did not bear with resignation the joyous spectacle of his happiness for flying high so haughtily, the old brigantine *Monckbarns* wound up in the coal yard in Corcubión harbor, the *Monckbarns* had a ghost on board, a ghost which used to light up the sea not with an oil lamp but with an electric flashlight, this ghost could be heard though not seen and would murmur the following phrase in English: Kiss the back of my hand as a mark of respect and the palm of my hand as a mark of gratitude.

"Do you know that for a fact?"

"Yes, sirree, it was told me by Susito, son of Suso the innkeeper in Xestosa, who is studying for the priesthood in Mondoñedo seminary, within two years he'll be saying mass, God willing."

The ghost forewarned of impending death by dropping heavy tools on deck, he was never wide of the mark, the irons would clang loudly and not a single death passed him by, the *Monckbarns* was broken up some years ago, breaking up a ship is like exhuming a cemetery which is always shamelessly carried out, and nothing further was ever heard of the ghost, maybe it died, nobody knows whether ghosts die like persons, animals and flowers, or maybe he went off to haunt some other habitation or even back to his home country, nobody can swear that that it is his own corpse because the dead are silent and discreet, ghosts are set in their ways but in spite of this they always vary their conduct a little, that's inevitable, men, too, although they copy one another a great deal, the dead smile only upon those who are about to die, it is like a forewarning that should be received with heartfelt thanks in a sincere and reverent spirit, Fabián Penela has been in the other world for at least three years now but he still appears each week at the spot where he was buried, in the Barizo graveyard, not far inland past the Co reefs, at times he appears dressed as a diver or a priest, or as Pierrot, this was where the yacht *Cachafello* foundered, her two crewmen were drowned, they were two young gents from Betanzos who had gone out for a spin, their bodies were swept away by the current and they were never seen again, Fabián Penela was known as the Moor because he looked like a carpet salesman from Murcia, swarthy with a little Moorish moustache, Fabián was always clumsy and uncouth, perhaps he had no finer feelings, Fabián mistreated Ofelita his wife and one day, when her turnip top broth turned out too salty, he pulled up her skirts to teach her a lesson, plonked her down on top of the red-hot stove and roasted her rump, they had to rush her off to the clinic where they dusted her down with antiseptic powder, Fabián the Moor has been dead for over three years now and his soul appears every week in the Barizo graveyard, it springs to mind that today, the Feast of St. Athanasia and St. Demetrius, is the anniversary of the battle of Aljubarrota in which King John of Portugal defeated King John of Castile, I touch upon such historical considerations mindful that wild rhubarb steeped in goat's milk whey serves to soothe itching in the male member of infantrymen, it was already in use in the infantry regiments of Flanders, this memory did not spring of its own accord but was triggered partly by Paulo, my seventh son, partner to Macías de Lourenza in the kiosk on Santa Isabel beach in Corcubión, which has a loyal clientele among the summer visitors, this son of mine got a clip on the ear from a skeleton in Beo graveyard, in the lee of Cherpa point, and it gave him a hell of a fright.

"Should the viaticum be administered to a racing cyclist?"

"Indeed, why would you not give it to him?"

"I don't know. What about to a footballer?"

"Him too, the viaticum may be administered to all dying persons who have faith in God."

"Is it usual for the dead person to appear to the priest when he goes to fetch the Holy Oil?"

"I don't think so, it happens from time to time but I don't think that it is usual."

One day on the stony slopes of Caldelaxes I spied a sorrel colt looking like a prince as he trotted majestically with his neck arched, defiant and proud, it is not the same to grow in patience and wisdom as in fear and ignorance, the just man rises each time he stumbles but the poor wretch wallows in infamy and never manages to get back on his feet again, the vessel *Boedo y Ponte* sank on the sandbar in the Corme estuary with her cargo of timber, her skipper and three sailors perished, the crew of *El Compostelano* had to abandon ship one day in a strong southerly gale with gusting crosswinds, only the ship's cat remained on board, *El Compostelano* drifted, narrowly missing the perils of the sandbar, sailed into Cánduas, went up the Allones or Ponteceso river, a manoeuver normally requiring some expertise and, skirting the island of Tiñosa, made it to la Tellería, nobody quite knew how, maybe the ship's cat, guided by the Virgin of Carmen, was standing at the helm, the English schooner *Adelaide* was sailing from Bristol to the West Indies with one passenger and thirteen crew on board when she ran fast in Laxe and they all perished save the skipper, whose wife and son also perished, the skipper ordered a tombstone to be raised beside the atrium of the church, but now it is languishing in a garage grimy and neglected, it is a sad thing to see how memories fade away, lunatics should be given dogs' brains to eat, the magnetic transplantable properties of dogs' brains are effective in correcting imbalances, the best is the brain of a local mongrel with a spot on the head, neither too big nor too small but, rather, medium-sized, they are known to have more harmonious transversal radiotherapeutic atoms and molecules, in contrast cats' brains may induce madness or epileptic fits because on many occasions they harbor the devil, there is no way of telling in advance, although it would be highly convenient and useful to know this beforehand, Insua point or Cape Laxe closes the Corme and Laxe estuary to the south, here the fishing vessel *Playa de Arnela* foundered and ten seafarers perished, from the sea you can see Laxe cemetery quite clearly, the far north of Insua point is a cliff, the Laxe do Boi and Lavandeiras shoals fill the air with spume, Catasol point provides shelter from northeasterly winds and Traba beach which is a mile and a half long may be approached only on a calm sea because it lies in the shallows, Moncho Mínguez had a stepbrother in the missions called Cristobiño, others called him Cristobaliño, who converted heathens under the merciful assumed name of Narcissus of the Divine

Bonaventure, Brother Narcissus used to sing Corcubión drinking songs in a fine voice, the Otavalo Indians would chortle when they heard him, allow themselves to be baptized without resistance, then afterwards they would get drunk on moonshine, piss and spit in the wineskins the better to ferment it, *Oh, St. Peter is a glutton who lets nothing go to waste, he eats the best of mutton and leaves bare bones upon his plate,* Cristobiño would have liked to become a missionary bishop, one of those fellows prancing around in white vestments returning home to Galicia every fifteen or twenty years to be interviewed in the local papers, Fabián the Moor and Ofelita fought like hammer and tongs, not that this is uncommon between husband and wife, it happens in many marriages and nobody bats an eyelid, that's just how things are, other couples don't get on well yet don't get on badly but restrict themselves to ignoring one another and resign themselves to their lot, now that she has been widowed she can breathe easy without fear, most women are widows because nature protects them and is on the lookout for them, not that the law does as much, nobody is obliged to become good all of a sudden, it's enough to become good little by little, Don Gabriel Iglesias, retired secretary to the town council, jailed after the war for being a sort of freethinker, argues that it is not couples who fail but, rather, the institution of marriage which is obsolete and functions poorly and less effectively all the time.

"It's ridiculous to enter into a contract for life, the limits of marriage should not exceed those of a lease, for instance, marriage should be for a period of three, five or seven years renewable by mutual consent, in order to avoid disputes the children would always remain with the mother unless by specific agreement to the contrary, that's the sensible way mammals behave, thus the male does not have to be the mirror of another male, furthermore the position of honorary spouse could also be instituted with all the benefits accruing from patience and privilege due, she would cede the nuptial bed, though not total control, to the executive spouse, one wife in bed and another in the dining room and wine cellar depending upon the agreement, marriage should be like a private company, family businesses require

renewal of structure in order to render them flexible and effective,"
there are five family businesses which affect us most: the whaling
station with its mystery and foul smell, not to mention blood, the
canning and salting works with their ups and downs, the sawmill
with its wounded screeching, the shipping company with its uncer-
tainties, and marriage with its attendant risk, wishing to work boxwood is a whim that carries its own cost, whims are not simply
dished out free of charge to anyone, everything carries its own consequences.

When a body renounces the principles of faith, they can wind up
excommunicated, oh, laurel that sprouted without our planting,
remove the hex from this excommunicant, the Forked Crag is also
known as the Cleft Crag, whatever takes your fancy, the three other
sacred mountains are the Tower of Moa, the Mount of the Moors and
the Castle, Don Gabriel Iglesias knows full well that the creation of
the universe is represented by the double helix which is in some way
related to the cosmogonic egg whence the serpent hatches, quaking
rocks sway and strike fear with their motion, Winkle knows of some,
the one in the Zapateira mountains in Canle de Laxe, the Swallow
Rock on Santa Leocadia mountain in Foxo beside the Sacred Spring,
the Rocking Stone in Mantiñán which rocks like a cradle and the
shelving rock below Castelo de Veiga with its Fonte da Virtude, quaking rocks have a magical air about them and seem to be moved with
great gentleness by the Holy Spirit without toppling over or tumbling
down, the Holy Spirit is the head honcho over us all.

"Good night to you, may God be with you, could you tell me
what time it is?"

"I have no watch, good lady, pardon me, but it must be about 8
o'clock, the sun is already high and has not yet started to grow."

On the beaches stranded rorqual and cachalot whales, some sickly and others wasting away, let themselves be torn asunder without
even pleading to be slaughtered first, the fowls of the air and beasts
of the mountain cannot finish off the rorqual and cachalot whales
but dismember them bit by bit, they cannot kill them cleanly and
humanely, if you pray to St. Bartomeu of Maceda swellings are

reduced and if you petition St. Bieito da Cova do Lobo at times the health of those suffering at the hands of the vile hobgoblin who spews forth spite improves and they even gain weight, an echo does not repeat the voice of a soul, nor can its face be seen in a looking glass or reflected in the waters of a spring, the boatmen of purgatory suffer as they weave their way through waves of remorse in their fickle, fragile barques of boxwood, which, as we already know, barely floats and smoulders slowly, Florinda Carreira, wife of Angel Macabeo Verduga, the Monteagudiño drug dealer, looked like the older sister of Joan of Arc, she had a gravelly voice, big boobs and feet, was tall and stoutly built, resolute, bold and fearless, all she needed was plate armor with a silver fleur-de-lys, nothing could stand in Florinda's way, Florinda would marinate partridges, quails, sardines and tuna to perfection, she was also a dab hand at baking sardine turnovers and puff pastries filled with angel's hair which she baked to a T, up Corunna way they call sprat brisling, Angel Macabeo died possessed by the devil in the throes of hideous torture and suffering, they had to tie him to the bed so that he couldn't smash the whole place to smithereens: the coffeepot, the portrait of Franco, the television, the refrigerator, the map of Spain, the map of Europe before the First World War with its border of little flags, just about everything, it was to no avail that his wife commended him to St. Euphemia of Arteixo, Pepa the Vixen has only to look sideways at pullets in order to kill them, she leaves them in a squalid state, and can sow a shoddy streak in folks without anybody being any the wiser, Celidonia Cabarcos, the Castriz healer, purges possessed people with julep and smokes them with gold, incense and myrrh which are luxury aromatics, Celidonia keeps a tame crow which can whistle the first few bars of a two-step, before that she had another one which she had to drown in a bucket of kerosene because he shat on the Holy Bible, Celidonia couldn't get the better of the demon in Angel Macabeo, he was truly headstrong, you can cure wasp and scorpion stings with wormwood which grows on the summer pastures of San Cibrán and when uprooted it withers straight away and lasts no time at all, Cassandra the witch has signed on for social security as self-employed and is also up to date with her municipal taxes, nowadays it is not like the old times and witches make both political and sporting predictions: Real Madrid will soon win the European Cup again, nowadays there is well nigh a register of witches, the wisewoman of Baíñas can even cure T.B., cancer, too, if caught in time, Pepa de Juana in Finisterre is a dab hand at getting rid of goiter, Ermitas in Portonovo makes barren females fertile: mares, heifers, she-asses, nanny goats, ewes, women, while Aurora in Caldas de Reis cures lumbago and rheumatism, Marujita in Pontevedra withers warts and shrivels fistulas however malign they be, witches can give the saints a run for their money if they ally themselves with the devil, though nothing of the sort may be supposed about any of the aforementioned witches, here on the outer edge of the world, on this very border separating what is from what is gradually coming to pass, only miracles allowed by God and those wrought through tradition handed down from father to son are believed in, you can ward off the devil only with prayer and fasting and in an alliance with him you always lose out because he pays buttons for souls, less and less every time, it is not the same thing to command veteran soldiers as sheep or swine, when an infantry captain is killed in the war his loyal troops do not douse their torches until his funeral is over, you mull things over and suddenly you realize that Don Gerardo's Marina transformed inertia into swift efficiency, you can put back the clock if you rock it to and fro wisely and lovingly, Don Gabriel Iglesias is a friend of my brother-in-law Estanis, once one of them said to the other, it doesn't matter who said so to whom, that the art of homely, hierarchical, municipal, idle, remorseful, maybe even solicitous daydreaming is unworthy and too bewildering, there are certain things which, out of compassion, cannot be requested, more than likely whichever one of them it was was perfectly correct, Feliberto Urdilde, Fabián Penela, Fideliño the Pig and Floro Cedeira the cowherd gather to play cards on the rocky shores of Arou where the English collier *Daylight* foundered without loss of life, their ghosts flit through the air and the sea spray does not drench them nor is their deck of cards blown away, this business of the dead playing cards is a sure sign that the soul is

ready to leave purgatory, it is a common state of affairs among people with names beginning with the letter 'f'': Francisco, Feliberto,
Filemon, and others, they do not engage in promiscuity, indeed the
ways of the dead seldom allow for this so it hardly ever occurs, the
dead have great respect for traditional ways and are not generally par-
tial to innovation or license, Macías de Lourenza, the fellow who has
a half-share in the beach kiosk with my son Paulo, is marrying a very
beautiful girl of means by name of Lucila who is studying pharma-
cology and is the granddaughter of Don Eudaldo the registrar, Macías
is thinking of giving up the beach kiosk and setting up a restaurant
on the highway, I see my son Paulo out and about, granite is the
noblest of rocks, even nobler than marble and quartz, granite is the
only rock respected by sea, wind and rain, lightning may split though
never destroy it, granite is destroyed only by gulls, God grew weary
of keeping Chubby Manteiga, the Prouso Louro half-wit, among the
living and summoned him to his presence, before this he told St.
Peter:

"Reburdiños no longer requires an oracle, Chubby has done his
duty, so send him off to burn in purgatory for a few days, then bring
him up here and you can put him in with the cherubim."

Father Xerardiño the priest smokes like a chimney, we pals of his
hold that he'll wind up with lung cancer, Father Xerardiño the priest
never stops smoking, ever since he went blind for farting while saying the Our Father, Liduvino the traveling laborer wanders around
romerías singing ballads about criminals hanged on the gallows and
begging alms for the love of God, the whales continue on their way
paying no heed to the monotonous misfortunes of men, in that
respect they keep their own counsel, there are no sharks swimming
in these seas for they seek out warmer waters, Don Sadurniño uses
green ink to jot down wise sayings in his notebook, scores of folk
pass off cuttlefish as squid, souls always play card games with a
Spanish pack, French cards suit them less, hereabouts nobody speaks
French, swallows are revered because they plucked the thorns from
Christ on the cross, whoever harms a swallow spits in the face of the
Virgin Mary, there are some who say that God cut short the life of

Chubby Manteiga because he saw that he was just one step away from getting out of line, but I don't believe a word of it, to my mind Chubby was always obedient and respectful, it is frowned upon for black people to foretell the future or restore whites to health, everything in its rightful place, that is something which would be frowned upon by anybody, if a black man cures a white man of bad luck the cured man is mocked while the black man is reported to the Civil Guard, what people dogged by bad luck must do is to steer clear of tomfoolery and light a candle to St. Lazarus and another one to St. Vitorio of Begonte, you cannot trifle with your health, your health is more readily lost than regained and may take some time to recover or perhaps never return, your health is no lottery but a tussle between life and death, you need presence of mind in order to care for your health and administer it to best advantage, the soul dwells at peace within a healthy body, Belarmino Bugallo retired from sailing because he was growing long in the tooth, now he's on the lookout for an obliging, shapely lass to keep him company, you know what I mean: knead dough, simmer broth, fry eggs, roast rumpsteaks, stew squid, wash clothes and selflessly keep him warm at night, she also has to be hale, hearty and able to play dominoes and parcheesi, Belarmino now works as a locksmith in his brother Pepiño's forge for he has a flair for metal work, he has the knack of gauging weight by the eye, a kilo more a kilo less, more often than not he is spot on, Belarmino and Pepiño have another brother who is the wealthiest and most respected in the family: Father Xiao the priest in Esclavitude over Iria way, they knackered his nag so now he lumbers to funerals on the back of a lad from Lampai, St. Polonia is the patron of toothpullers and bloodletters, Laracha leeches were famous all over the world until they went out of vogue, nowadays leeches are hardly ever used to lower blood pressure and stabilize the system, some twelve or fifteen years ago there was a spook in Almendralejo, some two leagues from Torremejía, Pascual Duarte's hometown, who would slip into houses in the early hours of the morning and grope the balls of men in their marriage beds—genitals was how the newspapers put it—so the locals formed a militia to patrol the area but they never managed to capture the spook for he invariably gave them the slip, between the Condemned Men reefs and the Castrillones shoals shortly before the First World War there foundered a Normandy barque painted blue and white, *la Belle Ginette* or *Jeune Ginette*, I'm not quite sure which, to my mind nobody really knows because some say one thing while others another, she had a tame crow on board which used to perch upon her mizzen mast, not a jaunty storm petrel but a lugubrious land bird which lived off the sweet, scented worms in the timbers, for over a year *la Belle Ginette* had been crewed by dead men who, by dint of a miracle wrought by the Virgin of Carmen, were not thwarted by maggots so that they could continue blindly sailing their day's run, when at last the vessel struck the rocks and began to sink, the souls of the dead sailors crouching on the poop deck—nowadays it is generally called the quarterdeck—leaped ashore and set off for purgatory, not one soul among them had to go knocking at the gates of hell, in some mountain villages, Vilachán, Morquintiáns, Touriñán, the ghosts of these Normans kept prowling around for a long time, they also pilfered eggs from hencoops, some nights they would get into bed with folks, not with a view to sinning but just to keep warm, when big, fat Celso Mancelle, coachman to Don Fiz Labandeira, killed his wife by suffocating her with a pillow, some ghosts from the crew of the barque appeared to him in prison to frighten him and poke fun at him, every night they appeared to him two by two and would draw a gallows on the wall and a cross upon the ceiling marked R.I.P., on this coast facing the endless ocean we can all acquire patience and wisdom, Germans of old used to say that two nights prior to reaching the Dark Star of Finisterre the sea would destroy sailors on the coast, almost invariably on Regala Point, that is what has been happening for a long time now, across from the Paxariño de Fóra and Turdeiro rocks, a little southeast of the Centulo with its lamenting.

"Shrieking?"

"Yes, shrieking and howling, too, sometimes."

The unfaithful mermaid who was not forgiven by the oarsman from the fishing smack *Xibardo* told him the last time she saw him:

"I never thought that you would make me pay so dearly for my unfaithfulness which was not caused by lack of love, Farruquiño you shit, I never thought I would do so but now I curse you and wish you dead, may you drown in the selfsame sea where we were so happy! I'm off to Ireland and may I never lay eyes on you again!"

There are highly passionate, vengeful mermaids who swim south of the 43rd parallel in particular which crosses the Finisterre peninsula from Alba point in the Outer Sea to the Crags of the Crows, almost in the inner bay, in the Outer Sea every summer some tourist or other drowns, swept away by the current, Miguel hated his father and Amadeo empathized with his son, it is easier to despise a son than to admire a father, you cannot laugh at the funeral of your father though indeed you should weep, however unwillingly, at the funeral of a son dead and destroyed through a misfortune as widespread as smallpox, at the funeral of his son Miguel who was found dead from an overdose with the needle still stuck in the crook of his arm in the gents in the Bar Martin, heroin is a hard taskmaster, Amadeo Gosende's mind was elsewhere and thinking of this, philosophy scrawled in human excrement, excrement of body and soul, serves little purpose for in the end stubborn death is preferable to humiliating repentence, which is generally insincere, also to the monotonous path of righteousness.

"Could you tell hatred from pity?"

"I don't believe so. What about you?"

"No, not me."

In Niñones bay, north of Escorrentada point, Miss Elvira López Villalba drowned on the eve of her wedding day, that afternoon she went to have her hair permed and to visit her grandmother, Enriqueta, her mother's mother, who could no longer stir from her rocking chair, Elvira's body was swallowed up by the sea and was never seen again.

"Could you tell disdain from admiration?"

"Yes, perhaps I could. What about you?"

"No, no matter how hard I try, I certainly couldn't, you have to be highly ingenious to solve these moral mazes and I'm a tad on the dimwitted side."

It is only reasonable that the haughty, fortunate man is tolerated while the foolish unfortunate is not, when the waters erode the earth's crust a cove, or rather a very small bay, is formed, the last ones to burn in the Cove of the Scorched Corpses were the twenty-three crewmen of the Russian oil tanker *Vladivostock*, they didn't even have to be buried, that morning the dolphins were leaping strangely in a way that was hard to interpret, like goats turning pirouettes or slavering lapdogs, the French fishing vessel *Noll-Zent* went down without loss of life on the Arou reefs, the English freighter *Saint Marc* sank without loss of life on the Pedra do Sal, *virgo fidelis ora pro nobis*, the Greek collier *Maria L.* sank without loss of life also on the Pedra do Sal, *per omnia saecula saeculorum*, the English cargo vessel *Ribadavia* sank without loss of life on Capelo point, the German vessel *Barcelona* laden with casks of wine sank without loss of life at the very same spot, the sea bass tasted of wine for quite some time, the Dutch dredger *Rosario no. 2* sank without loss of life on the Santa Mariña shoals, it's a relief to stop reeling off the dead, the seafarer's trade is already tough enough in its own right, Policarpiño, skipper of the coastal cutter *San Fernando* was swept away by the sea on Cagada Point, three sailors drowned with him, the English collier *Trevidere* was also lost on Cagada Point, one man perished, the colliers *Modesto Fuentes*, a Spanish-flagged, and the *Alekos*, a Greek vessel, went down in the Cagada roads, what a pain! though without loss of life, Pierre Durand the boatswain and Nocencio Estévez the galley hand on board the French packet *Saint-Malo* wrecked on the Aforcamento rock were the only two drowned, all the others—the skipper, officers, seamen and all the passengers— were rescued but the galleyhand could not escape, he was staring through the captain's porthole when he realized it was too late to make his getaway, the boatswain fractured both legs so it was impossible to move him, the fishing boat *Julita* struck the same rock as the *Serpent*, a fisherman was dragged overboard by a purse seine which was too heavy and got trapped beneath the net, master netsman Farruquiño Quintáns plays the march of the Ancient Kingdom of Galicia better and better, there is nothing he cannot play on the pipes, he has a masterful touch, Farruquiño Quintáns also likes

Mexican tunes but doesn't say so to anybody so as not to cause a distraction, it was night in the lonesome October and my memories were treacherous and sere for we knew not the month was October, why did we not know that the month was October? without a doubt the verses of Poe sound better in Galician, what Farruquiño cannot play is the accordion, will the notes of the accordion sound far and wide? will the cachalot and rorqual whales hear them? Farruquiño Quintáns made himself a new redingote last year and always sports a plaid peaked cap, between the Yugueiz and Moteiz mountains there lives a sturdy Marco Polo sheep called Alexander, I named him Alexander the minute I laid eyes upon him, you could tell straight away that this was his name, nobody can catch Alexander for he can scale heights where a man can no longer catch his breath and his courage will fail, Alexander is five years old, with enormous horns and a defiant or pleading look in his eye depending on the time of day, the temperature or his spirits, at twenty-five Alexander will have died of old age if he isn't killed before then, at twenty-five years of age you should no longer play rugby, in the Hunslet Boys there are only three players older than that, winger James E. Allen gave up playing for good at twenty-five years of age because he felt himself getting on in years, a quarter of a century has a more solemn ring to it, with a quarter of a century behind him a man may be youthful depending what for, for a bullfighter indeed though not for a rugby player, my cousin Vitiño Leis is courageous, tough and daring, my cousin Vitiño Leis is Doña Dosinda's obliging male friend and he also accepts gifts, males of all species accept gifts and let themselves be loved, the wolf, the fox, the wild boar, it is a way of showing their strength, the stones speak a language which is not always understood, there are men who have better hearing and men as deaf as the stars in the heavens above who speak only through signs, the rain and hail also speak a mysterious, garbled, almost impenetrable language, Trece Cape is also known as Tosto Cape, it lies at the end of Boi point where the rocks cover and show and confound the seafarer, the Baleas de Fóra and the Baleas de Terra rocks where the sea sorely lashed the ensign flying on the English freighter *Iris Hull* which lost thirty-seven men, the Quaking Rock in Muxía sways only if you are in a state of grace and remains motionless if you are skulking about in a state of mortal sin, but to return to what we were talking about: one night in a northwesterly gale the English steamer *Diligent* split her propeller shaft and her crew had to abandon ship, that they reached the coast in lifeboats was as much a matter of good luck as dogged endeavour, by hook or by crook the German tugboat *Newa* managed to tow her to Corunna where she could not make it over the Guisanda shoals and sank, Don Antonio Maroñas, owner of the freighter *Vicente Maroñas* which was wrecked on the Espiritiño rock, became a wealthy man by dint of hard work, scrimping and saving, "When I was a poor slip of a lad they all called me Tony, now that I lack for nothing I'm Don Antonio," his father, Vicente Maroñas, is still alive and kicking, he can neither read nor write but smokes a clay pipe and likes to listen to the wireless, he can hardly see the television because it makes his eyes smart, during the First World War—I was one year old at the time—cod fishermen from the Finisterre trawler *Aurora* saw a German submarine detain the Portuguese cargo vessel *Cabo Verde* in the Arboliños fishing grounds and blow her sky-high when an English cruiser hove in sight, her entire crew came ashore in Santa Mariña, some say that when the *Iris Hull* was wrecked, a long century ago, her crew lashed a harpoon fast to a line with a bowline knot and cast it into the sea so that people watching from the shore could catch it but the villagers—let's hope this is merely malicious gossip and has no grain of truth in it—severed the rope and took it home with them while the Englishmen drowned one by one, the captain of the *Iris* took his own life by slitting his throat, the English steamship *Loss of the Trinacria* struck the Lucín shoals, seven men were swept away by the sea and washed ashore alive and well while thirty others perished and their bodies had to be set on fire because they could not be disentangled from the mangled metal in which they were trapped, these were the fellows who lent their names to the Cove of the Scorched Corpses, the last to burn there were Russians from the *Vladivostock*, around the area the story goes that a dog helped the shipwrecked men until it collapsed from exhaustion, Celso Tembura invited me to have snow crab, baked sea bream, fried songbirds, pork pasties followed by pancakes, then afterwards presented me with a stuffed owl, I brought the wine, the *aguardiente* and cigars, a fresh breeze was blowing from the sea and apart from the fright of my companion suddenly being taken ill—later on we realized that it had been nothing of any great consequence—the feast we sat down to was second to none, thanks be to God for letting us enjoy life! we sent to Santiago for girls, the red-light district boasts quite a variety, the girls were Portuguese for we didn't have the dimes for French women since they charge a higher price and are more demanding, the other three present at the feast asked me not to divulge their names since they have no wish to get into trouble and I understand them perfectly.

"Do you go to confession every time?"

"No, not every time, every two or three times, there's no need to exaggerate, discretion is the better part of valor."

Father Xerardiño, the priest in San Xurxo, works miracles as easily as you could steer a bike with just one hand, all very naturally and almost smiling, Father Xerardiño is dead but hardly anybody notices, Father Xerardiño hears confession from whomsoever has sins to confess, plays cards with all and sundry, dusts the cobwebs from the two frying pans he keeps hanging on the wall and sings free of charge at masses for lost seamen, and cooks hake Galician style: you chop it into chunks and fry it over a high flame with some sliced onions and a few bay leaves, you almost scorch it while separately you prepare the fried onion garnish—garlic sauce is what Father Xerardiño calls it—with fried garlic, a dash of olive oil and sweet paprika.

"You can say what you like, but to my mind this all seems very jumbled, well, garbled, really."

"No, it is not garbled at all."

"As you wish, I won't gainsay you."

One of the friends at the party—and there is no need to name names—took a turn for the worse and we had to drive him to the doctor's in Corcubión, we traveled in the Dodge belonging to Micaela's Carliños which took ages for the car was leaking oil and also had a slow puncture, along the way the sick man was shivering, vomiting and bleeding from his ears, there were moments when we were scared stiff yet at other times we were laughing merrily, Dolorinhas, one of the Portuguese girls, came with us for she was some sort of a nurse and knew how to take his pulse and administer injections and enemas, my brother-in-law Estanis is very tall, it gives me a crick in the neck just to look at him, to be a schoolteacher you don't need to be very tall but in order to become a basketball player stature is a great help, my brother-in-law Estanis is a pal of Recesinde the priest and has a preoccupation with sins of the flesh which may incur dire consequences: blenorrhagia, syphilis, eternal damnation, nowadays there's also AIDS, of course, when the *Maria Laar* was wrecked a Civil Guard pilfered a cheese almost the size of a grindstone and gave it to a sailor to send home to his girlfriend, nothing further was ever heard of either the cheese or the sailor, the Civil Guard was trusting rather than suspicious and lost the cheese as a result, on stormy nights country people scour the coast in search of flotsam and jetsam, Father Xerardiño smokes like a chimney and hides butts all over the place, Rosa Bugairido took her own life by throwing herself into the sea, in midair she had no time to think of anything because her ears started ringing, though this is merely a supposition, we would all like to understand the mystery of death, the thing is that God remains tight-lipped and doesn't usually tell men anything, perhaps this is free will and we all clutch at doubt like a straw, my uncle Knut Skien hunts the rorqual whale with ancient skills and conducts experiments in recreative physics burning phosphorus under water.

"I drink the animal's blood because I respect it, I mix it with rum to strengthen it and remove the venom, I kill not for killing's sake but in order to live, the soul of the rorqual whale is released with the last drop of blood in its body and mingles with my soul."

Fideliño the Pig sneaked like a fox up to the Five Fingered Woman rock and shot himself in the mouth, he tumbled down the slope and the birds of early morning pecked out his eyes and tongue, Floro the cowherd believes that the sound of the sea comes and goes with the pulse of the veins in his head but it isn't true, the sound of the sea has always come: whoosh, whoosh, whoosh, the cyclist Gumesinde was killed in the Civil War and did not live to see the

Allied victory, the cyclist Gumesinde was a sort of Anglophile, like a colonial big game hunter, but he kept this under his hat because there's no need to express such sentiments, now there's good breeding for you, when he stopped playing rugby for good his uncle Knut Skien took overseer James E. Allen off to hunt Marco Polo sheep, Knut Skien was also my uncle but he never took me along.

"You've enough on your plate what with horseback riding and dancing the two-step, you can't have it all."

"True."

"Marco Polo sheep harbor within them the soul of a Mongol warlord.

"Manchurian surely?"

"Alright then, Manchurian."

"Afghan even?"

"Alright, Afghan."

Behind their horns Marco Polo sheep conceal the fury of ancient warriors from those mountainous parts and surrounding countries according to the four points of the compass, those borders are highly confusing, the Altai and the Alatura have neither beginning nor end, some ancient women from Arévalo still recall Timoteo Gutiérrez-Enciso, St. Paul's disciple who wrote the diaphanous *Book Of Splendor* in Aramaic, on the Lesser Lobeira island the English vessel *Derventwater* was wrecked laden with fruit and two of her sailors drowned, Antona Vougo the Campelo witch is known as Stag Beetle because she always dresses in black, mourning is the color of respect.

"What about contempt?"

"Contempt too."

"Weariness?"

"That too. As well as intolerance, obstinacy and indifference."

Antona cures the flux by placing upon the kidneys of the patient cobwebs stewed in wine vinegar with a thimbleful of dust from the baker's oven, if the blood is flowing from the nose the remedy is placed upon the nape of the neck and if the bleeding is trickling from the mouth, in other words, if the patient is spitting blood, they should confess to a stoutly built priest, not a scrawny priest—where consumptives are concerned one skinny person is already more than enough—and do penance with certain devotion and unction, Marco Polo sheep can scale greater heights than any other land animal, as high as any soaring bird of the haughty heights, some birds of prey and carrion eaters weigh up to seventy-five pounds, on the Great Lobeira island the Spanish vessel *Francisca Rosa*, laden with salt, and the English vessel *Skuld Stawange*, laden with minerals, both foundered, Antona Stag Beetle told my uncle Knut to be wary of the laborer Pauliños because he wanted to poison him with laboratory products, some substances destroy the body without even leaving time to vomit them up, the Norwegian freighter *Blus* sank without loss of life off the Caneliñas factory, when James E. Allen gave up playing rugby Moncho Méndez, I mean Mínguez, had not yet castrated Dubliner Johnny Jorick, the event became a great talking point and in general Moncho's conduct came in for severe criticism, James E. Allen, the overseer, red-haired and freckled, is English although he looks like an Irishman, he also has willpower problems and ups and downs in his understanding, James plays the accordion masterfully perched upon the wall of the whaling station gazing out over the sea, which you should never turn your back upon, James patiently plays jigs, polkas and rigadoons, with both enthusiasm and resignation, he's like the Grand Old Duke of York, a little farther north the fishing vessel the *Río Tambo* foundered and two seamen were lost, my uncle Knut told James and me what Antona Stag Beetle had warned him:

"That is what the woman told me, it's surely true but I believe you should be somewhat cautious with laborers, indeed, though not overly so because they are not dangerous, they are just mean, but what you must not do is to allow them put on airs and graces, I don't believe they are dangerous Bolsheviks but you must not let them get above themselves, an uppity laborer can be a nuisance and you may have to give him a lash of the whip, Pauliños is not a bad sort, merely shy and bashful and wants to fight against his way of being, against his tendencies."

Off Cape Nasa which lies just above Carrumeiro island, there sank without loss of life the Spanish coastal cutter *Nuestra Señora del Carmen* and the English steamer *Country of Cardigan* with her hold crammed with corn, the dolphins grew sleek and contented.

"There are two types of men: the ones who upon waking believe that their dreams were pure, vain illusion and the ones who dream while awake, and these are the most dangerous because they believe themselves capable of anything and would let themselves be killed for an idea or a whim even, that Pauliños is just a wretch who gets above himself from time to time."

Through Cornwall, Brittany and Galicia there wends a way strewn with stone crosses and nuggets of gold.

II

ANNELIE AND THE HUNCHBACK

(WHEN WE GIVE UP TENNIS FOR GOOD)

ANNELIE FONSECA DOMBATE, known as the lass from Mosquetín, although hardly anybody calls her that nowadays, widow of the philatelist Don Sebastian Cornanda, the man who was killed by a freight train when he was sauntering along on horseback over the Osebe level crossing, his mind was elsewhere you see, is having a love affair with a hunchback who smokes grass, knows every single star in the firmament and understands a thing or two about the mysteries of astrology, is a good pastry cook—his almond custard and tiramisu are becoming quite famous—can read palms as well as cards, is knowledgeable about wines and cheeses and can juggle seven oranges or seven bottles all at once without dropping them, he now looks after the late Don Sebastian's stamps, the wealthy man in my family was Dick the brother of Cam, my maternal great-grandfather, Dick hunted whales off the Azores and wanted to build a house with boxwood beams but didn't manage to because time ran out on him, in the Corcubión area the Spanish freighters *Ereza*, *Gijón* and *Maria II* sank as well as the Greek colliers *Constantino Pateris*, *Manoussis* and *Mont Parnass*, no lives were lost, in the waters around Carrumeiro the sea is treacherous and surges strongly, Annelie's hunchback is called Vincent Goupey and he is a Frenchman, well, he is presumed to be French even though he has no documentation for he lost his papers in the shipwreck though neither the Civil Guard nor the naval headquarters have ever asked to see them, we'll take your word for it, there are days when Annelie calls him Vinny or Vince, this hunchback was an ordinary seaman on board the brigantine *Aurore Chaillot* when she foundered off Mozogordón beach in Ponte do Porto and he was the

sole survivor, while a foul fate befell the others, even though it is a
sheltered spot and fairly safe, not that the sea was surging there but
the dynamite which the ship was carrying exploded on board and
they were all blown sky-high and sent hurtling to purgatory together, Dubliner Johnny Jorick was castrated for treading on the toes of a
municipal guard, well, he wasn't a guard quite yet, shortly before
reaching the Camariñas anchorage, between Insuela and Lingundia
points under the lee of Trasteiro peak the coastal cutter *Bonitiña* ran
aground and broke up, leaving the cabin boy—who was the owner's
grandson—trapped down below, his name was Nuco Gundiáns and
he was twelve years of age, Vincent Goupey speaks both Castilian
and Galician fluently, hunchbacks generally have a flair for languages
as well as for games of chance, the lottery, sweepstakes, dice, bingo,
they also bring happiness and ward off misfortune, Vincent allows
lottery tickets to be passed over his hump in return for tips: five
cents, ten cents, or twenty cents, in bed Annelie tenderly calls her
hunchback "my wretch," once Annelie's needs have been met, she
folds down the sheet and Vincent creeps off to sleep on the rug, he
wraps himself in a blanket and uses a cushion from the sofa as a pillow, when Annelie taps him with the flyswatter Vinny passes her
slippers—that's one tap—or the chamber pot—two taps—some
nights Vincent fondles himself by candlelight because Annelie likes
to watch him jerk off, now it seems more appropriate to call him
Vinny.

"What about Vince?"

"That's more appropriate for discussing his character."

Vince is shyly capricious but obliging, he likes to serve and obey,
Vince is compliant and enjoys submission, perhaps he harbors a cautious criminal within his breast, he becomes calm when serving and
obeying orders.

"Without reserve?"

"No, with a certain reserve."

My Norwegian uncle works in the Caneliñas factory, he is also
the uncle of James E. Allen who no longer plays rugby because he is
getting on, he now plays tennis and can do so until the age of forty or
forty-five.

"What then?"

"Then we'll see, that all depends."

The Pedras de Xan sandbank and the low-lying Galiñeiros shoals hoodwink seafarers and punish the imprudent, the coastal cutter *Bitadorna* went down in these waters with her six crewmen.

"There were seven of them."

"Alright then, with her seven crewmen."

Vincent reads Albert Camus and has autographed photos of Edith Piaf and Catherine Deneuve, Annelie allows him to keep them but does not let him place them on display, Vincent likes to assist at masses for the dead whenever they are held, to place flowers on the high altar, accompany the viaticum and play checkers, the cloud demon is scared away by the pealing of bells, while the thunder demon is held in check with a sprig of sweet bay which has been blessed, hobgoblins give us nightmares while wicked elves sap the health of animals, the devil appeared to Vincent one night while he was saying the rosary with Annelie, but Vincent scared him off by praying louder and lighting a lamp to St. Pito Pato, patron of stuttering pilgrims, St. Pito Pato is more shabbily attired than Carafuzas or any other cacodemon but he doesn't give a hoot for he has always turned his back upon human considerations and stories of agathodemons, St. Pito Pato was struck off the martyrology by the second Vatican Council along with St. Fiz of Valois, patron of the lame, and various others besides, Braulio Isorna told his neighbour Leonor that he wouldn't hang about with Ricardiño since he was a sort of a halfwit, you cannot even take simpletons to mass because they run around the choir and giggle and piddle during the sermon, when the devil spits in the baking flour or upon freshly laundered bed linen it is a sure sign that you should first of all air out the house and then have it blessed, the book of St. Cyprian recommends taking two lion's eyes aired by the light of the moon in crescent quarter, etc., now that's hard to do for there are no lions along this coast—not that there ever were any for the sea scares them away—every year Vincent sets off for San Andrés de Teixido, where everyone goes on pilgrimage once in a lifetime whether alive or dead, Annelie and Vincent are not married because he has no papers nor does he wish to apply for

them, Dorothy, my great uncle Dick's wife, is a woman of strange
ways, her husband shows great patience towards her, preferring to
bend over backwards, maybe she'll wind up throwing herself out of a
window, you never know, my great uncle Dick had three brothers:
Cam, Shem and Japheth, I'm descended from Cam, my grandfather
and father were also called Cam, the three of them hunted whales
and never got on well together, none of them was of good character
and all three were greedy and avaricious, the Chinaman Li Piang-
tung took the name Adrián Brenaing alias the Uzbek because he pre-
ferred to pass unnoticed, an ancestor of his reached the Caroline
islands before the explorer Toribio Alonso de Salazar but didn't
breathe a word to anyone, a century later Papin invented the pressure
cooker, Braulio was a pal of Vincent's and used to swap stamps and
even prephilatelic marks—his house was full of them—in exchange
for Lugo chorizo—great, big sausages bursting with onion—and
Arzúa cheese, the fishing vessel *Siempre Perales* sank on the Sisarga
islands, her five crewmen were rescued alive, Ricardiño was a brother of Leonor's and somewhat slow on the uptake but he attended
school and knew the names of a number of European capitals, could
add, subtract and multiply though not divide, although he never got
as far as the three times tables, there are five names which are
accursed: Barabbas, Satan, Cain, Herod and Judas, and they are all
lurking around these latitudes: Barabbas on Farelo mountain, Satan
on Fonfría peak, Cain in Facho Lourido, Herod in Leixón de Xan Boi
and Judas at Casa Santa point, each one of them disguises himself as
best he can, as animal, vegetable or mineral, makes no difference, in
the San Xurxo graveyard will-o'-the-wisps hover and glide, to see
them so much at ease brings respite to the soul, the sailing ship *Bella
Edelmira* sank with her cargo of cookies on the Fusisaca rock which
the tides cover and show north of Roncudo point, three sailors perished, not by drowning but when the foremast split and struck their
heads, the Sedes sorceror cures cataracts by beseeching assistance
from St. Peter and St. Rufina, Hail Mary full of grace conceived without sin, I am not vengeful though rancorous indeed, I am like an alli-
gator and seek revenge without resentment, coldly seeking revenge

just for the heck of it, the three pillars of Spain are the Christians waging war, the Moors tilling the land and the Jews trading, as well as gypsies buying and selling horses, rogues cheating and missionaries baptizing heathens, the art of playing the accordion is quite confusing, Vincent is nimble-fingered but cannot play the accordion, he's a better hand at the mandola and in particular the banjo which is an up-to-date agreeable instrument, the bodies of the wife and son of the skipper of the *Adelaide* appeared locked in a tight embrace, clutching one another lovingly even in death, in Ponte do Porto, too, the women make lace, Annelie deftly clicks her lace-making pins while Vincent reads bestsellers aloud to her, taking care with his intonation and even gestures, Camariñas lace is made all along this coastline from Corme to Muxía, Annelie chuckles quietly as she thinks of Vincent and the pleasure he gives her, oh, love of mine with your twisted legs, little rounded belly and the hump upon your back, a sailor from Noya whose name escapes me inquired with great respect:

"Did you know, sir, that the Devil appeared in the Goa stream last year, just above Gómez point? He took the form of a medium-sized turtle with his head engulfed by St. Elmo's fire, with flames streaming from his eyes and lightning flashing from his tail, he sank two flat-bottomed punts just by looking at them, did you know that?"

"No, I did not. Nobody told me about that."

On board the *Aurore Chaillot*, a small but splendid ship, a well-appointed vessel, Vincent kept the galley shipshape and knew how best to stow the provisions, Vincent always provisioned with oranges and lemons in order to prevent scurvy, the gums of the men on board never rotted however long they spent at sea, in the village of Aplazadoiro all the dogs were found dead one fateful morning, that was an ill omen because afterwards the children—not that there were many to begin with—began to die one by one, their dead bodies revealed a clean bite mark with three perforations on the throat, nobody had heard any commotion and the Civil Guard in Vimianzo were unable to get to the bottom of it, Vincent told Annelie that he suspected the culprit was a shipwrecked mariner from the Russian submarine *Igor Yavlinsky* who had turned into an owl and was lurking about those parts, with their black arts the officers turned themselves into owls and the ordinary seamen into jellyfish, Annelie told him that it was better to keep this under his hat for nobody would pay him any heed, there are certain matters in which outsiders should not meddle, plantain is a magical herb which grows in the gardens of certain witches, if you bind the feet of a sick person with plantain leaves, you stem the flow of collywobbles running willynilly down his leg.

"Do you know where to find Leonor's brother Ricardiño's pet crocodile?"

"No. It hid in one of the three springs in Tufiones and nothing has been heard of it ever since."

Pedro Chosco cures warts with the greatest of ease, Pedro Chosco throws open both doors of his house, the person with the wart enters through the door on the north side, casts a handful of coarse salt into the fire in the hearth, leaves a rye loaf and a quart of *herb aguardiente* for the healer, says what is required of him: Warts I bring, warts I bear, warts I doff, now I'm off! and then he departs, as clean as a whistle, through the south door.

"Did you know that St. Vitus' dance in widows may be cured by eating cod braised with new potatoes, red peppers, carrots, onion, garlic and parsley?"

"So Adega told me but I don't believe it."

If the Holy Ghost were a bat instead of a dove our religion would not be the one true faith and there would be fewer Catholics, and if he were a magpie or a jackdaw there would be none at all, the devil appears in the guise of a billy goat whose rump you kiss as a mark of homage and respect, the Holy Ghost could have been a swallow but not a cormorant, the form taken by the Holy Ghost is well thought out, you immediately see the hand of God in it, Father Xerardiño, the priest in San Xurxo, supposes that the form might also have been a butterfly in all the colors of the spectrum, between the Curbiños shoals and Escorrentada point there lies the Pedo Muiño rock which shows at low tide, the brothers Teodoro and Leoncio Quindimil play dominoes and card games better than anyone, they are true masters of the art, Vincent believes they cheat but wisely holds his tongue for you can never be too prudent, the Holy Ghost never took the form of a land animal, he must have had his own reasons for not doing so, to have followed that line of conduct, the Holy Ghost could only have become a lamb or a rabbit which are shy, gentle creatures, I do not overlook the fox or the haughty, quarrelsome rooster, proud and pugnacious, the Christians drew a fish on the wall of the catacombs but that is a very ancient representation and is no longer understood, Teodoro Quindimil is a master builder, he now has the contract for the slaughterhouse and the school building, his brother Leoncio has a store selling domestic appliances and a gymnasium with a sauna, they gave my cousin Vitiño Leis a gift of a new radio, everybody knows that it was Doña Dosinda but he won't admit it, James E. Allen has many years ahead of him in which to play tennis, Vincent would also have liked to play tennis but he does not have the physical capacity for it, hunchbacks cannot play tennis because they hit the ball sideways, it's quite funny to watch, the most they can play is badminton since the amusement caused is more charitable and indulgent.

"Shall we play a game of badminton?"

"No. I'm French so I prefer bowls."

Annelie dines upon fruit and curd, she likes greengages and peaches as well as strawberries and blackberries while Vincent eats string beans with bacon or fried sausage and boiled chestnuts, he seldom varies, he has to be careful not to fart because he would get a lambasting, Annelie is persnickety and won't allow anything gross or coarse, Annelie can blow her top without warning, a sudden outburst, and then she calms down once more, the Lesser Carrumeiro island is known as the cemetery of Greek ships, for many came and perished here and their crewmen came ashore spick, span and beaming from ear to ear, with their jackets just so and smart new suitcases, they did not look like shipwrecked men, but maybe Lloyds of London has some information up its sleeve about that, Corpiño mountain up in Muxía ends in the spur where the Sanctuary of Our Lady of Barca stands crammed full of votive offerings, there is no room to squeeze another one in, the Virgin appeared to the Apostle with the Baby Jesus in her arms in a stone boat rowed by two blonde angels with cropped hair, then they all flew out and the boat turned into the Dos Cadrís Rock, if you pass beneath it you can cure any ailment of the bones and certain complaints of the spirit, as well as afflictions of the lungs, belly and other innards of the human body, three sailors perished while another five were swept away by the sea in the wreck of the Danish merchant vessel *Charm* outside Spanish territorial waters, four crewmen managed to survive, Vincent is careful with the stamps which Annelie inherited, he does not handle them but lifts them with tweezers and tries to store the albums in a dry place, Vincent grows tobacco and marijuana, dries the leaves in the hearth and smokes them in roll-me-owns, he adds a little sugar or honey to his cigarettes and rolls them flawlessly, with great precision and poise, Ptolemy called the constellation of the Swan the Bird and Vincent knows that, as the stars move, so the passage of life and the ups and downs of love and death may be divined, Cósmede Pedrouzas the deaf-mute was holed up in his shack for several days with a fever, his wolf brought him back a wild rabbit which he ate, while the bear fetched him a cabbage and some potatoes, he kept the fire burning in his shack, embers glow for quite some time and if you throw pine cones on them you can fan the flames back to life, Ricardiño was exempted from military service on account of being rickety, Ricardiño is not too bright although you couldn't say he was a half-wit altogether, only a sort of a dimwit, Ricardiño works in Leoncio Quindimil's store loading and unloading goods, he cannot drive the delivery van because he is not allowed to nor is he fit to do so, once he cranked up the motor and drove the van straight through the shop window, after that they kept him working for two years with no pay and gave him a beating to boot, they tanned his hide, kicked his ass, shouted abuse at him and drowned him in spittle, they also rammed his head down the toilet to teach him a lesson— all quite natural—Ricardiño sweeps the store, runs errands, brews coffee and cooks up goose barnacles and blue crabs, Ricardiño has neither contract nor social security and some Saturdays he does not get paid at all though, in general, they treat him well, viewed from the north from Cape Trece and the Baleas de Tosto, Cape Vilán looks like the backdrop for a Wagnerian opera, solemn and theatrical like a cardboard cutout, it cannot be far short of a hundred meters above sea level, the lighthouse is perched at the very top while halfway up the hillside looms the silhouette of the old ruined lighthouse, on the stony ground of Arneliña large-uddered nanny goats with huge horns crop the grass, glaring warily at any passerby, Cape Vilán ends in the Estrufo, a quirky outcrop of rock with an imposing outline, while a short distance offshore there lies the islet of Vilán de Fóra where only small boats can slip through the channel separating it from the coast and that only at high tide, farther offshore lies the perilous, hazardous Bufardo rock, Farruco Pedrosa, the Merexo mariner who fell overboard from the motor launch *Three Pals*, spent an entire night there, Farruco was swept overboard in a sudden squall but latched on to the rock like a limpet and held out until the following morning when they managed to throw a line to him and rescue him, nobody can figure out how he lasted so long, how he did not weary of being more dead than alive, drowned men float belly up, drowned men indicate currents and tidal streams, phenomena which can sometimes be variable, some drowned men return to land of their own accord while others have to be fished out once it is possible to do so, though sometimes not even that is possible, there are also those who are lost forever and later forgotten or disintegrate into the sea little by little, the unruly nature of the sea throws a spanner in the works of legal proceedings, the Civil Guards have certain forms to complete yet sometimes they aren't able to, parish priests and County Hall secretaries also require evidence and proof, Barnacle is an inveterate liar, he spends his life spinning yarns which hardly a soul believes, although he himself does, Vincent pares a few slivers of local cheese, then spreads a dallop of quince jelly between two slices, coats this with flour, beaten egg and bread crumbs, deep-fries it in oil, leaves it to drain, sprinkles it with cinnamon and sugar and eats it hand in hand with Annelie who, as a reward, often allows her breast to slip from beneath her dress, on Cape Vilán the English colliers *Begoña*, *Tumbridge* and *Travessie* foundered without loss of life, as well as the aforesaid *Loss of Trinacria* which lost thirty men, while seven were rescued, her boatswain hanged on his own belt, the Norwegian coastal lugger Sirius with seven lives lost, the Italian colliers *Ciampa* and *Brignetti* without loss of life, the coastal cutter *Lourido* from Arosa with the loss of five men, the Finisterre dragnet trawler *Loliña* with her entire crew of seventeen drowned and the Spanish freighter *Duró*, the Liberian freighter *Yaga*, the Portuguese coastal cutter *Yale Hermoso* which was carrying tobacco and a French floating dock which broke her moorings because they misread the signal: the fellows on the tugboat raised the A pennant: Is the mooring holding? and the fellows on the dyke replied using the same pennant: The mooring is holding, which wasn't true, some of these vessels were spared loss of life, the end to this litany is still unknown, indeed it probably has no end, the ships of the sea carry their stories with them, some even their tales of love, hate, commercial, political and maritime intrigue, the history of the world could be told with deadly accuracy by totting up self-denial and resentment, envy and altruism, but the history of the world will never be written because man is an impatient, highly-strung creature thriving upon sensation.

"Do you know anything about church history?"

"Not a lot."

"Do you know anything about natural history?"

"No."

"Do you know anything about general history?"

"I don't, I hardly studied at all."

Ariadna, the sweetheart of skipper Don José Eutelo Esternande, drowned off Caldelaxes point, the skipper could not find happiness thereafter and arranged for his body to be buried at sea when his time came, Ricardiño had a pet crocodile but lost it in Tufiones, he slipped it into one of the Mouriño springs and it was never seen again, it was as happy as could be, Leonor is Ricardiño's sister, the two of them live together and she takes care of him, sees that he washes and eats properly, Leonor works as a house cleaner wherever she's needed and at times she sleeps with Teodoro and Leoncio Quindimil, generally on Mondays, they shut up shop, send Ricardiño off on some errand or other and dally with her upon a piece of oilcloth spread on the floor of the store to ward off the damp, they pay her sixty *duros**, give her chewing gum and chocolate, they've also paid for two abortions, for Leonor wouldn't have been able to care for a child, Adega carries out abortions, all very hygienic too, Vincent can read the lines in the palm of your hand, he can interpret their length, their shallowness or depth, the sudden breaks and ruptures in them, he is generally right for this is a highly scientific skill, he also reads the cards but does not always disclose what he sees there for Vincent has no wish to be a harbinger of doom, Adega has faith in the healing powers of certain foodstuffs, especially cod, Floro Cedeira cures rheumatism, lumbago and cramps with raw octopus, though you've got to chew it well, Adega cures respiratory complaints with raw cod, digestive disorders with fried cod, waterworks trouble with baked cod and nervous complaints with braised cod, neither spinach nor Swiss chard should be overlooked for they have great thermodynamic, reflective value, over two hundred years ago, just below Cape Vilán, the frigate *Cantabria* sank, H.M. the King's Mail from Corunna to Buenos Aires, and the body of her skipper was washed up in Coenda still clutching the tiller in his hand, having perished on board ship as was his duty he would not relinquish command even after death, fifteen other men also perished with him, Vincent has a fine palate for wine and strives to keep it in top form, Braulio Isorna does not hang out with Ricardiño but does not turn his back upon him if he chances upon him, Ricardiño enjoys company but is almost always alone, nobody willingly seeks out the company of a half-wit or dimwit, the first thing you have to do in order to win the heart of a mature woman is to spruce yourself up, young lasses are less demanding since they are more needy, Telmo Tembura tells me that the French naval dock did not sink on the Baleas shoals, she didn't get as far as sinking because they man-

---

* *duro*: five-peseta coin

aged to save her first, what happened was that she was unable to ride out the northwesterly gale, the high winds chafed through her moorings and cast her adrift but when the storm abated this monstrosity was towed to Ferrol, her crew made landfall on the Dor da Man rocks, amid the goose barnacles and wrack which the sea bestows, in these waters where the *Cantabria* was wrecked the Moroccan flagged vessel *Banora*, with a cargo of oranges on board, also ran aground, the sea changed color because it was awash with oranges, also the U.S., formerly German, steamship *Black Arrow* which was used in part-payment of debts from the '14–'18 war, with general cargo, passengers and over a hundred crew on board, all of them were spared, they managed to refloat the *Black Arrow* and she was repaired in the Ferrol shipyards, during the civil war there was an Italian division called the *Black Arrows* which was not held in high esteem, the French know a thing or two about cheese and Vincent was no exception, Galicia has good cheeses if you know where to source them, not a wide variety but good nevertheless, although somewhat unpredictable, somewhere in these isolated parts—though nobody can tell me where exactly—the famous Captain Tiengo, an adventurer from Tenerife who stood up to Drake, had his hideaway, Don Anselmo Prieto Montero, Professor of Latin in the Corunna Institute, penned a highly entertaining novel about this character and his seafaring escapades entitled *The Diving Bell* which was well written, flowing, graceful and captivating, his narrative style would remind you of Pío Baroja, what a pity that he could not find a publisher and that on his deathbed he ordered the manuscript to be burnt. I was unable to dissuade his heirs, they assured me that to alter the last will of the deceased, etc. etc., toads that have their eyes stitched up must be burned so that they do not wreak cruel revenge, toads with their eyes stitched up are rancorous indeed, that business of the sinking of the tanker *Aegean Sea* was a real catastrophe, like a curse from God: the *Aegean Sea* struck the Torre de Hércules rocks as she was heading for the oil company pontoon and spilled almost eighty thousand tons of crude oil into the sea, those black waters tainted nearly two hundred miles of coastline, Vincent also reads modern novels aloud to

Annelie, she is fond of love stories for they are the same over and over again, just like love itself but that is no bad thing, out in the open sea there were other more minor shipwrecks: the sailing ship *Rosario*, the Portuguese pilot cutter *Delfina* which went down on the Boliños da Fortuna rocks with a group of actors on board, when the thespians saw they were doomed they all got drunk and dolefully sang *fados*, the collier *Luz*, the schooner *Santa Rosa de Lima* and the captain's two wives, both called Consuelito, and maybe another one besides, you ward off the devil by making the sign of the cross, the world and his mother know that, the ghost of the Chinaman Adrián Brenaing the Uzbek slumbers on Farelo mountain hidden by Barabbas, some young priests like to request a little light petting in the confessional, it's both fun and reassuring to see how young girls blush, some chuckling softly, some young priests reek of smegma and hair oil, Vincent is a nimble juggler, no orange ever falls to the ground, he is also a conjurer and can pull a rabbit out of a top hat, though he's not so skilled at hypnotism, hunchbacks have many uses, but perhaps they're not much good at hypnotism, Micaela's Carliños is clumsy at tennis, he would like to play better but he does not apply himself so that's out of the question, James E. Allen has difficulty finding a tennis partner, you need to devote time and a certain enthusiasm to this sport, Micaela's Carliños drives a ramshackle old Dodge which barely trundles along, he will have to repair it before it is too late, the repairs could cost a pretty penny and may not be worth the trouble, Carliños' Dodge is put to multifarious uses, both decent and indecent, it stands outdoors in the lee of a rounded boulder and some nights the wind shakes it to bits, it is a delight to have the windows tight shut and your arms around a woman, even an elderly one, at the height of the storm that's the least of your worries, Vincent teaches French to children in the municipal school while in exchange he learns Galician and speaks it quite fluently now, the children in the catechism class are the same as those from the public school but their ways are different, Vincent knows nothing about French grammar but he skirts around it and gets by, Annelie's slippers have a colorful lotus blossom embroidered on the toe, when

Annelie taps him once with the flyswatter Vinny fetches them for her, Vinny likes to obey, it yields the conscience great serenity, submission is the mold which shapes character, scapulars filled with verbena blossom help win battles of love, the French brigantine *Franlla* was sailing from Havana and she sank on the Villueira reefs, below the Virgin of the Mount point and Portocelo cove, the corvette *Constancia* struck the rocks on Carnicería point, Vincent cooks vegetables, fish and meat just to Annelie's liking: greens in salad or plain boiled—hereabouts overcooking is generally the order of the day— fried fish, roast meat, he roasts the beef to a T, like the English, his stews are spot on, not to mention his desserts, he is renowned for his rice pudding and custards, he also runs the house like clockwork, hunchbacks are highly intuitive, he keeps the store cupboard shipshape and allows nothing go to waste, you can chuck whatever you like into pasties and croquettes, look after the pennies and the pounds will take care of themselves, Vincent pronounces it "cocrettes" and so does Annelie, in this cooking business you can say whatever you want, Annelie is not exactly respectful to anybody but she has no hidden perverse tendencies, she is just slightly off the rails, Annelie was widowed by a freight train, Don Sebastian Cornanda might have paid more attention to where he was going, fewer and fewer people call Annelie Fonseca Dombate "the lass from Mosquetin", some nicknames fall by the wayside, fall into disuse, a wave swept a Philippine sailor overboard from the deck of the Panamanian vessel *Aruba Jade*, Moorish pirates have not been the scourge of the Galician coastline for several centuries now, Saracens is what Don Anselmo Prieto calls them, later on the English came, Captain Tiengo also fought bloodthirsty Harry Pay, the man who hanged a prisoner before breakfast each morning because he liked to watch them wriggle and writhe, we Galicians fortified Louro mountain and other dominant points, culverins have an accurate aim and are readily moved, we also managed to bury the bells so they were not stolen to melt down for cannons, it's all the same bronze, bronze is a noble metal with many uses, in Minorca they even minted coins from bells, it was a delight to hear them ring out when they clinked

against the counter, Vincent is a dab hand at games of chance and is
lucky in the lottery, this is the case with all hunchbacks, San Simón
cheese is smoked with birchwood, it vexes Vincent that greater care
is not taken with Cebreiro cheese, James E. Allen plays tennis, before
that he used to play rugby, when we give up tennis for good it will be
a sign that we are growing old, getting on in years, the calendar never
goes backward, you can tell straight away that it harbors ill will, St.
Tramunda from Pontevedra lends encouragement to the heartsore,
you light a candle to her so as not to be overwhelmed by the blues,
the Moors of Abderraman II abducted her from the village of San
Martiño and carried her off to Cordova, after many years the blues
got the better of her and the angels brought her home once more and
deposited her in Poio, Floro Cedeira the cowherd cannot see himself
in the mirror because he is dead, dead though not buried, Micaela's
Carliños has a natural inclination, although he lacks the means, to
live as a gentleman of leisure, will undoubtedly counts for a great
deal though it's not the full story, will is but a tool which brings
things within man's reach, you need other merits besides determina-
tion, Micaela's Carliños is not overly fond of hard work, they had to
turf him out of the factory in Caneliñas as a lazy layabout, he did not
a stroke of work so they were left with no option but to boot him out,
dead rorquals stink to high heaven and attract swarms of flies, rats
scurry up the ramp, the dogs kill as many of them as they can,
smooth-haired fox terriers are clever, courageous and cunning fight-
ers too, there are lucky dogs and ill-starred dogs, it's the very same
with people, just as there are good-natured dogs and cranky dogs,
some old rats stand up to them while others plunge into the water or
scuttle beneath mounds of guts, the fishing vessel *Rey Alvarez II* was
wrecked northeast of Corunna, two fishermen plummeted into the
water from the rescue helicopter and were drowned when the winching gear broke down, the other six crewmen were rescued, Vincent
was born on October 26 so that makes him a Scorpio, the newspaper
says that his horoscope is still under the influence of the goddess
Fortune, boosting his thyroid gland and bringing a surge of optimism
and high spirits, hunchbacks bring good luck and ward off misfor-

tune, Annelie calls him my little shred, my little tatter, and whips up
eggnog with port wine to give him strength, the German tanker *Nord
Atlantic* sank in the Camariñas estuary, tainted the waters and killed
off a great many shellfish, on Buitra point the Liberian-flagged
steamship *Bristol* and the *Monrovia*, with her cargo of several million live silkworms in their cocoons, were wrecked, her entire crew
of twenty-two perished, all of them black except for the captain who
was an Irishman with the Ursa Minor tattooed upon his forehead,
accordions from the *Salier* still wail across the waters down off
Corrubedo point, my friend the canned food manufacturer Jesus
Martínez tells me that in these waters there swim jellyfish with
umbrellas five meters in diameter and huge octopus which prey upon
sea bass and angler fish in deep water and which only come up to the
surface to bask in the sunlight, though there is not much sunshine
hereabouts, there is one gigantic octopus which he has named the
Fawn Fox, which greets him by waving two or three of its tentacles,
Jesus Martínez and I do not know whether octopus hunt or fish their
prey, at times we think one thing while at other times another, Jesus
also tells me that there are also gaudy, highly voracious female
sharks but I don't see that this could be true, I never heard tell of it
from anyone else, Besta Cantigueira the bird is as big and as noisy as
an airplane and has wings sheathed with nerves of boxwood, she flies
only on moonless nights and steals lambs, kids and small children,
she can swoop down the chimneys of houses, the Greek vessel
Ionion with a cargo of scrap iron on board sank on the very same spot
as the *Bristol* with her silkworm cocoons, the *Inogedo* from
Santander ran aground on the Habilidosa shoals, something strange
must have occurred for it was a clear day with a calm sea and fishermen working in that area warned her that she was heading off course,
but boats have their whims and do not always respond, the helmsman of a sardine smack even fired a warning flare but the *Inogedo*
took no notice, one day when Annelie was in a bad temper, and
sometimes this can arise as a result of constipation, the water in
which splinters of boxwood have been boiled is often a good remedy,
well, one day when she was in a foul mood, Annelie sought out the

photos of Edith Piaf and Catherine Deneuve and drew moustaches on
them and spat on their autographs, Vincent pretended not to notice
and slipped off to arrange the flowers on the high altar, Jesus
Martínez had highly fanciful notions, for him the sea was like an
open book where everything was recorded and might easily be read,
the pity is that Jesus died an ill-starred old man without jotting down
his findings and inventions on paper, St. Crispin is the patron saint
of cobblers, St. Crispin converted the poor to Christianity by repair-
ing their shoes free of charge, in some places it is customary for Jews
to become shoemakers and tailors, my great grandfather Cam and his
brothers Dick, Shem and Japheth were always at daggers drawn and
never treated one another with either affection or respect, those who
lingered on in this world prayed for those who departed for the next
world but nobody ever saw them weep, the hunting of whales sun-
ders a family and sows countless seeds of doubt, fostering neither
sense nor style since nobody ever wants to back down, whales have
names which are not always recalled by the harpoonists and quarter-
ers, my great grandfather gave me a gift of a fob watch, a compass, a
sextant, a barometer and a thermometer, resolve was all I lacked, the
Panamanian steamer *Nuño Galante* with general cargo on board
foundered on the Forcados islets off Cubelo Point, her entire crew
were rescued except for two seamen who were swept towards
Carnota beach, the Xures half-wit runs errands for Father Xerardiño
who slips him a lemon candy when he goes to confession, the
Norwegian collier *Svea* foundered on the Buxeirados shoals and her
thirteen crewmen were rescued, the collier *Antonio Ferrer* ran
aground on the very same spot and also foundered without loss of
life, Jesus Martínez was knocked down and killed by a taxi in
Santiago, he was well over eighty but still in fine fettle and had gone
to Santiago to have his eyesight tested, the *Alfonso Fierro* foundered
on those selfsame shoals, her twenty-eight crewmen did not manage
to save their belongings but indeed their lives were spared, that was
back in 1933, and some years later, in '75, the oil tanker *Ildefonso
Fierro* with her port side breached listed into Llagosteira for survey
and to decide what course of action was to be taken, with appropri-

ate precautions and assistance she managed to make the shipyards in
Ferrol where she was then repaired, the mishaps involving these two
boats with such similar names gave rise to confusion, Vincent assists
almost unctuously at mass, masses for the dead are the most heartfelt and affecting, the lust in people is stirred at masses for the dead,
awakening gently at first, then turning feverish, capricious even,
Vincent also plays checkers and dominoes and plays patience with a
deck of cards, Jesus Martínez's widow sold me some of her late husband's personal effects: a telescope, binoculars, opera glasses, a lady's
lorgnette, a pair of reading glasses, a blue glass eye, some charts from
the Naval Hydrographical Institute, a beautifully bound edition of
National Episodes by Pérez Galdós, and two sets of false teeth which
were in good condition although a shade on the small side for me, she
could have given me these mementos as a gift, that's true, but she
didn't, though I should add in her defense that she was not comfortably off, on Barca or Xaviña point the collier *Mina Sorriego* foundered
and her eleven crewmen perished, also the fishing vessel *José
Antonio Lasa*, with the loss of another eleven souls, only her skipper,
swept overboard from the bridge, was rescued, and the *María del
Carmen*, another fishing vessel from which two men perished, sometimes the difficulty lies not in reaching land but in not being swept
offshore once more, seaweed makes the rocks slippery and it is hard
to keep your balance until the bitter end before exhaustion wears you
down, Don Gabriel Iglesias believes that marriage should be for
renewable legal terms, at the burial of my friend Jesus Martínez there
were three priests singing with a throng of mourners behind them
and everybody, not just the neighbors from the parish and surrounding villages, trudged to the graveyard and attended his requiem mass,
people loved and respected him for he was always openhanded, charitable and helpful to the needy, Pelegrina Romelle was a keener and
forewoman of keeners, she hired her keeners on favorable terms and
conditions and then made them weep ceaselessly and with great feeling, funerals at which Pelegrina keened were renowned for their
solemnity and resounding send-off: Farewell my little saint! Father to
the poor and wretched! My treasure! My good man! Light of my life!

at any moment, when everybody least expects it, the question can
crop up just like a flower or a seashell and somebody asks:

"Tristán or me?"

I can't remember whether it was me or Tristán, Celso and Telmo
Tembura's cousin, who said that at times the whales swim so close
together that you cannot fish with a boulter because the hooks
become entangled and get destroyed, to my mind this does not appear
to be an exaggeration although perhaps to others it does for folks are
distrustful and suspicious, the collier *Emilia Mallol* ran aground on
the Garrido shoals in Touriñán without loss of life, on Boi point the
Spanish cement ship *Begoña* foundered and five men perished, the
English collier *Begoña* which we have already mentioned was in
point of fact named *Punta Begoña* and she foundered over half a century earlier in Cuño cove at the very spot where the poet Bernaldín
de Brandeñas heard the trilling of the last goldfinch in the west, as
youngsters in Iria we used to play a type of baseball without a ball in
which we would ask, Is there smoke in your house? and answer, No,
in my house there's only light!, and then scatter like hares, forearmed
with patience and a hunting knife, James E. Allen carved a boxwood
skateboard as a present for Luquiñas, Tomasita Silvarredo's boy, she's
the woman from A Gudiña, everyone has their reasons and ideas
about things, as well as their own ways of courting the mother in
order to win the daughter, from time to time James E. Allen heads up
to Corunna to play tennis at the club, A Gudiña produces hale and
hearty lasses as well as fine sausages which cure well over there since
the weather is inclined to be cold, they also produce a tasty goat's
cheese, A Gudiña lies in the Tameirón area on the very fringes of
Galicia, it was the birthplace of San Francisco Blanco, later crucified
by the Japanese, *San Francisco Blanco born and bred in Tameirón,
tired of herding goats went and croaked it in Japan*, the three-
wheeled skateboard which you can sit on, used to be carved from
pine with an axle of willow or oak, but James E. Allen wanted
Luquiñas' skateboard to be made from boxwood, the whale has weak
eyesight and no sense of smell, on the other hand it has sharp hearing and brains to burn, why, it is nearly as smart as a wildcat, Tristán

Suárez Tembura spent some time in Buenos Aires and now works in
the Caneliñas whaling station, on building maintenance, or main-
taining what is left of the buildings, he dances the tango awkwardly,
though he claims to be a good dancer but it isn't true, Florinda
Carreira, wife of the drug dealer Angel Macabeo Verduga, knows that
her husband was poisoned but with proud compassion she holds her
tongue, there is no call for the judges to find out everything, and
there are certain matters which not even judges should know about,
men are not reaching agreement with regard to whaling and will
wind up wiping out the entire species, when he wishes to talk to me
seriously my uncle Knut invites me to have a glass of sweet vermouth.

"I've told you so many times, Cam, all we know is killing whales
and once we polish off the last of them we will starve, nowadays we
have nowhere to fight beneficial wars, wars are waged only among
the poor who are already well used to suffering. Here in this whaling
business either countries reach an accord and comply with it or we're
all doomed and will be scuppered for sure, I know the Japanese have
to eat but I also know that they cannot eat everyone's share, the
whale has a more placid nature and sincerer ways than man."

At the Lourido leading light, between the Buitra and Cachelmo
hills, there lived one winter a French hermit called Brother Anselm
who was swept away by the wind one stormy night, they say that he
was last seen flying past in the direction of Touriñán.

"Did you know that only Cornish, Breton and Galician hermits
can fly on the wind?"

"So I heard my father say."

"Did you also hear him say that the devil serves hermits from
those three countries as a trusty retainer?"

"No, I never heard him say that."

"Small wonder, for it isn't true."

Maybe it scares Vincent to have his papers in order, while you do
not have to there's no reason to comply with the regulations, the second Vatican Council struck many names from the sanctoral calendar
especially those saints who came in pairs: Cibrán and Xustina,
Modesto and Crescencia, Xeminiano and Lucía, or in a group:

Eustaquio and companions, Martiña and companions, Ursula and companions and so on.

"Was there a surfeit of saints?"

"It would appear so."

The bird Besta Cantigueira's wings creak as she flies, some women miscarry on hearing her flight because the sound gives them the creeps like scraping whitewash on the wall with your fingernails only louder, Jesus Martínez, the canner, shot an entire roll of film of the octopus Fawn Fox but declined to show the photographs to anyone, his widow told me that she had never seen them, Oliviña Lousada, the jellyfish, would speed through the water, and when she came to a halt she looked like a Japanese woodcut, delicately shaded in subtle hues, the goose barnacles used to sing a lovely song to Bastián the rorqual whale: *Bastián, Bastián, riding on a hound, the hound then fell and tossed him down a well, the well made him shiver so he tossed him in the river, the river was all surf so he tossed him on the turf, the turf was all shorn so he tossed him in the thorn, the thorn made him sore so Bastián let out a roar, and the good hound ran no more,* Eudosio the cachalot whale used to devour squid galore, at times he even gobbled up sharks, though dolphins are not so easy to catch for they are agile, swift and very smart to boot, Eudosio also used to tell dirty jokes in English and could whistle into the bargain, these five happy campers of the great outdoors and the stricken, windswept sea are neither friend nor foe, they each know the others' strength and their territories are clearly defined, they do not seek strife but prefer peace and pretense which are civilized virtues, the sea always remains and does not move from where it is, it sways to and fro but does not edge beyond its borders, the sea does not come and go but has always come: whoosh, whoosh, whoosh, like the old age of man and beast, of oak tree and gorse, if Leonor were willing Braulio Isorna would allow Ricardiño to hang out with him, but Leonor was not willing and Ricardiño continued to hang about on his own, whistling and scuffing the stones, over a century and a half ago now throughout Galicia there roamed many an outlaw of greater renown than generosity, more infamous than virtuous, none robbed the rich to give to the poor—let the poor fend for them-

selves or go hang!—and they came in unruly, bloodthirsty bands, the
names of some of the leaders still spring to mind: many a tale was
told of Mamed Casanova, the Sullen fellow, Ciledón Noutigosa,
Gafento de Erviñou and Xan Quinto, one night my grandfather
chanced upon Xan Quinto at the Four Elm Trees, near our house, but
all he had to do was produce his revolver, and also Pepa the She-Wolf,
who got her name because at the age of twelve she hacked a wolf to
death with a mattock, indeed she well and truly made her mark and
the wolf was paraded throughout these parts on the back of a donkey,
she received gifts of foodstuffs and was showered with rewards, I
always thought that it would be good for history to be able to understand ghosts, Tristán Tembura swears by his ancestors that the
ghosts of the six aforementioned outlaws meet up on the last
Monday of each month to chat and play a game of cards in the hold
of the coastal cutter Simeón Gutiérrez which foundered with her
entire crew at Cape Prioriño Chico, they all perished and their skeletons still lie beneath the sea, along with the skeletons of a dog and a
parrot, Mouro and Cubanito, the bones can be seen but not removed
for burial as they ought, the bones of dogs and parrots should be
buried though not in hallowed ground, there is no reason to leave
them lying in the open air, Cirís from Fadibón died spliced on to the
devil on Cabernalde hill, he died of hunger and thirst, there are shipwrecks where seafarers perish from hunger and thirst just as there are
other startling, eerie fates, everything which the devil touches is
tainted with cautious reserve and great fear, events do not always
have to be explained because that might give rise to complications,
the Coyiños half-wit took leave of his senses when he saw the
shenanigans Cirís and Satan were up to, certain impressions send the
senses out of kilter, the church fathers hold discussions about
whether demons and the Devil are one and the same or whether
there are many demons each with its own name, or whether it is just
one which is called one thing or another depending upon what fits
the bill, it's not my place to pronounce upon this thorny topic which
could lead to excommunication and eternal, or at least semi-eternal,
flames, Vincent is fond of music played upon stringed instruments

which is delightful and brings great satisfaction, when the sea lashes
and the wind howls the lighthouse at Touriñán looks as though it is
about to fly away and, even when the sea is not surging and the wind
is not buffeting, those rocks at Touriñán command respect, all it
takes is to recall the magnetism which sends the compass awaver, I
cannot confirm this for I have no wish to spread gossip but indeed I
do take it as true that, in these waters upon a glassy sea, though
maybe it happened just a shade closer to Finisterre but nobody recalls
the exact spot for it took place many a long year ago now, the passenger steamer *Europa*, an English-flagged vessel sailing from
Gibraltar to Liverpool, ran foul of the *Stafford* and sank within a few
minutes of the collision, it happened in broad daylight on a glassy
sea, as I've said, and occurred in the month of July, both passengers
and crew were rescued, less fortunate was the collision between the
passenger steamers the *Irurac-Bac*, a Spanish-flagged vessel sailing
from Corunna to Cuba and Puerto Rico, and the *Douro*, a British-
flagged ship coming from Lisbon and making for Liverpool, the
Douro belonged to the English Royal Mail, the company on board
whose ship there always traveled the tailor to the squires of
Villagarcía de Arosa who were the best dressed gentlefolk in all of
Galicia, in 1902 my grandfather founded the Galicia Yacht Club—
since 1913 it has been known as the Royal Yacht Club and is the old-
est in Spain—and gave the people of Villagarcía their fondness for
whisky and tea, anyway the two vessels I mentioned sank swiftly
with a great many casualties—thirty-one from the Spanish vessel and
forty-two from the English ship—while the steamer *Hidalgo-Hull*,
also an English-flagged vessel, managed to haul one hundred and
forty survivors from the water, they say that in the throes of this
tragedy all participants acquitted themselves well.

"Do you believe that chivalrous conduct at sea has been abandoned?"

"It grieves me to say so, but indeed I do, modern navigation
equipment has no feeling and upsets man, who, in his haste to ideal-
ize machinery and confuse the technical with the spiritual, has abdi-
cated the realm of will. And without will, Don Leandro, why, neither

dignity nor elegance can be upheld, nor are survivors rescued."

Shipwrecked sailors from Russian submarines turn into owls or jellyfish, depending upon whether they are officers or sailors, into ghostly, cold-blooded owls and jellyfish which never ever die, Vincent knows this but he does not wish to breathe it to a soul so as not to cause offence, the Norwegian collier *Balduvin* was sunk without loss of life by a German submarine, it was the third time her skipper had been thwarted in such a manner, the Farelo is a rounded rock which shows at low tide, some folks call it the Basking Shark, it lies directly offshore from the hermitage on Farelo mountain and various vessels have struck it, the English freighter *California*, the French collier *Meguellan*, the Norwegian steamer *Caracas* with a cargo of cooking oil and the Portuguese sailing ship *Maria Alice* were torpedoed by the Germans more or less off the Farelo rock, nobody heard a sound from the dogs and children killed by a chomp from Officer Yavlinsky turned into an owl, the *Gumersindo Junquera* stuck fast on this rock but was towed to safety by the tugboat *Salvamento* summoned from Ferrol, Teodoro and Leoncio Quindimil probably cheat at cards but it is hard to tell, the coastal cutter *America* with her cargo of salt and the German collier *Madeleigne Reig* also perished on that selfsame rock, it is unfair that hunchbacks cannot play tennis but they've no option but to grin and bear it, sometimes justice is but a thin disguise, the Spanish freighter *Venus* went down with the loss of two lives in these waters, imagination often runs riot and legend manages to muddle or blot out history, in Touriñán they still speak of the horrific bloodshed of the *Embaka* catastrophe but at the heel of the hunt nobody knows anything for certain, there was an English collier of this name but her foundering without loss of life was not of major importance, last year Vincent won 286,414,866 pesetas in the lottery, a real fortune, the combination which reaped such rich rewards was as follows: 6, 14, 16, 20, 26, 30, all even numbers, which goes against the law of nature, the state of nature, the inertia and even nostalgia of nature, Vincent bought a lucky lottery drum, placed the numbered balls inside it and—Bob's your uncle! When Vincent told Annelie about his winnings they agreed to keep it under their hats, they thought of taking a trip to Paris but Vincent would have had to apply for a passport and he balked at that, so then they bought gold, two whole sacks crammed with gold sovereigns and guineas which they had to purchase in dribs and drabs so as not to attract attention, and hid this loot beneath the kitchen floor so they could tread upon it, sense and feel its presence at all times.

"What do I care that the price of gold goes up and down? With any luck both of us will be dead before we have to think of that."

"Yes, and with any luck whether richer or poorer than before will cross nobody's mind for the time being."

In the village of Figueroa, which lies in the Matamao point area above the lower skirts of Pedrouso mountain, lives Damiana Buiturón Dominguez, the woman who cures the trots by washing the belly of the sufferer with an infusion of chamomile steeped in sweet milk from a local cow and then anointing the belly with mutton fat: brave man, gentle woman, soft blanket of bracken, remove the runs from me as God ordains, an Our Father and a Hail Mary for the intercession of the Virgin Mary, Amen! you have to say this for three days in a row, starting on a Wednesday, but not during menses, in order to cure cancer you place upon the affected spot ashes from the head of a rabid dog steeped for nine days in vinegar with a handful of goatsbeard leaves, on the rocky shores of Bolal point a little south of Laxial point just before Parede point—hereabouts it's all points and entrances and exits—the Greek freighter *Annubis* foundered carrying bales of cotton but they managed to rescue her crew although they spent the night in the open air perishing with cold, you must not let misfortune become a bad habit, the Milky Way strews the heavens with beacons which we do not always choose to see, over towards Monte Gordo below As Negras point the English merchantman *Rivera* foundered with her cargo of fruit, wine and bundles of pelts though without loss of life, hereabouts the English collier *Richard Robert*, disoriented by the fog, also foundered without loss of life, just off the rocky shores of Cusiñadoiro or Vela point the Portuguese vessel *Illa Madeira* with her cargo of iron, the Maltese steamer *Tierra*

Santa transporting Danish pilgrims, and the *Eight Brothers*, a sailing
ship from Villagarcía de Arosa, were wrecked, all three without loss
of life, the Danish pilgrims spent many hours drifting on life rafts but
in the end they were rescued, the German steamer *Madeleigne Reig*
was navigating by eye and split the Villagarcia coastal cutter right
down the middle twenty years before she ran on the Farelo rock and
sank herself into the bargain, it smacks of revenge, Maruxa from
Queiroso keeps an owl in her hearth which roosts in a copper cauldron hanging from a beam and feeds upon oil, figs and maize, at times
it catches the odd rat, lizard or bird and gobbles it up, Bentiño and
Nicolás, Maruxa from Queiroso's two sons, perished in the sinking of
the coastal cutter *Ruadeiro* off Percebeira head while making from
Vigo to Gijón with a cargo of briquettes, Maruxa from Queiroso was
unable to bury her sons for their bodies never reappeared, shrouded
by fog the sea swept them away forever, Bentiño had always been a
great one for frequenting prostitutes, Nicolás less so, Nicolás was one
for sentiment and bragging, south of Nemiña beach lapping against
Barra point, after it flows through the village of Lires—yet where it
rises nobody knows—the del Castro river meets the sea, Lires was
the birthplace of the famous adventurer Crispinián Anobres, nicknamed Stripling, who became king of the night in Rio de Janeiro
before Chico Recarei, a friend of Moncho Vilas and a friend of mine,
Crispinián made his fortune in the white slave trade with a range of
pick-up joints and a well-organized distribution network, his mulat-
tas were tall and shapely and he drove around in a gold Rolls- Royce.
  "Don't you think that this is a little garbled?"
  "A little, no doubt, though not overly so, it doesn't do to say so
lest you confuse missionaries or the young, but life and death are
never too much in tune."
  The virgin Locaia a Balagota was badly abused by the heathens
and the Apostle St. James, so in order to teach them a lesson and to
assert her rights, she sent the pox to decimate them, that was the
onset of their downfall, it would have been better for those seven lads
accursed, those seven lads who defied God, to have been swept away
by the sea: Noah, Chelipiño, Doado, Froitoso, Lucas, Martiño and
Renato, one for each of the dead foxes in the parish of San Xurxo,

who now wander with the Holy Company along the banks of the
river Maroñas where trees spring from the shadows, mystery and
solitude, they know that they have a long stretch of penitence and
chastisement ahead.

"Can you imagine a hunchback hunting whales?"

"Not really."

"Playing rugby then?"

"Even less likely. Hunchbacks are all elderly."

"What about tennis then?"

"Nope, the ball swerves off at an angle and makes people laugh."

"Jerking off in front of a mirror?"

"Yes, indeed I could, hunchbacks are very fond of masturbating
in front of the mirror, they like to spray the mirror with semen,
Annelie likes Vincent to jerk off before the mirror in front of her and
rewards him with the sweetest of smiles."

"Can you imagine a hunchback dreaming of building himself a
house with boxwood beams?"

"God would not allow it for it would be an unpardonable impertinence."

Box produces small greenish flowers, boxwood timber is lemon-
colored, hard and polishes beautifully, boxwood violins sound better
than any others, they are a delight to listen to and even herring gulls
fall silent to enjoy the sound, Dick's wife, Dorothy, would never listen to the music of a boxwood violin because emotion grieved her,
the little French steamer *Nouveau Conseil* carrying a cargo of
Portuguese wine struck the reef at Touriñán and sprang a leak, her
skipper struggled valiantly for nineteen days and finally managed to
run her on to Rostro beach but the sea got the upper hand of him and
she languished there finally fading to a pitiful hulk, the English collier *Turret* was wrecked on Arnela beach, between the Gavoteiro and
Arnela or Robaleira point, the *Turret* was a strange vessel, at first she
was believed to be a French torpedo ship, Floro plays ancient airs on
his flute and tends his dun heifers with great care, Floro's cows are
swathed in the very wind which sweeps in from the sea and rebounds
from the mountain, truth to tell, Floro's heifers are a sight for sore
eyes but they give milk and draw the ox-cart just the same, Spirito

Santo Vilarelho taught Winkle to sing *fados*, song forges links between men even though they hail from different countries and lends them the strength to contend with life and await death without losing sight of it, without losing face.

"Without losing patience?"

"That too, if you lose patience everything goes awry and there's little can be done about it."

In As Pardas, east of the Sinchouza shoals, the *Silva Golveira* was lost without trace, there are times when misfortune seems to grow ashamed and hide its face, Annelie and Vincent go to mass on Sunday, nobody knows that Vincent studied for the priesthood in the seminary in Saint-Etienne, but he did not get as far as saying mass, maybe there is no seminary in Saint-Etienne, indeed there is one but the seed of doubt is sown so that the reader gains confidence, these matters are always muddled and confusing, he might also have studied at the seminary in Perpignan, maybe there is no seminary in Perpignan either, indeed there is one but the seed of doubt is sown so that the reader is left bewildered and cannot make head nor tail of it, Vincent is full of fancy, at times he is outspoken, even impudent, but he is no liar, now the fellow who is a liar is one Celso Tembura, a man who cannot tell two truths in a row, one day in the Mariquito cafeteria in Finisterre, surrounded by couples watching television, Celso Tembura told me that, while he was having a few drinks in the Flor de Melide tavern in Santiago, he made the acquaintance of the brothers Estanislao, Estagüisco and Extremado Carkuff along with their cousin Etelvina the whore, he was introduced to them by his friend Toribio Berrimes, they were on their way to receive a plenary indulgence so they were taking her along in order to sleep with her, thus forearmed they would save money and avoid vexing situations, all this was untrue because those odd bods and their names were made up, they had never existed and were but a figment of Barnacle the sacristan's imagination, the story did contain a grain of common sense but was untrue from start to finish, the Yugoslav schooner *Split* struck Petón Bermello point when sailing from Sydney to Brest with a cargo of sheep, though there wasn't space for too many on

board, they managed to refloat the vessel and she continued on her
way, the skipper ran her on Nemiña beach where she was patched up
and after a week and a half's work she was in a fit state to make for
El Ferrol with the assistance of two tugboats, when the fodder ran out
they tossed the sheep overboard, some of them survived for quite
some time while others drowned straight away, peasants in the out-
lying villages rescued many of them, dead or alive sheep still come in
handy, if it has not yet started to rot they bleed and thoroughly dis-
embowel a sheep that has just died, dry the flesh and air it well, cure
it over the hearth, nor do the skin and fleece go to waste either, the
mutton can be stewed, roasted or fried, it always tastes good, even
raw drizzled with a little olive oil and garlic, the English steamship
Cardiff II ran onto Mixirica point while transporting timber and rubber and her cargo wound up strewn on Nemiña beach, thereabouts
goods given up by the sea or ownerless property is known as flotsam
and jetsam, in this shipwreck the entire crew perished, nor was the
captain's ladylove, an eye-catching black Tobagan woman, spared, on
the Outer Sinchouzas the Dutch brigantine *Westkapelle* foundered
with a cargo of fine costume jewelry, her entire crew perished too,
from the Berron de la Nave to Oidos point the signal from Finisterre
lighthouse is not visible, these shadowy zones should not be sailed
after dark because the stars do not always give due warning,
Gavoteiro point—there is another one farther north—and the Outer
Sea beach lie within this zone unseen and exposed, limping Telmo
Tembura despises folks who eat ice cream and doughnuts, his friend
the priest Father Xerardiño Aldemunde laughs at him but Telmo falls
silent out of respect, just before Matamao point the Cuño river flows
into the sea where the Ribeira de Biceo shore rises steep and sheer,
truth to tell, it is all very topsy-turvy, as are the thrashings doled out
by the sea, this is where the Danish steamship *Hirtshals* went down
with her cargo of bananas without loss of life, San Xurxo is the patron
saint of barbers, hair can be made to sprout on bald pates with
Costanza de Evanxelina's remedy: rinse the pate thoroughly with
rose water and two or three scant drops of ammonia, the shinier the
scalp the better, whip thirteen egg yolks and blend in soot from the

hearth to form a smooth paste, spread this paste upon the bald pate before retiring to bed, the head should be swathed in brown paper or plastic because it must not breathe, recite the Holy Rosary and repeat this procedure every twenty-one days then wait another few—it is important not to lose count—the thirteen unbeaten egg whites should be taken on a fasting stomach, it is a good sign if the bald man vomits, the family must laugh at him in order to teach him a lesson, the thirteen egg whites must be taken even though the bald man starts to throw up at the second or third, the two questions which I ask which nobody has been able to answer are: how many souls might there be within the Holy Company of mariners? one thousand, two thousand? and: What does a soul weigh? Maybe souls are weightless, Cape Touriñán starts at O Carrexo with a filthy, perilous sea, suddenly there appeared on the scene the nephew of Don Sebastian Cornanda poking his nose in, well, he seemed to be poking his nose in and in the end it was all entirely cleared up in a roundabout manner but without beating about the bush: "My name is Froilán Fontecha, are you Mr. Vincent Goupey? I neither seek nor request anything, I am here simply to visit Doña Annelie, widow of my uncle Don Sebastian Cornanda, and to pay her my respects, I live in León but I've come to Galicia on business so I took this opportunity to visit my aunt, I am told that you are her administrator...", on the Farelo shoals you can make out the wreck of the *Gumersindo Junquera* broken up by the sea, the edges of these shoals are unclear and deceptive, the Chinese ship was called the *Cason*—now I remember—and she blew up and then caught fire some fifteen miles off Finisterre within waters which are an exclusion zone for the passage of hazardous cargo, but the maritime authorities are accommodating, or perhaps they just turn a blind eye so as not to have to work too hard, the vessel ran aground at Rostro point, the wind drove her onshore and she wound up wedged on the Anzuela reef, between Castelo and Pardiñas points, she had thirty-one crew on board and eight of them were rescued, she was carrying a cargo of chemical products and throughout the area it was feared that the air would be tainted and destroy us all and that the sea would be polluted and kill

off the fish we eat, the five-gallon cans bore the skull and crossbones
and were marked Inco 6 which is stamped only on highly hazardous
items the identity of which is known solely to the skipper who, in
this instance, was one of the casualties, the population of Finisterre
was evacuated amid great confusion but things turned out well
because God willed it so, it might equally have wound up in catastrophe, the turtle adorned with St. Elmo's fire which appeared last
year to certain seafarers in the Goa stream was the demon Barrabas,
as you know, who is in the habit of sleeping on Farelo mountain, a
spot which should not be ventured across after dark for it could prove
dicey, virtues are not lost but relinquished and fear of the devil can
be held in check by going through life forever chewing cloves of wild
garlic, the radio which Doña Dosinda gave my cousin Vitiño as a gift
works a treat and it's a delight to listen to, it is always playing lively, tuneful music, up-to-date, catchy tunes, my cousin is most grateful and repays Doña Dosinda with his utmost endeavors in the art of
hanky-panky, gratitude is more heartfelt from the vantage point of
misfortune than of fortune though this does not fit with my cousin's
character, on the Sisarga islands the Greek tanker *Andros Patria*
caught fire one New Year's Eve and spewed fifty thousand tons of
crude oil into the sea, there were thirty casualties and three survivors, near where the *Cason* perished the fishing vessel *Cizurquil*
from San Sebastian collided with and was sunk by the Iranian
freighter *Iran-el-Ham*, her seven crewmen went missing and the sea
gave up the body of her skipper, although people usually conduct
themselves better at sea, the fishing vessel *Josal* from Muxía was
rammed and sunk within minutes by a cargo vessel which then fled
the scene and nothing was ever heard of her again, there were three
casualties and five survivors from the *Josal*, the same thing happened
to the dragnet vessel *Hermanos Diez Colomé II* which was rammed
some twenty miles off Corunna by a large freighter which never even
stopped, her skipper perished and her eleven crewmen went missing,
if Vincent knew about mesmerism it would be well-nigh perfect,
Annelie would really like it if Vincent could hypnotize her but there
is no way, disproportion does not generally make for a happy match,

children at the municipal school know less French than Vincent does Galician, the children can utter odd phrases with fairly good accents though they cannot construct sentences, nor do they pay much attention, that's the reality, Micaela's Carliños should have been born with a silver spoon in his mouth, aptitude and presence he had aplenty but luck was not on his side and he was born into straitened circumstances, though his family was not pitifully poor for in his house no one went hungry, Micaela's Carliños has no papers for his Dodge, so in reality it no longer exists even though it is still driving, so long as the Civil Guards do not stop him on the highway, though truth to tell he goes out very little, the Dodge belonging to Micaela's Carliños has unexpected though reasonable uses, just like people, both chastity and lechery have their ups and downs, one day Leonor relented and Braulio Isorna started to hang about with Ricardiño, condoms don't come cheap but if they are rinsed thoroughly and stored in sawdust they may be used several times, on her feast day Braulio Isorna presented Leonor with two kerchiefs embroidered with flowers.

"Where did you get your hands on those?"

"That's none of your business."

"Mercy, what manners the creep has!"

The Bilbao-registered freighter *Dauka* collided with the Polish freezer-ship *Harmattan* at Cape Vilán, three men perished, ten went missing and there was one survivor, a fellow from Galicia called Ramón Cambeiro, Feliberto Urdilde hailed from Baxantes and used to arm wrestle my cousin Vitiño, the poor fellow was killed by a blow from a bottle of gin, it split his head in two like a pumpkin and he was dead upon arrival at hospital, now he appears to widows and they cannot sleep in peace ever after and continue to overdose on coffee, it is a vicious circle, or at least an uphill battle, which not even valerian can break, it would have been a beautiful sight if the two masts of the brigantine *Aurore Chaillot* had remained visible for five winters but they were blown to smithereens in the explosion, the Virgin of Pastoriza slipped up badly that day, the Virgin of Pastoriza keeps an eye out for ships and on the high seas parts the waters before them, but the *Aurore Chaillot* was not on the high seas and the Virgin of Pastoriza failed to save her from the flames, she either could not or would not, though maybe fire wasn't her thing, saints set limits to their area of protection because anything else would be bedlam, Nuco Gundián the cabin boy was twelve years old when he perished on board the coastal cutter *Bonitiña*, trapped in the hold unable to escape, his grandfather was the owner and he then became a monk in the Samos monastery because he could not face the sea again, nor talk to anyone, either about the sea or about anything else, sorrow is best borne in silence far from surging seas, the worst thing about sadness is that it scares off the wish to give it up, the son of *Bonitiña's* owner, that is Nuco's father, also perished at sea, in the wreck of the coastal cutter *Novo Pardemarín* which struck the Carballosa shoal and went down with all hands on board, not a single man was spared, the Benedictines, *ora et labora*, pray and toil, sing Gregorian chants, till the land, raise cows, make cheese and brew liqueurs, Moors crossing the Gibraltar strait crammed aboard little speedboats say that wind, fear and life all pass away but that the sea, land and deception remain, together with grinding poverty and sleep, the poor are always drowsy, but they have nowhere either to lay their heads or to die, nowhere to fall asleep or pass away, a sleeping man occupies the same amount of space as a corpse, everybody knows that it is not the same thing for the brains to simmer in the swamped cauldron of the skull as to be scorched in the red-hot heat of the heart, there are as many types of death as dead men, some cities are swept away by the wind or swallowed up by the sea while others are wiped out by earthquakes or buried because of their licentious ways, the Swiss-flagged yacht the *Pirate* was wrecked off Ortigueira, far from here, there were nine drownings and three survivors, Winkle does not tread upon the cracks between the paving stones on the quay lest he mock the holy cross which is our defense against misfortune and sin, whoever treads upon the cross tramples upon the Son, Jesus, who is the second person in the Holy Trinity, the voice of the sea scares even those who are accustomed to hearing it as well as heathens, heretics rather, there's no reason to let them off lightly, come what may.

"All heathens should be put to death, all heretics starting with the Protestants who are the worst, whether or not the death penalty is a deterrent makes no difference to me, I don't give a toss about this business of punishment, the death penalty brings solace, I think they should all be put to death."

"I don't disagree."

"Chop off their heads or garrote them?"

"What difference does it make? Listen to what the experts have to say."

Time is the spy of man, the confidant of man, the crutch and compass of man, Carmeliña has rosy cheeks, blue eyes and blonde hair, Carmeliña is the widow of a fisherman drowned off the Casteláns sandbar, Carmeliña is the image of dignity itself, the priest in San Xurxo of the Seven Dead Foxes is left-handed but he blesses his parishioners and serves communion with his right hand, Father Xerardiño doesn't give a hoot about money and shares what little he has with others, when wolves roamed over these hills goats, sheep and newly farrowed piglets had to be protected, nowadays only hens and ducks have to be protected from the fox, James E. Allen played rugby and now he plays tennis, he plays the accordion and recites eerie poetry by Poe in Galician, it's no secret that Poe gains greatly read in Galician, gazing out over the sea.

Here once, through an alley Titanic
Of cypress, I roamed with my Soul—
Of cypress, with Psyche, my Soul.

Do any of you know whether whales can hear the accordion and the verses of James E. Allen? María Flora, housekeeper to Father Socorro the priest in Morquintiáns, hides from the devil by covering her head with a Manila shawl.

"Do you think that the devil has a prick like a man?"

"Hail Mary, Mother of Grace, what a thing to say! Yours Truly believes so indeed only more pointy and corkscrew-shaped, like a boar's if you will, if you'll pardon me!"

Wormwood simmered in rainwater with a few drops of sweet

anisette alleviates many sicknesses but cannot cure either melancholy or indifference, the Basque tuna boat *Playa de Arrízar* was
struck and sunk by the French container ship *Artois*, one man perished, six went missing and there were five survivors, among seafarers a dead man is one whose body the sea gives up while a missing
person is someone the sea swallows up forever and never returns,
pancakes laced with *aguardiente* are the key to Telmo Tembura's
heart and memory, when you ply him with pancakes, *aguardiente*
and a cheap cigar Telmo Tembura tells eerie tales of Pindo hill and
the earthquake which altered the course of the river Xallas, people's
characters are like jam stains, like smudges of strawberry, blackcur-
rant, cherry, fig, bilberry or blackberry jam, each jam makes a different smudge and from its shape and color you can tell the timid or
forthright characters of folks, mermaids were the first lacemakers in
Camariñas, from the fronds and filigrees of seaweed, the feints and
cabrioles of seahorses, they fashioned graceful patterns, one morning
fishermen from the dragnet boat *Furelo* came across the drowned
body of a beautiful young woman, who appeared to be good-looking
even though she was a poor color, with a rope around her neck, when
they went to carry out an autopsy the pathologist could discover
nothing because the dead girl had vanished into thin air like a soap
bubble, all that could be presumed was that she had been hanged and
then thrown into the sea, there are unknown reasons for hanging a
woman and then throwing her into the sea, with the body of the
Furelo lass you could not have played buzkashi, the tribesmen in the
Pamir mountains require something tougher, more solid and wholesome, Marco Polo sheep live and die in that remote corner of the
world where death scoffs at others, man maybe not, but death does
indeed scoff, garbled news from the rest of the world does not reach
the remote mountain passes inhabited by Marco Polo sheep, there are
various places on Earth where the same thing goes on happening and
nobody changes their tune, gets het up or starts to cry, anybody could
die of a heart attack and not find it reasonable, hanged men, consumptives, the envious, cuckolds, excommunicants and dead half-
wits can spread their blight to the innocent, you must tread warily in

these matters, the Greek tanker *Galini* caught fire following three explosions on board and sank far offshore from Cape Ortegal, three men perished while nine went missing, everybody knows that the story has an uncertain beginning and a muddled ending, if this was remembered nobody would put out to sea, the horns of the Marco Polo sheep which my uncle Knut slew are encrusted with cobwebs, that's because nobody passes a duster over them more's the pity, you don't notice at first but later on when you do it grieves you and even grows to be a weight upon your conscience, although there is no reason why it should, the English cemetery fell into neglect and that, too, is a pity to see, so dignified yet dilapidated, Cain felt himself scorned by Abel and unearthed the jawbone of the ass in order to set matters straight, brother can be the bitterest enemy to brother and it is sad to see families decimated by outsiders who do not want peace but rather to foment bitterness, you should be able to say prayers you can make neither head nor tail of for miracles have no call to obey any law, the ghost of Minguiños the Poltroon's father may appear to him any night now to enquire about the alarm clock, young Bardullas restores the sick to health by virtue of powers granted to him by the Immaculate Conception and the Holy Trinity, Father, Son and Holy Ghost, amen, Lord Jesus, he is also a born miracle worker, known for his goodwill and upstanding conduct, it's important that circumstances fall into place.

"Have you heard that Modestiña Fernández, Don Julio's wife, gave birth to a largish, hairy octopus instead of even a black baby?"

"That cannot be true, folks say more than their prayers and, since he is always ready to deceive true believers, the devil never misses an opportunity to ensnare Christians even though they are in a state of grace."

"And to confuse assumptions from the outset?"

"That too, of course."

With the laying on of a hand which has slain a mole, better still if it is the left hand, you can alleviate stomachache so long as the pain is not from colic or overeating, Barnacle would like to speak Latin but he has no call for it, sacristans have no reason to have too

many needs or costly whims, humble patience and resignation suffice for their calling, sacristans should be easygoing and sober by
nature, Barnacle would also like to have been able to do geometry but
that's only for lighthouse keepers, poets and musicians who play per-
cussion or wind instruments, musicians who play stringed instruments are carried along more by instinct since the hand follows its
own course, the patron saint of musicians is St. Icia who was cruelly
martyred, the hangman had not done for her when he delivered the
three slashes of the sword permitted by law, in Castile this martyr is
known as St. Cecilia, palmers journey to Jerusalem and return bearing palms, romers go to Rome clutching pilgrim staffs and clad in pilgrim robes and return with the Pope's blessing, while true pilgrims
journey to Santiago de Compostela adorned with cockleshells and
return with their souls sluiced by the rain, Spirito Santo Vilarelho,
the cross-eyed Portuguese, taught Barnacle to sing *fados*, the Finnish
ketch *Kemi* sank on the Sabadelle weedbank with seven students of
rorqual whale behaviour on board who all drowned, I met them in
Malpica just eight or nine days earlier, we downed a few beers in the
London bar where I paid for the drinks, then later on they invited me
to dine at the Casa Elías restaurant where the stuffed quails were
exquisite, these students were well-heeled, the Cypriot cargo vessel
Erika II went down between Ferrol and Ribadeo, now that's quite a
different stretch of sea, nine of her crewmen went missing while two
were rescued, the Good Lord does not take kindly to man building
tunnels and bridges and ports and reservoirs, nobody likes to have
their plans amended, that business of the river Xallas drove the Good
Lord to the end of his tether, it was the straw that broke the camel's
back, Telmo Tembura knows the story well and at times he tells it to
whoever will listen, some folks do so with their eyes shut as a mark
of respect, Doña Dosinda and my cousin Vitiño Leis get tipsy together in the hut at Calboa point, she can drink him under the table, what
they like above all else is Dutch gin, they light a fire in the cabin and
are very cosy and comfortable, sometimes they spend two or three
days there at a stretch without going out, getting drunk, screwing,
vomiting and sleeping, the *Happy Return* was a fishing vessel from

Porto Son which went missing with her five crew, they were all related and not one of them was laid to rest because the sea did not give them up, it is hard to hold the gaze of a one-eyed person because they grow confused, it's also rare for one eye to be one color and the other another as happened with my uncle Knut, nor can you look at such people face on because it is disconcerting, Don Anselmo Prieto, author of the unpublished work *The Diving Bell*, used to thrust out his chest, straighten his bowtie and say, "My novel deals with certain historical facts which do not allow me excessive poetic license," folks loved to hear him, people love a sentence to start and finish as it ought, Don Anselmo quoted a verse from Antonio Machado as the epigraph to his novel: the man who talks to himself aspires to talk to God one day, barnacle is the name for the crustacean which clings to the hulls of boats while winkle is a small pointed seashell also known as periwinkle, I mention this because my neighbor Sonsoles Asenjo, the dressmaker, a rather strange woman from Segovia, enquired about it, she is the wife of Portela the assistant pharmacist, the Carkuff brothers were Czech and hailed from Karlovy Vary on the German border but they dressed like Bavarians in their waistcoats, lederhosen and Tyrolean hats sporting red and green feathers, Estanislao, the eldest of the three, was a watchmaker, he had great patience and could work wonders with his hands, Estagüisco, the second brother, worked as a clerk in the social statistics section of the Prague city council, before that he had been a glassblower, while Extremado, the youngest, was studying for the priesthood but when things went to hell in a handcart he took a job as a fireman and spent his days off doing gymnastics, he was like a circus acrobat, Etelvina, the hooker cousin, was not a good-looker though she had goodwill aplenty and was desirous to please, Etelvina was taller and more portly than her cousins and ate and drank more than they did, Etelvina would not stop eating or drinking until she was told to do so and as she was obedient she would then stop, they had already been in Santiago for just over a year, living in Cacheiras on the outskirts of the city, where they make such delicious potato omelettes, and since they were skilful and reliable they managed to live in meager comfort, cousin Etelvina refrained from practising her trade so as not to offend sensitivities and toiled long hours as a house cleaner wherever she was needed, her employers were delighted with her because she was indefatigable, her only drawback was that she smoked like a chimney but they had to put up with it for it was her own tobacco she smoked, she was never to be found snitching cigarettes, Barnacle, or rather Winkle, the sacristan also told me that they were putting their papers in order because they wished to become Spanish citizens, at first they encountered certain difficulties but it now seems that things are working out and progressing apace, the dogs in the factory in Caneliñas are fierce and spend their lives ratting and scaring off tourists, there are no thefts from the factory since, after all, there is nothing to steal, Estanislao, Estagüisco and Extremado all bowl really well, also Estagüisco is a chess player of some note, nobody in the area can beat him even though he pawns a rook, the Carkuff brothers speak both Castilian and Galician fairly well, though you can tell from their accents that they are not from hereabouts but they are almost fluent in both languages, when folk left Finisterre fleeing the perils of the *Cason* the dogs nearly starved to death, they polished off the hens and tame rabbits first, the streets were strewn with feathers and chunks of fur, I would like to have met the Carkuff brothers and Etelvina but Winkle evaded me with excuses that were not always logical, it took some time before I realized that it was all a tall tale and that these foreigners had never existed, it is not hard to fool us people of goodwill for we are generally credulous and trusting, rather than reproaching the sacristan for his yarns I invited him to have a few glasses of Ribeiro wine with me because deep down I like him, it is true that lying is an ugly vice but liars can be entertaining (when they are doing no harm) and above all unavoidable, I once asked Winkle if he found it an effort to tell tall tales and he told me it was not, that they flowed from him naturally, the sixteen men rowing on board the traíña *Joven Elenita* were rescued when she split in two after running on to Percebeira head, there was great anxiety in Camelle for the rescue of the shipwrecked seafarers took over six hours and darkness was closing in, none of the crew could swim but they held out like lions, clinging on to whatever they could, you have to hold out at sea, there's little use being able to swim and most fishermen cannot, what would be the point? the fishing vessel *Bonito* foundered around about the Lesser Berrón islet, exactly where is not known, just north of Cape la Nave and the Ventoliña rock, eleven fishermen perished and the sea swept away or swallowed up each and every last plank of her, the Swedish freighter *Svtford* sank above and beyond the Carraca, nine men perished, and the English vessel *Denewell* foundered without loss of life below the Carracas just before you reach the Mañoto rocks, the asbestos sheeting of Cósmede's shack is weighted down with stones so that it cannot be swept away when the wind buffets Gures beach, though no more than anywhere else hereabouts, Cósmede the deaf-mute makes kites which he gives as gifts to the children in the villages, he smiles and allows himself to be helped out with scraps of food or a couple of cabbages, once he was given a whole cheese, he also sets snares for rabbits, keeps three hens which are wary of the wolf and the bear, prises goose barnacles from the rocks and fishes for octopus, I think I've already mentioned, although I am not certain, that the wolf and the bear slip off to the garbage dump by night and always find something to scavenge, dogs bark at them but the country people know them and let them go undisturbed, the dragon at Uña de Ferro point sings folk songs and makes many a sinful, indecent utterance, folks are kind of scared and scarcely venture forth by night, Froilán Cornanda Fontecha, nephew of Annelie's late husband, lost no time in revealing his intentions in a furtive though tortuously insistent manner, what he wanted was money: I neither request nor seek anything but have come simply to visit Doña Annelie, widow of my uncle Don Sebastian Cornanda, Lord rest him! I would have liked to have had a few masses said for him but that was beyond my means, for, truth to tell, I am going through hard times at the moment, Annelie and Vincent agreed to give him a modest amount in return for his departure, after much haggling the sum was set at one hundred guineas, and Annelie told him: "Sebastian left me one thousand guineas but as a token of goodwill towards you I am giving you one hundred, dentists pay good money for gold, after all gold is gold, now, sign here," the document stated: I, the undersigned, Froilán Cornanda Fontecha, a Spanish citizen, of legal age, a married man and domiciled in León, etc., hereby declare that I waive my claim to the portion of my uncle Don Sebastian Cornanda Estévez's inheritance which might rightfully accrue to me, etc., and Vincent hid in the attic for three days so that Froilán would believe that he had gone to Corunna to fetch the filthy lucre, the Panamanian flagged steamship *Commodore Iván Petit*, with general cargo on board, went down off the Besugueiro Mascota rock, her twelve crewmen—all of them black—were drowned, the skipper was an Irishman, it is not uncommon to find black seafarers serving under Irish skippers, some things should be borne in mind and never forgotten, dead blacks who have conducted themselves well in this life leap from branch to branch or from wave to wave to reach the happy hunting grounds situated in the nooks and crannies of the Milky Way, blacks play diabolo and spin yoyos in their paradise, or perhaps it is limbo for it is not eternal, as well as hula hoops, and strum dainty musical instruments, when they have been there for one hundred centuries they return to life as white men, the Milky Way is a huge river where the righteous repair in order to savor all imaginable pleasures, in his notebook bound in black oilcloth Don Sadurnino made the following note: there are only three pure colors, red for blood, yellow for gold and blue for the sea, all the rest are base.

"What about green for grass and the ink he writes with?"

"I know what I am saying."

Some twenty years ago now, in December 1978, the Pedra de Abalar Rock in Muxía, which weighs about eighty tons, was swept up into the air by a huge breaker and split in two when it crashed down, since then the sea has brutally buffeted that coastline and for the time being nobody has succeeded in putting back the clock, time goes by sifting and unraveling lives, handing tools to the vengeful and ropes to those about to hang themselves, it is all a matter of patience and never meeting anybody's gaze, never looking at anybody joyfully and straight in the eye, Fideliño the Pig gave Xan from

Labaña a terrible fright when he hollered at him to bury him in hallowed ground, life is lengthy and squalid and opportunity always presents itself even though it comes hobbling along for time both conceals and reveals everything, ponder it carefully, time meddles with and ruins everything, joy is swifter than misfortune and the years still to come bring both sacrifice and benefit, that is the poor man's consolation, Marta the Scad did not bat an eye when she found out that her husband had shot himself in the mouth, what puzzled her was why he had traveled so far afield, Xan from Labaña found a Norwegian cod fisherman's boot on the beach, Norwegian cod fishermen are the best shod on the high seas, the handsome boot of a well-heeled fisherman, a quality boot with an almost knee-high leather upper and a timber sole.

"Boxwood?"

"Maybe."

They say that a pair of cobblers from hereabouts make similar footwear, St. Crispín and St. Mariña of Obre, patron saints of shopkeepers, inspire true, effective and practical vagaries in those they protect and strive to help, Jews are rumored to be compassionate, the worst thing about those boots is that they are very expensive, hardly anybody can afford them because they are so pricey, Fideliño found the cod fisherman's other boot and Xan got wind of it, things work out more smoothly when properly thought through beforehand, Xan waited for a stormy night to slip under cover of the wind and roaring of the sea up to the Pig's house where he crept up onto the tiled roof, then putting on a voice from beyond the grave, he boomed down the chimney: "Give me the boot, Fideliño, give me the boot, for I cannot leave purgatory without it!" The Pig got such a fright that he tossed the boot out of the window, without even daring to open the door, then he began to weep and tremble like a leaf, crouched in a corner of the hearth munching slivers of pork sausage on corn bread, lit a cigarette and fell asleep, Botelo sausage is the sausage of poor men and the mysteriously ill which is made by stuffing the intestine of a pig—though wild boar is even better—with well-mashed backbone with a dash of salt, it is then cured, smoked and served to all and sundry, the Pig's wife's house was built upon the ruins of an old windmill which her father-in-law paid forty *duros* for, an elderly lighthouse keeper, now retired, recalls the sum from the loan with which his father helped to purchase it, his great grandson told me so, and when she was widowed Marta sold it for fifty thousand *pesetas*, now they have opened a discotheque beside the graveyard, in the old days folks did not dare to pass by there at night and even the bravest of men went to great lengths to avoid the howling of the dead in mortal sin and will-o'-the-wisps, the serenest of old folk say that you cannot leave off believing in something all of a sudden, stop being fearful of something all of a sudden, you have to believe and you have to be fearful, you also have to move little by little and accommodate yourself to the idea of speed and lulls, things changed with the advent of electricity, footwear, the pill for women and divorce, in the old days it was all very different, during the war a German plane nose-dived into Cachelmo hill, it was not being harrassed and the fuel must have run out for it did not catch fire, both crewmen died, they were dressed in the best of clothing with standard issue boots, jackets and wristwatches, one airman even had two watches: one on either wrist, and silk scarves wrapped about their necks, parachute cloth makes stout, sturdy sails, navigational instruments are little use but you can always take them home as keepsakes, by the time the Civil Guard arrive at a crash site the cockpit is generally stripped bare and the dead airmen stark naked, the English steamship *Streamer*, sailing from Mohammedan lands to Portsmouth with a cargo of citrus fruits, Maltese goats and Moroccan whores, foundered off Chorente point, at the mouth of Merexo bay, nobody knows what happened for it was broad daylight at the time and the weather was fair, the citrus fruits were washed away by the sea and carried to Borreiros point, while the goats and the whores remained afloat, soon the water was dotted with flat-bottomed punts, some folks rescued goats while others rescued women, all depending on their particular tastes and requirements, several goats drowned but all the whores were spared, *Porvenir Portuario*, the Villagarcía schooner with general cargo on board, was driven by high winds on to the Barreira sands, there was no loss of life and the vessel was refloated without difficulty, Maruxa Mórdemo reads the cards and foretells the future in Ponte do Porto, she has a sizeable following for in many instances she hits the nail on the head, before this she wrought cures with medicinal herbs but gave that up because sick people turned her stomach, Maruxa had a love affair with Don Arturo Catasol, a cargo skipper who suddenly went missing without a trace, some folks claim to have seen him in Montevideo but Maruxa could never prove it, sometimes Annelie and Vincent make love on the floor, Vincent was passing cloudy urine for a while and Annelie called Maruxa on the telephone, you must pray to St. Liborius and Nosa Señora da Barca, dose him with sand spurrey one day and with strawberry corn the next, when he is cured he should drink rosemary tea every morning with a green salad made from hedge mustard and olive oil, but don't add vinegar to it, you must not lose faith or hope and should steer clear of fizzy drinks for the bubbles stick to the body and throw it out of kilter, hunchbacks generally suffer from urinary tract problems but nothing more sinister than that, the stinging cleared up straight away and Vincent soon recovered, Vincent believes that the Quindimil brothers cheat at cards but he keeps this under his hat for discretion is the better part of valor, nothing is ever resolved by shouting it from the rooftops, things sort themselves out or else are never sorted out, silence is a help, you've got to understand it this way from the outset because that it is also how it is from the outset, it all depends upon how you go about things and what the nature of each individual is like, in the sporting club in Corunna there are three or four tennis players whom James E. Allen can never beat, everyone should know their own sporting limitations, if the Holy Ghost were a bat or a praying mantis instead of a dove, or maybe a turtle dove, our religion would not be the one true faith and we Catholics would not have left the catacombs, many years ago they used to sing a Charleston tune, the words of which went: In the catacombs of New York City that horrible sect of terror has its hideout, this was referring to the Ku Klux Klan, blacks are killed in various ways all of which serve as a deterrent, though never by poisoning which is an unspectacular death, by tying them to the tail of a horse which is ridden off at a gallop or the rear bumper of an automobile driven at speed, hanging, burning, kicking, flogging, stoning, etc., whether God is black or white is not known, the K.K.K. believe that he is white as do most blacks too, the Portuguese collier *Cristelo* struck Percebeira head and sank with the loss of three lives and three survivors, they were all picked up by *Virtudes* the coastal cutter from Palmeira which was dredging down Vigo way, Annelie calls the shots when she is in bed with a man and Vincent follows orders when he is in bed with a woman, everyone has their own ways and their own crows to pluck, and nobody will change that because there are no two miseries and no two wretches totally alike, it is like the law of universal gravity, at times Vincent is lonelier than a child but it comforts him to think that loneliness is the opposite of melancholy, when Ricardiño grows old, though maybe he won't live that long, he still will not know that grinding poverty does not kill but scars the soul, Leoncio is even more vile than he is wretched although he is unaware of this for he is the one who opens and closes the shop door, and that gives great verve, virtue is more monotonous than truth though not more wholesome, nor less either indeed, the Italian steamship *Fortoreto* laden with aromatic spices ran aground on Arnela beach, the tugboat *Trafesa IV* refloated her and she continued on her way, Vincent knows all Maruxa Mórdema's wiles but keeps them under his hat so that they aren't used against him, the German steamer *Zingst* with her cargo of onions struck the Xan do Norte rocks, also off Arnela beach, and was driven back onto the Muñiza shoals where she swiftly sank, her entire crew perished except for one man who spent several hours clinging to a cork life buoy, the octopus Fawn Fox heartily greeted my friend Jesus Martínez, it is preferable for God's creatures to get on well together and treat one another with consideration, the bird Besta Cantigueira has been flying hereabouts for several nights marauding and thieving lambs, though she hasn't carried off any children for some time now, the Portuguese sailing ship *Sesimbra* sank on the Castelo sandbar, without loss of life, my great grandfather Cam never got along well with his brothers, we all know whose fault that was but nobody breathes a word, outsiders are the undoing of families because they have ways which feed ingratitude and clothe it in the hues of virtue quivering and beckoning like a false beacon, the five men aboard the *dorna** *Loliña* were rescued by Fawn Fox the octopus who righted the boat and hoisted them back on board one by one with no harm done, when they returned ashore nobody believed a word of their adventure, the bard Bernaldín de Brandeñas saw the last nine-colored rainbow in the Western world.

"Do you know that it shows itself only to consumptive artists (poets, watercolorists, violinists, though not to bagpipers because they have strong lungs) from certain countries?"

"Cornwall, Brittany and Galicia?"

"Precisely, and Ireland, too, sometimes. Tell me now, in all seriousness and sincerity, do you follow what I am asking?"

"Yes, of course, I do, many years ago I heard it said by red-haired Elisabetiña de Casiana, my father's ladylove."

"Have you also heard it said that those artists commend the health of their flesh and blood muses to St. Casilda?"

"Yes, I've heard it said over a hundred times, and at daybreak they have to kneel down and look out over the sea, this is so that the first ray of sunlight enters their behinds, and they have to pray: oh, St. Casilda, preserve me from the womb and from lust, Amen, Lord Jesus!"

On the Ferretes rock, between Finisterre and the Lesser Lobeira island, Beelzebub bathes with his lover the she-devil Buttercup of the Golden Pelt, who plays waltzes upon a conch shell, luring boats to their doom when the skipper's gaze is distracted and his eyes stand out like organ stops, hunting whales is known to sunder families, money always keeps families apart, I did not inherit my great grandfather's resolve so the squalls of life have buffeted me hither and thither and forced me to toady to the dreary stickler who serves the

* *dorna*: traditional single-masted vessel, often with a lateen sail, used for inshore fishing in the Lower Estuaries since ancient times.

soup kitchen swill and doles out the dreary convent soup with a huge
pewter ladle, widows keep many a secret under lock and key and seldom wash, they reek of greasy old woman even though they are not
yet elderly, Verdugo the druggist's widow is called Florinda and she
never looks you in the eye, her husband died of poisoning but that's
neither here nor there, nor does it contribute anything to order when
judges know more than is good for them, Oliviña Lourida the jellyfish, Eudosio the cachalot whale, and Fawn Fox the octopus, the bird
Besta Cantigueira and Bastián the rorqual whale dwell in peace and
harmony because they seek refuge in pretense, therein lies their great
wisdom, timber boats withstand sea monsters better than steel vessels, which are led astray by magnetism, when a swordfish pierces
the hull of a coastal cutter you have to tie it fast so that it cannot
swim off and open up a leak in the vessel, the best thing is to chop
off its head and secure its sword with lines, Damiana Buiturón kills
tapeworms with southernwood, thyme and another herb which she
does not disclose, she has never mentioned it to anybody, she killed
a three-foot-long tapeworm in Don Glicerio the secretary and cures
incontinence with infusions of hops and yarrow, Don Glicerio no
longer wets himself, and she treats prostate problems with a brew of
nettles and goldenrod, nettles do not sting us Iria folk if we hold our
breaths while we pick them, Florinda Carreira, widow of the druggist
Angel Macabeo Verduga, has a whole chest of silver *duros*, Florinda
seeks out men and pays them in silver *duros*, one for dallying a short
spell with her, three *duros* and breakfast for a whole night long, the
battle against loneliness does not cost the earth, she prefers outsiders
who are just passing through, she lives alone but keeps a Leonese
mastiff called Turk who blindly obeys her and would spring to her
defense the moment she gave him the word, when Florinda is in bed
with a man, Turk gets randy and rubs himself, he tries not to get in
the way because he is heavy, he licks the couple's behinds and humps
wherever he can, frequently against Florinda's legs which, for reasons
of amatory strategy, are generally on top, the compass governing the
posture of lovers is lodged in the clitoral gland or third crevice of the
woman's vulva, have no fear, all he wants is to enjoy himself just as

you and I are enjoying ourselves, Florinda does not allow herself to be addressed by the familiar "tú" when she is in bed, nor does she address anyone informally, the widow likes to fondle the mastiff's balls, to the touch they are very like those of her late husband, R.I.P., when my uncle Knut invites me to have a sweet vermouth I start to tremble, I do complicated exercises so as to establish order in my head and say: I like to learn about dying on my own but solitude also frightens me, sometimes I walk to the window and even though the rain is beating against the panes I can see that someone is alive and is eating or drinking or smoking or dreaming or fucking or dying somewhere, nothing further was ever heard of Brother Anselm, the French hermit who was swept skywards, maybe he is over in Newfoundland or on the Labrador coast now, unusual events occur all over the world on a daily basis, I won't list them for it is not worth the trouble, the great thrill is to gamble with the unexpected and always get it wrong, the Greek steamship *Kiparissia* laden with walnuts foundered on the Casteláns Norte rock, one man perished while five others went missing, nobody knows the evil thoughts of anybody else and within the head of the person who is about to do harm confusions pile up so that nobody can read them clearly, the sailor on the verge of drowning does not think of death but of life and the woman who is about to be strangled does not think of pain or anguish but of the boozy breath of the man, that willy-nilly executioner, that somewhat sinister puppet who grows ashamed of his role, the worst is when somebody skips lightly over the barrier separating horror from pleasure.

"What about duty?"

"Yes, duty, too, sometimes."

On the seven rocky shoals of Escordadura, trapped between the fourth and fifth reef, the Camariñas coastal cutter *Estrelamar* foundered coming from Noya and did not make it to Ferrol with her cargo of briquettes, her skipper and two men perished, the Escordadura shoals are not marked on any chart, between the two northernmost rocky shoals mermaids bathe when the weather is fine, Vincent claims to have seen them on more than one occasion, mermaids allow themselves be watched by hunchbacks for they are known to inspire trust, Pepiño Tasaraño, the Queiroso half-wit, vociferously explains that the best mermaids are the ones with haddock tails, the ones with hake tails are not yet mature while the ones with whiting tails are undersized, Pepiño swears that almost all mermaids are called Rose, the priest called me Rose and I replied: "No roses like these, mister priest, ever bloom in your bower," Pepiño Tasaraño was not exempted from military service and was packed off to war, his company captain had more sense than the fellows in the recruiting office and set him to peeling potatoes rather than firing a gun, mermaids sing *fados* and other love songs in tuneful, theatrical voices, it is no wonder that seafarers are struck dumb when they hear them, Galician, English and Portuguese mermaids are the same, though Breton mermaids are perhaps slightly taller and haughtier, nobody, not even his widow, ever saw the photos which Jesus Martínez took of Fawn Fox the octopus, it would be very handy if the roll of film were to turn up so the photos could be studied by experts, only the poor in heart murder one another, that is the wretchedness of the weak, Leonor usually has sex with the Quindimil brothers on Mondays, first one brother then the other, they send Ricardiño off on some errand or other, shut up shop and cavort with her in the store, they spread a piece of oilcloth on the floor to keep off the damp, Leonor almost always has a good time, though some days she does not because her privates are smarting and she feels disgusted and close to tears, but she smiles gratefully when they hand her sixty *duros* and some candies, do you know what a word is for? for precious little, it seems to me that a word serves for precious little, do you know that a word is the reflection of life, the very shadow and silhouette of life? no, nobody told me so, for goodness sake! do you know that beneath each word an idea slumbers its feverish sleep? no, I didn't, I don't know anything unless they tell me, the ghost of her husband often appears to Florinda, she keeps it at bay by burning rosemary alcohol, reciting a Hail Mary and fondling Turk who is ever compliant for he is a grateful beast, Florinda lives alone but does not bar the door for Turk only goes out to do the needful and returns

straight away, the criminal is not the one who slits your throat but
the fellow who whets the knife, my late friend Jesus Martínez's
stamp collection is not as good as Don Sebastian Cornanda's but it
has its own merits, nonetheless Martínez's stamp collection was sold
off too cheaply by his widow who was tripping over herself to turn
any memento of her late husband into hard cash, sometimes widows
are overcome by a demonic desire to suppress memory, that spring
which never dries, would anybody dare to put their hand in the flame
and swear that the pardoner is not the accomplice? my late friend
Jesus Martínez never said so to anybody but he believed that within
the soul of the sinner there might slumber the sparrow's egg of the
saint, both in the soul of the criminal as well as in the soul of the
saint there throbs (or may throb) the cicatrix of that selfsame bloody
dream for life is not loved with greater vehemence than death, Doña
Dosinda caught a dose of crabs in Corunna from a Norwegian sailor
called Olaf who lost his boat as a result of a drinking spree, Doña
Dosinda and my cousin Vitiño were splitting their sides with laughter as they doused the crabs with Crabesol, the Portuguese steamship
Felgueiras, which was sailing from Leixoes to Gijón with general
cargo and a Maltese woman passenger with an almost newborn son
on board, foundered on the Cantarela rock which covers and dries
and they were all drowned, the bodies were washed up on Rostro
beach, the Bible says one thing and then another: a brother helped by
his brother is a fortress and also a brother who is the enemy of his
brother is a fortress, a brother too similar either slays his brother or
kills himself, for a double is hard to bear, hardly anyone understood
the paradox of Cain and Abel, there was a poet who spoke of the
errant shadow of Cain, the selfsame shadow that killed him, while
Don Antonio thought that it was envy of virtue that turned Cain into
a criminal, Doña Dosinda copied out verses for Vitiño in her beautifully rounded copperplate hand, people get confused on their own
because they close their eyes each time they stumble into something,
I will never tire of repeating that it can be alarming when my uncle
Knut invites me to have a glass of sweet vermouth with him, Uncle
Knut is not a skinflint nor is he a big spender but a shade canny

where money is concerned, the Maltese lady from the *Felgueiras* was also traveling with a Pomeranian, God made man in such a way that he can confuse life with death, and vice versa and then it transpires that the dead man they are about to bury is still alive and he turns over in his coffin, close your eyes, say the Credo and hold your breath, Liduvino the traveling laborer did not hold his breath, why, he even farted while praying and the Good Lord smote him blind in order to chastise him, so nowadays he sings ballads and other songs at *romerías*, St. Xulián of Luaña, whittled from buckthorn, has more strength in his pecker than my porker in its snout, God metes out punishment without recourse to sticks or stones but at times he loses control of himself, such lack of restraint is proper to gods, it must be very difficult to measure up the fragility of man and fit the punishment to match the offender, lack of restraint is not an irrelevance but a matter of huge importance not easy for man to grasp and therein lies the seed of faith, there are folks who say that Annelie and Vincent have not been getting on at all well for some time now, that they bicker over petty trifles and that Vincent is no longer as respectful as he once was, more than likely this is not true, well, more than likely this may or may not be true, folks say things just so as to have something to talk about and do not pay too much heed to what they are saying, the air enveloping the crime is no more unbreathable, no lighter, the worst thing about crime is that it seeks out the company of another crime, alongside the Fonte Raposo saltworks carpenters from the Finisterre coastline ply their chisels hewing timber, the living should not battle with the dead, burying them and having a few masses said is sufficient, there are men and women without a story such as Farruco Roque the fellow from Celanova or Rosa Bugairido wife of the male nurse Roquiño Lousame and men and women with a great deal of history, not that I am about to name them since nobody is asking me to, Farruco Roque never laid eyes upon the sea, what for since the land was already enough for him? Rosa Bugairido threw herself over the cliff at Cape Vilán where her body did not fall directly into the sea but bounced off the goose barnacles, the person who finds Queen Lupa's treasure will be richer than the rest of us

Galicians put together, but for the time being nobody has found it, gold and silver do not perish and the fire that broke out in the oak wood on Pindo mountain neither hid it deeper nor brought it to light, the wild horses of the rocky plain of As Negres kick out at the breeze to warm it and also to rid it of damp, nowadays there are hardly any wolves around here, Chonchiña Casal says that on All Souls Day she spotted two of them from her house in Fumiñeo, loping along the road to Villastosa at a leisurely pace, gold is costlier than virtue but the virtuous man does not love but fears it, although Annelie does not realize it, she enjoys humiliating Vincent, a scornful scowl is worse than making someone sleep on the floor, Annelie dines on fruit, one night she popped cherries into Vincent's behind so that he could later shit them into her mouth, but that is a somewhat murky episode in which I have no wish to implicate anybody, within the head of an obedient person at times there hatches without warning the spider's egg of revenge, it generally aborts before bearing fruit but if it hatches death and disharmony may ensue, the killer instinct can take shape from one day to the next, no lengthy maturation process is required because nobody knows that he is a murderer until he feels it to be so or the devil whispers it in his ear, the devil is murmuring into your ear: Give up mass and give up the Rosary, go on sleeping, long live Mary! long live the Rosary!, long live St. Domingo! by blessing yourself with holy water you can ward off evil thoughts, the devil tempted St. Anthony by appearing naked in the guise of a lustful woman, the worst thing about some paths is that there is no going backwards, if Dorothy had not been fearful of emotion she would have attended religious services like any other woman and a great many men, it is unhealthy to ignore the graves of grandparents, parents, children, grandchildren and domestics, families should return to the earth of their own soil so that the oak trees and chestnuts grow strong and solemn, so that the boxwood breathes harder and more deeply, this business of being buried abroad, surrounded by dead you do not even understand, is undignified, upon the land which covers the bones of my father there should grow a currant bush wherein the nightingale sings its song of despair at midnight, hope should not be confused with desire because it is more noble, it is only right to know that families should not move around too much, women should understand the language of the males with whom they fornicate because the sin of bestiality yields no fruit and it is all a matter of giving birth, always giving birth, in order to predominate, the flesh of men is like the land shaded by the chestnut trees and also requires patience and serenity, Vincent has no papers because he has no need for them, Annelie believes that Vincent would need to have his papers in order if she were to die before him, Annelie is drawn to danger, although she is not aware that this is so, Annelie wrote in her own hand on pink paper embossed with her initials that, if she were to predecease him, she left everything to Vincent, Annelie also thinks that her decision is elegant though not timely or even reasonable, Annelie has no relatives, her late husband's nephew is related only by marriage, you can appoint someone your heir for reasons of hatred, contempt or love, as well as from pity or for amusement's sake, you hate and also love what you despise, you despise and also hate what you love, you love and also despise what you hate, it's a highy irregular game with treacherous margins, Don Gabriel Iglesias wanted to let the law of inheritance lapse and to regulate marriage along the lines of a lease, abolish the death penalty, disband the Civil Guard, prohibit prostitution, grant women the vote, set up a mounted police force and turn Spain into a federal republic presided over by a triumvirate of life members, the fishing smack *Espiñeira* went down on the Vespereiro weedbank, the weed was stronger than the oars and all the fishermen were strangled by the trailing weed, that is a cruel death, the Vesporeira weedbank is like a forest of blind, cruel, venomous vipers, the French sloop *Grande Pélegrine* sank on the Farelo weedbank, the weed was stronger than the wind in her sails, the seven dead foxes of the parish of San Xurxo saunter forth to kill chickens in the villages of Grixa, Porcar and Lagoa, they surely roam farther afield too, country folks say that smallshot and even buckshot pellets glance off their pelts, that they can be slain only with a knife like the wild boar or with a rifle like the wolf, there is nothing sadder than a sickly wild boar or an old wolf, in some houses they still have firearms from the war, the mauser and the musket are reliable weapons, it is against the law to have them, at the end of the war they were to be handed over at the Civil Guard barracks, the souls of the seven lads who didn't give a toss about the sermon are now burning in hell or in purgatory, some were more blameworthy than others, at times they wander with the Holy Company along the banks of the river Maroñas, the devil does not shepherd souls according to type as the Incas herded cattle in a fold, hereabouts almost all souls are birds of a feather, there is no great confusion in that, Vincent does not want to think of Annelie, it is enough for him to obey her with waning enthusiasm and greater resignation (not less resignation), certain times are ripe for crime while others scare crime away like a timid, fragile fowl, Vincent would have spit with fury and rage upon the heart of that wretched witness which God places at each crime as a lesson to the last innocent, nobody minds hanging the last innocent, Luisiño Nannestad the Norwegian was married *in articulo mortis* to Catalina from Andalusia who inherited two nearly new overcoats, a reindeer pelt, two pairs of boots in good condition, twelve tobacco pipes, nine of them clay and three meerschaum, a fortune in silver *duros*—nowadays they would be worth more—and five doubloons, Luisiño the Norwegian was a wealthy man, upon the stone bed of San Guillermo all barren sterility is banished, it is a good sign if at the moment of pleasure with the man on top—not with the man underneath—the woman dreams of a cachalot whale with a beak like the antlers of a deer, like the cachalot stranded on Traba beach, they say that years ago another one was stranded on Pedrosa beach, over towards Forcados point, Celso Tembura the sacristan catches herring gulls with a fishing hook, he knows that it is an offense but what does he care? cowardice can be cloaked in cruelty, Martiño Villartide is a heretic and blasphemer but he figured out in time that crime is not a vocation but a circumstance, although he did not figure this out with ideas nor did he say so in so many words but he felt it in his throat and in the throbbng of his temple, Celso Tembura the sacristan serves a glass of wine to the man who slays a wolf and is merciless with the body of the wolf that kills a man, it is customary to hang it after death and leave it dangling until maggots strip the bones bare and flies alight on it only to rest, the children of summer visitors drown on the O Cuarteirón weedbank, one every year, but news of it no longer makes the newspaper, Father Xerardiño smokes like a chimney, sometimes he even smokes during mass, Father Xerardiño is so skilful that he can work miracles with just one hand, everybody knows that, Father Xerardiño does not work major miracles but ones that are indeed useful to his parishioners never-theless, he does not resuscitate the dead who have already begun to stink but scares off the devil, dries up pus, reduces swellings and brings comfort to the heartsore, Father Xerardiño is kindly and com-passionate and more than once he gave a herring, a crust of corn bread and a glass of wine to the Xures half-wit, landlubbers call the rorqual whale the finback, the finback is the humpback whale, James E. Allen is going to have to give up tennis for good because it is a sport for which he has little aptitude, the years take their toll and the old ticker runs out of puff, it does not fail but runs out of steam, my father set Elisabetiña de Casiana up with a student boardinghouse for it behooves a body to be generous with those who give, or have given, you pleasure and because everybody needs to live in a dignified man-ner, Elisabetiña has dyed hair, big boobs and feet and a wistful, melodic voice, Elisabetiña likes to play the saxophone with the Snowstorm band, previously known as the Hell Raisers ensemble, Elisabetiña was married to a Uruguayan fellow who ran off on her, Don Sadurniño Losada says that Uruguayans are given to running away, but there is a great deal of exaggeration in many things that are said, that was before Elisabetiña got involved with my father who was already advanced in years, she also had an affair with Uncle Knut and with Verduga the druggist, too, or so they say, Elisabetiña was always a woman who cut a great dash and could stand up to anyone, Florinda pays men with silver *duros*, and some of those selfsame *duros* came to rest in Elisabetiña's coffers because money does the rounds and maybe even passes through the same hands seven times, I would like to be able to die with dignity, not frightened or running scared like a lizard, the English cargo vessel *Scarborough* was sunk by a German submarine off the outer part of the Quebrantas rocks, almost all the crew were rescued but not one of them would talk, nobody can read a tight-lipped mouth and the eyes can lie readily, barefacedly even, the battle against loneliness is just as lost as the battle against death and the skirmish with indifference, against which it is customary to resort only to the light cavalry, almost all man's battles are lost in advance, more than half do not know that they are dying nor when they are lying upon their deathbeds or in the throes of death, a drowning man clutches at life even though the water slips through his fingers, Pepiño Tasaraño knows a great deal about mermaids and when he is in a cheerful mood he plays old anthems to them on the harmonica, Cósmede the deaf-mute is as happy as a clam in his shack on Gures beach, the love affair between Annelie and Vincent the hunchback may be going through a sticky patch or may be gradually on the wane, Annelie is most demanding but she is starting to weary of monotony, mermaids love stout, sturdy, strong-hearted seafarers, but they are so decent that they allow only the weak to glimpse them, mermaids with whiting tails are no good for anything but frying up in the pan with their tails tucked neatly in their mouths, it's a pity for them but law students and student teachers have to eat too, Elisabetiña serves her lodgers fried whiting with their tails tucked in their mouths, widows like to choke back memory and more than one fondles herself while whistling revolutionary marches, it is generally a hymn they whistle when fondling their little nephews to send them to sleep, Annelie is well on the way to being a dead woman although she is unaware of it, nobody knows that they are about to die—not even when they are dying, saying an Our Father to the Holy Company is as good as an alarm clock, this business about the Finisterre and Corcubión fishermen seems to me a little exaggerated, fishermen from the Azores and Shetland islands, too, are said to know each and every whale by name, though clearly it is a beautiful sentiment, chronicles are always written after the unfolding of the events recounted, nobody knows the pain of anybody else, the evil thoughts of anybody else, and within the dizzied head of the criminal proud excuses and timid, faltering arguments jostle and collide, it is not hard to turn an ordinary run-of-the-mill man into a criminal, all it takes is to place a weapon in his hands and convince him that God is on his side and that he is following the serene designs of God, crimes takes shape with great clarity within the head of the criminal, the worst thing is the testimony of God's cautious spy, only three sailors were saved from the *Serpent*, spewed upon the land by the sea, they did nothing, nor could they have done anything, at times a man with one foot in the grave senses that life is holding him fast, he does not have to do anything beyond letting himself be carried along.

"I insist on telling you, I'm growing tired of drawing it to your attention that this is very muddled and confusing."

"No, it is not even sort of muddled or sort of confusing, it is going its own way in orderly fashion, please understand that it is not my fault that it is beyond you."

"All right, I won't gainsay anyone for it isn't worth the trouble."

Dolorinhas, the Portuguese who was some sort of a nurse and knew how to administer injections and enemas, accompanied us to Santiago in the Dodge belonging to Micaela's Carliños, we would all like to unravel the mystery of death but, once your ears start to hum, good intentions are set aside and not only the most muddled desires but illusions, too, fall by the wayside, Uncle Knut likes to conduct experiments in recreational physics and eat fried birds, he also likes hefty brunettes, Uncle Knut combats rheumatism with a potion brewed from cloves of garlic steeped in *aguardiente*, five drops on a fasting stomach, you can supplement this with an infusion of maidenhair and bay leaves, the greatest courtesan in history looks the worse for wear lying in her coffin with a bandage strapped beneath her chin, it is not the same thing to die of tuberculosis as by stabbing, suffocating or strangling, each guise of death has its own mask and even coiffure, the dead battle against the common grave, they flee the common grave although they do not always win this senseless war, at this moment in the present chronicle a vacuum may be created in almost all heads, Annelie is known to have been killed because these lines were written after her death, it is also known how and by whom, though not why, nor do the judges care and in this they are mistaken, her body was not found until several days after her death, I had to content myself with dancing the two-step and riding horseback because Uncle Knut did not take me to hunt Marco Polo sheep, now I am too old for such a trip to so remote a country, the traveling laborer Pauliños was a starveling whom my Uncle Knut was able to bring into line by giving him a couple of belts across the face, Antona went a-begging in return for her confidences and Uncle Knut gave her a carton of kippers, Antona always goes around dressed in mourning because she does not wish to take liberties, she is deeply respectful and always tries to keep to her place, before Mínguez castrated Dubliner Johnny Jorick the fishing vessel *Tarambollo* went down on the Turdeiro rock, one man drowned, another went missing and the rest were spared, Vincent vanished without trace, hunchbacks are very sneaky, some folks say that he left on board the French steamer *Noirmoutier* which was tied up for several hours in Ponte do Porto unloading domestic appliances and cooking utensils, before leaving he dug up his gold coins, he also took along Annelie's jewelry and the stamp collection, I've said it once and I have yet to say it three more times: through Cornwall, Brittany and Galicia there wends a way strewn with crosses and nuggets of gold.

III

LEFT-HANDED DOÑA ONOFRE

(WHEN WE GIVE UP FISHING WITH FORBIDDEN SKILLS FOR GOOD)

B ETWEEN THE TURDEIRO and Petonciño rocks and the Parede shoals, south of the Finisterre promontory, the *Ulster Duke*, an English merchantman under tow, foundered and her masts can still be seen, five of her crewmen perished, also the French sailing ship *Brignogan* with a cargo of Argentinian wheat, her masts can still be seen, seven of her crewmen perished, Celso Manselle smothered his wife with a pillow and never felt a twinge of conscience, there is no need to be overly considerate with whores for the law of God is fair and grants everyone their just deserts, Viruquiña had been unfaithful to her husband with Salustiano García the fellow from the gas company and with Respiciño Baldomero, son-in-law of Santibirión the Rumpus Rouser who walked with a slight limp, Salustiano had a huge prick that was whorled like a wild boar's, and Respiciño, who delivered telegrams by bicycle, gratified women by hypnotizing them and giving them a sup of a corn-beard brew, will the whales hear tell of such dimensions and abilities? in the Arosa estuary two smugglers' speedboats collided and Manueliño Durán, also known as Kubala, was killed, he was the most famous of the traffickers because of his skill in handling these small craft, Breixo Vázquez, son of Mermeladas Baamonde, was seriously injured, Blessed be St. Breixo, hewn from birchwood, full cousin to my wooden clogs and blood brother to my 'baccy box! James E. Allen sometimes sings in English, when we forgo outlawed skills we return to the source and it is as though we were left naked with nothing to eat or drink, we gave up those outlawed skills because we were forced to, manly arms may battle against sea breakers, but against the Civil Guard there is no way of doing battle, the worst will be the day when we are forbidden to grow Jerusalem artichokes and teach blackbirds to whistle scales, goldfinches and nightingales trill naturally and are hatched knowing how to, James E. Allen played rugby and tennis, and sings verses from Poe, always Poe.

Thus, in discourse, the lovers whiled away
The night that waned and waned and brought no day.

Doña Onofre Teresa de Todos los Santos Freire de Andrade y Reimúndez, widow of Cela, Don Celso Camilo de Cela Sotomayor, retired notarial official, noted in her diary the words quoted below, Don Celso Camilo was no bright spark although indeed he hailed from a well-to-do family, well, fairly well off, besides his grandfather, his father and he were the men of the house, Don Celso Camilo was fond of reading although he was no bright spark, mention should now be made that the Portuguese brigantine *Carrapichana* crewed by Angolan seamen was fetched up on the cape off the Mañoto rock while waiting for the storm to abate, her cargo became dislodged and no matter what he did the master on board could not stop the sea from gaining the upper hand and wrenching the helm from his grasp, the brigantine foundered and her entire crew drowned, heathens made the virgin Locaia a Balagota eat her own vermin steeped in fox pee, a foul-smelling liquid steeps from the stinking soul of olives and serves solely to humiliate.

"Don't you believe that heathens should be condemned to death?"

"You may be right."

Doña Dosinda and my cousin Vitiño never tire of sipping gin in the hut on Calboa point, Doña Dosinda generally brings along chorizo, bread and coffee pastilles, she simmers a can of condensed milk for three hours which makes a delicious dessert which would remind you of chestnuts roasted in their skins, Cósmede thinks that at the bottom of the sea there strut not only peacocks in myriad colors but also birds of paradise which pluck the lyre with romantic inspiration, some twenty years back the Greek-flagged merchantman Anna

caught fire four miles off Finisterre—but that was a different vessel
from the Singapore-flagged *Anna Leonard*—and was spotted swathed
in smoke by Antonio Martínez Cambreiro, skipper of the fishing vessel *Arrogante* which came alongside, her five or six crewmen were up
on deck and had launched a life raft, the machinist threw himself
overboard and was killed, well, he drowned, Cambeiro was able to
catch hold of the line which they threw him and the crewmen slid
down it, Cambeiro ferried them ashore and raised the alarm among
other vessels in the area, the fishing boats *Sea Date* skippered by
Manuel Sar Vilela, the *Santa Rosa* skippered by Manuel Silva Castro,
the *María Teresa* skippered by Gervasio Martínez, and the *Gelkucho*
skippered by José Antonio Martínez, all from Finisterre, and the
Cabo Noval from Porto do Son, though the name of her skipper
escapes me now, all of them came to the rescue and towed the *Anna*
into Finisterre where she burned out, her hull remained afloat and
was later towed to Corcubión, listen to me now, Cam, you could turn
everybody's dream into reality, build a house with boxwood beams
and gold faucet fittings, but you are neither steadfast nor in great
health, you could also grow chili pepper, which are good for dispelling wind, don't forget, Cam, that the worst thing about dying
abroad is that you could wind up buried in a common grave in a
cemetery where you understand neither the language nor the
motives of the other jumbled-up dead which would lead to fawning
sorrow, you still have time to request that they cast you into the sea
with a stone tied to your feet, it would be beautiful to descend upon
the remains of the *Blas de Lezo*, that glorious wreck, Johnny Jorick
came down with typhus in hospital, or maybe it was viral pleurisy,
they never would tell me which, there is no call to castrate anybody
for a bet, pranksters should answer for their capers before the courts,
Idalio Zamora the fellow from the slaughterhouse was well-known as
a scrounger, he might have been a Frenchman: "Paco give me some
tobacco!" "Ismael give me a bit of paper!" "Evaristo give me a light
now that I've got my fag end rolled!", the *dorna* belonging to
Manueliño and Simeón was lost on Palleiro point, Simeón drowned
but Manueliño was rescued alive, they sent him to hospital and with-

in a few days he was as right as rain, what Doña Onofre wrote in her diary was as follows: the nuns of Saint-Joseph of Cluny slapped me because I was left-handed, they forced me to write with my right hand and then beat the living daylights out of me because my handwriting was poor, the Spanish cargo vessel *Carreño*, carrying ballast to Gijón, struck the treacherous Socabo rock where the seas seldom even break, four of her crewmen perished while three disappeared, nobody ever gets used to going hungry and God forgives those who steal food, the dead do not eat but the dead buried in the earth are devoured by maggots, while the sea's dead are devoured by the water which destroys them as if they were bread, sea bread, some twenty years ago now the body of José Velay Rivas hove in sight with his feet entangled in fishing tackle, he was found by Juan Traba el Monacho, skipper of the *Ulloa*, close to the Lobeira islands, he in turn alerted the skipper of the *Lorchiño* who called Finisterre by phone to raise the alarm, the engineer and four crewmen were swept away by the sea never to return, José was the eldest of ten siblings who all earned their crust from the sea, the fishing vessels *Santa Rosa*, *Hermanos Silva*, *Lorchiño*, *Beatriz* and *Hermanos Velay*, owned by the skipper's father, all joined in the search, while the other son, Juan de Tuno, weeps when he recalls his dead brother with a wound on his forehead, the family owned two other vessels, the *Hermanos Velay* and the Vulcano, Uncle Knut knows many things besides hunting whales but he doesn't say so, one day there will be no more whales and then we will all go hungry, whales have long memories and may cruelly avenge themselves upon us, people with no conscience have already begun to ban us from fishing the way we have always fished, they want to push us to the very brink, Doña Onofre recorded her troubles in her notebook: in the needlework class I always pricked my fingers because they would not allow me to embroider with my left hand, in the dining-room they shamed me if I stained my smock, which invariably happened, and Sister Julienne even said to me one day: Behave yourself, young lady, and use your hands like everybody else, good Christians and fine folk in general do not use their left hands for anything because it is the hand of the devil, every night implore the

Lord Jesus to help you ward off vices which sully good manners and
entreat him to help you to use your right hand, say a Hail Mary for
this special intention, in Christ Jesus there are two natures, two wills
and two understandings, one single divine person, who is the second
member of the Holy Trinity, and one single human memory, because
God as such has no memory, four crewmen from the fishing vessel
Planeta perished when she foundered off Finisterre, it would be no
easy matter to check whether Bourton, Gould and Lacsne had any
children or grandchildren, many years have gone by and they are likely to have lived cradled by fear with the sound of the Bois sea echo-
ing through their heads, the skull makes a good soundbox, tobacco,
tobacco, like that, twice, it seems that the one who started that rig-
marole was Alejo Salmer Estévez, the fellow from the Pastor Bank, in
his house they spoke Castilian because both he and his wife were
from Valencia de Alcántara, seafarers, some seafarers, maybe hardly
any seafarers because this too may not be true, call out "Tobacco,
tobacco!" like that, twice, to the slivers of stone they scrape from the
backs of dead or dying whales, on the Outer Sea beach one night nine
whales were stranded and it was impossible to return them to the
sea, they took several days to die, people took photos of them and
plundered the flesh from their backs, slicing it off with bayonets and
handsaws, Damianciño Wolf Rump came armed with a cavalry saber,
in the wreck of the French barque *Biscarrosse* the Italian tenor Guido
Valtelini drowned, swept away by a breaker while singing the aria
from Act One of *Nabucco*, it is a lovely thing to die with theatrical
dignity, on naval charts the islet which is almost always shrouded in
dense, clinging, poetic fog is marked as the Centolo, northwest of the
overhanging Finisterre cliffs midway between the Mañoto rock and
Oídos point, though to my mind and in Don Benjamin's view
Centolo is a misprint for Centulo, many vessels foundered on the
Centulo, some of them historic events like the wreck of the *Blas de
Lezo*, gannets, hardy birds, nest on the Centulo, in the monastery of
San Xiao of Moraime knights swore loyalty to the Swabian kings and
swung from the boughs of oak trees in order to get a breath of fresh
air upon their chests and private parts, fresh air is good for keeping

misery at bay, cattle on the stony slopes of Touriñán must be hungry for they are scrawny and lackluster, it may be that the devil stalks these parts stealing milk from cows and eating quail eggs, one morning on this rocky land a dead body was discovered wearing a watch that was still ticking, the dead man had passed on just a short time before, the body was stiff and cold but had not yet started to decay, and bore no traces of blows or even needlepricks, and folks soon forgot all about it, someone stole the watch, what did need did the dead man have for it anyway? shortly before Viruquiña died smothered by her husband, thoughtless Celso Manselle learned to say the pi logarithm formula and repeated it constantly, rorquals navigate by describing regular orbits which may be studied using the pi logarithm, Viruquiña did not say this, nor did Sister Julienne because she is French, but Sister María who hails from Corcubión says of left-handed people that their fingers are all thumbs, Sister María had a sweetheart in the merchant marines who perished at sea, that was before she took the veil, the following conversation might have taken place at the very gates of hell, or even limbo, never let accuracy be a hindrance.

"Do you believe that it is a bad thing to be left-handed?"

"Why should it be?"

At Cape la Nave, the westernmost point in Galicia., more westerly even than Finisterre, between the beaches of the Outer sea and Mar de Rostro, the Cypriot cargo vessel *Troghodhos* foundered on Christmas Eve 1940, five of her fourteen crewmen were rescued alive, the gorse bushes have been Galician for longer than the hydrangeas and camellias, from the beginning to the end of the world the sound of the sea has always come: whoosh, whoosh, whoosh, Floro Cedeiro thinks that the sea comes and goes but he is mistaken, the lowing of the cows has always been coming too and has never gone away, the sea bellows like a chorus of a thousand calving cows, Pencho Ventoso tells tales of apparitions which speak through signs and live off the Sanctuary lamp oil like owls, Pencho starts to recount and when he stops, he pauses and then continues in a different rhythm, even with a different purpose, Moors and Christians in the village of Trez, perched on a hillside where the carts have to be tethered so they don't roll off on their own, hold a mock battle on the Feast of the Apostle, the Christians always get the upper hand, Cape la Nave is thus named because of its resemblance to a Greek nave or ship, according to legend all the heroes of the world embark for eternity there under the command of Hermes, not far from this spot lie the villages of Hermedesuxo de Enriba and Hermedesuxo de Embaixo, in both Hermedesuxo villages they bury wolves in quicklime in order to kill their souls, the world was born at the same moment as time but the world grows old and time does not, to the north, in Miñones Bay which lies within a stone's throw of Cormes, the *Nueva Elvira* foundered and all hands were lost: two men went missing while one man perished.

"Do you think it is a bad thing to be cross-eyed?"

"Could be worse."

On the Lesser Berrón the Portuguese coastal cutter *Filipinha Nova* went down, two of her crewmen perished and the rest were saved, today it forms the lonesome haunt of elderly mermaids and octopuses of licentious ways, octopuses are generally clean-living when young yet full of vice when they grow old.

"Do you think it is a bad thing to be one-eyed?"

"You have to thank God for the fifty percent remaining."

Two further coastal cutters were wrecked on this same rock: the *Roquiño* from Pontevedra with the loss of three lives and the *San Mamede* from Betanzos without loss of life, it is very funny to see the octopuses on the Lesser Berrón speaking pig Latin, the other type being more difficult.

"What about having a stutter? Do you think it is a bad thing to stutter?"

"Aw, I think it is cute!"

In A Muñiza the collier *Cabo Machichaco* went down without loss of life, they were unable to tow her because her lines snapped, hedge mustard sprouts on garbage dumps and lights up poverty with its yellow blossom.

"What about having one testicle?"

"Some folks aver that having three is worse."

"I don't know what to say! Better a feast than a famine, I would think."

On the Casteláns Norte sandbank lightning killed the skipper and all the oarsmen from the fishing smack *Forcaredo*.

"What about being a faggot?"

"That all depends on your tastes, it's like having a limp."

Some twelve or fifteen miles from Finisterre a South Korean-flagged merchantman collided with and sank the Spanish-Moroccan fishing vessel *Bnou I Shark*, her eight crewmen—four Moroccans, four Chinamen, well, Koreans they were—perished, the French cargo vessel *Saint-Cyprien* foundered without loss of life on the South Casteláns sandbar.

"What about being flat-footed?"

"That is the most painful of all because it is bewildering, a flat-footed man is under no obligation to love his fellow man nor to honor his father and mother, a flat-footed man can even be a faggot without anybody asking any questions."

On the Sambrea shoal a few years back there foundered a steamship the name of which nobody knew, it all happened so quickly that nobody even saw her afloat, her entire crew perished, the dance of intermediary states is lighted by virgin wax torches by the dwarves who keep order in the stage set of the seven deadly sins, then one of them raised his voice and said, life, no, but the tale of the climax of life is like a waterwheel which never wearies of turning upon its axle, when a donkey is hitched to the yoke of the waterwheel and its eyes are blindfolded it starts to walk and do rounds, Fiz o Alorceiro lost his wits when he saw the devil getting up to hanky-panky with Cirís from Fadibón but the priest from San Xurxo of the Seven Dead Foxes continues to conceal the fact that he is a corpse blessed by three patron saints, Our Lords St. Xoan, St. Peter and St. Antón have no wish to see folks sorrowful, in Muros there was an American who kept a peacock, Cósmede thinks that the bottom of the sea is full of blind, unobtrusive peacocks, no more secrets than are strictly necessary are going to be told of Doña Onofre, the last

time I spoke to her was in the Mariquito Café, when she asked me
for one thousand pesetas to have her highlights touched up at Cora's
hairdressing salon in Santiago, I later found out that the money was
to buy her medication, some folks are embarrassed to be on medication while others take pride in it and tell all and sundry, James E.
Allen gave up being a winger for the Hunslet Boys rugby team when
he turned twenty-five, Mariquito was the son of Mariquita and the
bar was always known as Mariquito's, when she died her heir carried
out some renovations and renamed it the Mariquito Café, Doña
Onofre used to breakfast in the Mariquito Café because her house
was just above it, they started to call Dosindiña Doña Dosinda once
she turned thirty, do you know whether the Apostle St. James could
forgive a man who sold the alarm clock he inherited from his father?
it is my view that he could for his power is far-reaching, the
Pontevedran coastal cutter *Penique* which was carrying ballast went
down on the Baralla sandbar, all it took was two slams to the bilges
for the breakers to split her in two, her entire crew perished, the virgin Locaia a Balagota is no longer keeping her eyes peeled for seafarers, so much indifference has made her grow weary, there was greater
solidarity, complicity even, in the olden days, a convalescent survivor was allowed to sleep with a woman of the house for a night,
Rosalía de Castro was never forgiven for saying so, some folks believe
that the Coast of Death runs from Corunna to the Stinking beach in
A Guarda, where the stench gets up sailors' noses, from the Marola
rock—once you cross the Marola rock you can cross the entire sea
they say—and the Torre de Hercules and Orzán bay down to the river
Miño and Camposancos beach just across from Portugal, though this
may be an exaggeration, although the sea is ferocious both in what
has gone before and in what is yet to come, Orzán bay peters out on
Riazor beach, country folks pile down to Riazor for the Feast of St.
Christopher, while swimmers come for the Feast of St. Catalina,
from Carreiro point and Burro point the sea loses something of its
wildness but this should not be taken to mean that it becomes calm,
in the Lower Estuaries the sea loses respect on the mussel rafts
which are now starting to be placed in orderly fashion, between the

fog and a fault in her rudder the *Nil* ran aground on Xan Ferreiro, on Arou beach, the *Nil* was carrying a cargo of luxury goods: French automobiles—Citroën, Renault, Peugeot—damask silks, pharmaceutical products and champagne, cases of champagne, her nineteen crewmen and passengers were taken to Camelle and thence to Corcubión, the captain held out as long as he could, he had no water so he made coffee from champagne, when he saw that the vessel could not be extricated from the shoal where she was stuck fast he moved into Camelle, the *Nil* was eventually stripped bare, in the village of Valdemiñán last year there died Estreliña de Rouca the witch who made people possessed spew forth the devil, by stabbing a black cat to death, a beast in which the evil enemy generally lurks in the guise of a basilisk, laden with porcelain crockery, the Italian steamer *Giulianova* struck the Chedeiro shoal, two of her crewmen perished while one went missing, until recently her masts could still be seen, the first thing Estreliña usually does is to crucify the cat with iron nails upon an olive log, then the person possessed should repeat aloud with their eyes wide open: perverse spirit, in the name of Jesus Christ I command you to come forth and torment me no more, the person possessed may be scourged with a rod upon the legs and shoulders to encourage him to speak forth, meanwhile the witch says the Credo and makes the sign of the cross as often as necessary and kills the cat with a knitting needle, Winkle the sacristan is a terrible liar but when he is spinning a yarn he twists his mouth in a way that tips people off and smirks like a lizard too, the Gaucho poet Hilario Ascasubi had a great fondness for civil wars and cultivated nostalgia, the Spanish Navy container ship *Delfín del Mediterráneo* foundered off the coast of Portugal lashed by a northwesterly storm, her fourteen crewmen abandoned ship in three lifeboats, one man drowned while the others were rescued two days later by marine rescue teams, Father Socorro's housekeeper, Maria Flora, gets up to hanky-panky with the dog but she douses the light beforehand, with general cargo on board the Yugoslav steamer *Rijeka* foundered on the Furatoxos shoals, one crewman was rescued with his dog but all the others went missing, pink-colored dolphins with a broad emerald green

stripe across their backs are seldom seen, the priest in Morquintiáns'
housekeeper swears she saw three of them leaping over the rocks at
Robaleira point, where the gulls were swooping overhead in curiosity, the fishing vessel *Vikingo* went down quite far away, up around
Cape Vilán, her thirteen crewmen were rescued, fourteen crewmen
from the English fishing vessel *Osako* were also rescued, a faraway
saint can work great wonders, that is not true and it is unhealthy to
believe it, the fishing vessel *Gondiez I* ran on the rocks at the Torre
de Hercules, three men perished while four went missing, the knitting needle pricks must be protracted so that the cat feels death more
keenly, the saint on your own doorstep cannot work wonders, this is
not true either and it is unhealthy to say so, the heart of the cat
should not be pierced because there is no need to be charitable to the
cruel enemy, in the Roibal weedbank the Portuguese coastal cutter
Murtosa went down, her entire crew drowned for they could not dis-
entangle themselves from the strands of weed, when the cat is dead
its eyes are gouged out, the body is placed in a sack together with a
snake, five scorpions, a foetus from a spinster who is not from these
parts—it makes no difference if the father is from hereabouts—the
sack is then secured with a guitar string and cast into the sea, for the
purposes of military manoeuvers the squadron was split into two
groups: the reds, charged with taking the Corcubión estuary by force,
and the blues, charged with its defense, the *Blas de Lezo* was the flagship vessel for the red group, on June 11, 1932 at half past three in the
afternoon, on a flood tide with wisps of fog gathering the *Blas de
Lezo* struck the shoals known as the Meixidos, between the Centulo
and the cliffs of Finisterre, she was trying to squeeze through a narrow channel where she could not fit, this rock is not shown on
Spanish Naval charts but is indeed marked on the British Admiralty
ones and local fishermen know it well, this is where the French cargo
vessel *Pierre Lavandoise* was wrecked, her five crewmen perished
and some years ago the cruiser *Cardinal Cisneros* went down there
too, the *Blas de Lezo* sprang a leak and started to list badly, the tugboat *Argos* came at full tilt from Corunna to stand by her but did not
make it in time, first there passed the destroyers *Sánchez*

Barcáiztegui and the *Lepanto*, then the cruiser *Méndez Núñez* which touched bottom and finally the *Blas de Lezo* which was scudding along when she ran on the rock bow first and tore her hull asunder, her entire crew scrambled to safety and the *Blas de Lezo* drifted half sunken to the entrance of the Muros estuary, where years before the *Cardinal Cisneros* had been lost, it seems as though ships select their watery graves alongside other vessels, my Uncle Knut is going blind, his pale blue eye is growing whiter while his green eye is losing its sparkle by the day, in the Caneliñas whaling station some nights you can hear the accordion playing and verses by Poe in Galician, though not in English, nine men perished and eight went missing from the fishing vessel *Os Tonechos* wrecked north of Baldaio beach, they wanted to run the *Blas de Lezo* up on Finisterre beach but her lines snapped and it all went awry, in this unfortunate incident mention was also made of magnetic phenomena which skewed the compass, the *Blas de Lezo* was the swiftest vessel in the Spanish Navy and the one which escorted Ramón Franco's seaplane, the *Plus Ultra*, to the island of Fernando Noronha, the *Blas de Lezo* finally sank off the Muros Estuary between the Lugo and Pordela shoals which are not marked on Spanish nautical charts but are shown on British Admiralty charts, local fishermen know them well, popular opinion condemned the *Blas de Lezo*, but it was the flagship's fault, sixty millions, Lord, what Spain lost! the *Serpent* was sunk by a northwesterly storm and all hands on board perished bar three, the *Blas de Lezo* was lost as a result of incompetence, what a pain, and all hands were saved, thank God! anybody hankering after the old ways is perhaps grieved that nobody got a bullet in the temple, from Gures beach Cósmede Pedrouzas the deaf-mute and his two animals stood gaping at this painful event, Cósmede Pedrouzas is no longer afraid of anything for he is used to losing, what good did it do Feliberto Urdilde to beat my cousin Vitiño at arm wrestling when in the end he was struck by a bottle of gin that split his head in two? Doña Onofre Freire had a love affair with a canon from Santiago called Father Sebastian Caramés Trillo, now this is a closely guarded secret which hardly a soul knows about and nobody, absolutely nobody, remarks

upon, my relation and Father Sebastian used to meet in Ponte
Nafonso, in the home of Purita Magariños, who had been a classmate
of Doña Onofre's, Father Sebastian had a cyst the size of peach on the
nape of his neck which he thought was funny, one day they met up
in the Araguaney hotel and had to beat a hasty retreat when they
were nearly discovered, some folks say that isn't true, at least nobody
could swear that it was true, they say that they both slipped in
through the garage entrance, one first then the other, he dressed as a
woman and she as a man, but that they had to beat a hasty retreat
because people were staring at them, women are highly courageous,
they may seem cowardly but are in fact courageous, their bravery
may even verge upon temerity and at times they do not draw back
even in the very teeth of danger but may even seek it out, Doña
Onofre, with her old-fashioned holier-than-thou look and her hint of
a shameful, mysteriously lascivious moustache, wasn't one to watch
her step but she was spared the scandal which such lustful encounters generally lead to because God is great and also discreet, discretion is the bulwark and bastion of honor, its very cornerstone indeed,
even more so than darkness or the tempest, two crewmen perished
and another two went missing when the yacht *Choliñas* was
wrecked after setting sail from Sanxenxo, Doña Onofre is left-handed and this is something which throws men off their stride because
they are caught off guard, Doña Onofre screws (if you'll pardon my
French), well, she makes loves more gently than Doña Dosinda, more
tenderly and cosily, it is also true that Father Sebastian rides (if you'll
pardon my French), well, mounts from behind less than my cousin
Vitiño, though we cannot generalize or reach conclusions upon such
matters because everyone is his own man and nobody ever learns
from anybody else, particularly at full moon Doña Dosinda likes
hanky-panky and wild fantasies, while Doña Onofre does not, Doña
Onofre prefers indefatigable, libidinous monotony, according to Don
Eudaldo Vilarvello, King Joseph Bonaparte was a close friend of
General Cabanellas and they met up at the outset of the 1936 Civil
War, more than likely to deal with matters of state, some say that it
was on the Lesser Sisarga island, where mermaids dally, and others

that it was on the Lesser Lobeira, where herring gulls gather, the
worst of it is that this matter will never be cleared up, the lads whose
souls went to burn in purgatory because they didn't give a toss about
the sermon cannot leave the Holy Company because nobody prays
for them, and it serves them right, dead men with gold teeth are highly sought after by beachcombers, the Scandinavians and the English,
as well as the Germans, the Dutch and half the French have top quality gold teeth, whereas crews sailing under a flag of convenience generally have mouths full of rotten stumps, soon after Annelie was laid
to rest nobody spoke of her death any more, nothing was ever heard
of Vincent again, everybody knows that hunchbacks are slippery fish
because their souls are smeared with snail spit, Don Sadurniño
Losada jotted down his pearls of wisdom in green ink, Cape Finisterre
lies southeast of the Centulo surrounded by rocks and other hazards,
this is a little studied corner, people are afraid even to look at it, at
the mouth of the Pontevedra estuary lie the islands of Ons and Onza
and between them at low tide you can see an islet which is also
called the Centulo, neither I nor anybody else could swear that the
beaked sperm whale which was stranded on Traba beach was the
devil, the spirit of the devil is always at the ready and is distrustful
by nature, Father Ireneo Serafín, the priest in Portela de Caldebarcos,
thought in his heart: I will not leave room in my heart for evil
thoughts and I will hold my tongue about what I think because what
remains unspoken dies within us, Father Ireneo Serafín took the
cloth after he was widowed, turning towards Finisterre we pass
Puntela point where the devil washes the dead departed in mortal sin
before dispatching them to hell, here the coastal cutter *Chafalleiro*
went down and five crewmen perished, her masts can still be seen,
may God forgive me but to my mind Dorothy has a liking for women,
maybe she cannot help it, the devil washes the eyes of the sinful dead
with turpentine and sluices their tongues with Dettol and permanganate in equal parts, this is followed by the Almirante shoals where
the lass Rosalía Silleiro drowned when her sweetheart left her—he
dumped her for a Zamora woman who had run away from her husband—Oídos rock and point where fish leap ashore to sunbathe and

relax, the stony slopes and rocks of Xastosa where the wind screech-
es like the skirl of the pipes, Regala point clustered with clumsy,
tasty pilgrim scallops, the Outer Paxariño rocks with their warm
waters, the Turdeiro rock as yet untamed, the treacherous Socabo
whence the dolphins flee because it sends out shocks like an electric
light, only charity can spare half-wits from rheumatism, around the
unrepentant Socabo there passes some nights the Holy Company of
mariners lost at sea, all wan and sickly, with spluttering coughs and
staring, wide-open eyes, the Parede shoals which separate limbo from
purgatory, the border runs to the river Bidasoa and even beyond, as
far as the river Garona, the Petonciño rock which produces the most
beautifully etched blue crabs in all of Christendom, the Centolleira
where the coast switches back and the sea bass disport themselves,
skipping and letting the diabolo fly, Porto das Moscas where the
number of poets who have committed suicide there, by slitting their
wrists and letting their blood flow into the sea, now stands at three,
King Amadeus of Savoy was reincarnated as the piper Lambertiño
Lestrove who was always cranky because his pecker itched and hurt,
Lambertiño was ailing with cancer of the prick which caused him
great suffering and setbacks, Lambertiño was some sort of relative of
Father Ireneo the priest but he claimed to be a Republican atheist,
maybe God ordered King Amadeo to be reincarnated in him in order
to teach him a lesson.

"And put him in his place?"

"Well, in a manner of speaking."

Whales are unified, indivisible creatures, it's the same as with
juniper in the plant kingdom: what appears to be one whale, or one
juniper, may turn out to be but the fin of a whale or the tip of a single juniper, a whole juniper wood may be just one single juniper
while a pod of whales may be just one single whale, this is no easy
matter to understand, neither is the mystery of the Holy Trinity for
that matter, nature likes to disguise herself in order to sow confusion
and the deity is marking her step, with even her head swathed in her
Manila shawl, María Floro, Father Socorro's housekeeper, starts to
weep for the shamelessness of sinners, one in every three widows is

utterly shameless and spends her evenings sipping coffee and smoking, Manuel Blanco Romasanta, the werewolf from Rebordechao in the Allariz mountains, was related to Father Socorro, he would tell young lasses that he was taking them to Castile to serve in good families and then would tear them asunder, between Paraisás and Pena Folenche which lie on either side of Pobla de Trives, a lustful young woman was cursed by her mother: "Away with you! May you be turned into a wolf and let that put a halt to your gallop!" and the young woman was turned into a wolf known as the people's wolf.

"Not she-wolf?"

"No, because nobody knew that she was a woman."

The damsel was rescued by a handsome young man who was watching over the land where chestnuts were spread out to dry, he burnt the wolfskin and then married her, women do not generally turn into wolves, Don Sadurniño did not know of any others, but all this has precious little to do with what we were talking about, a good Manila shawl is worth a pretty penny.

"Do you think that the Lord God can handle whales as readily as if they were halibut?"

"Indeed I do, the Lord God can always do whatever he wishes, that's why he is the Lord God, there is nobody above him."

The wind sculpted a wistful rod fisherman from the rock at Bufadoiro point, a pregnant woman missed her footing, fell into the sea and drowned at Inquieiro point where the river of the same name flows into the sea, the river Inquieiro flows into the sea at Cabanas beach, where the Wine-Stained rock stands with its red wine stain which never disappears, French fishermen gave a cask of wine to the hermit of San Guillén, or maybe it was Don Gaiferos, though others say that it was a Hungarian nobleman who had behaved cruelly in the Naples war, or also William of Acquitaine or William of Orange, nobody knows for sure, but the devil offered his assistance and halfway along the road he treacherously pushed both hermit and cask so that they hurtled downhill, nobody can remove that stain because by the will of God it is the symbol of the eucharist, on rogation days Finisterre folk would go to hear mass at that rock, halfway along there stands a boulder shaped like a frog with its mouth gaping open, this frog is said to have drunk all the water from the land and when they saw they were going to die of thirst men and beasts asked the frog to return the water but the frog did so only when an eel slithered by and then let such a guffaw that he could no longer contain himself, and that was the start of the Great Flood, on the road to the lighthouse stands the Cabanas water trough, there are two others in Finisterre: the Xuruxano and Mixirica, next to Cabanas beach is the enchanted cave which ends on the western side of the promontory, beneath the spot where herring gulls perch and which, in times gone by, served as both a storehouse and hiding place for smugglers, Cain slew his brother Abel because he did not read the Book of Proverbs nor could he gauge the scope of agreements, this farce of families poisoning themselves on the ephemeral spume of the pomp and vanity of auction sales leaves a bitter aftertaste, drama has an unknown ending and a hidden dénouement, whereas tragedy has a known outcome, it is just a matter of how this is arrived at, animals are dramatic, the domestic animal more so than the wild, both man and the fugitive animal are tragic, in a dolmen on top of San Guillén hill hewn from living rock stands the tomb of Orcavella, a witch of over three hundred years of age who ordered that she should be done away with when she saw that the hour of death was nigh, that knell which can neither be delayed nor brought forward for a single instant, the witch buried a shepherd alive in order to rest upon his body, his fellow shepherds wanted to rescue him but were unable to do so because one hundred rabid wolves and over one thousand enraged vipers were unleashed to do battle with them.

"Why will you not admit that this is garbled and unbalanced?"

"Because that isn't true, it is only slightly garbled and I believe that it is better and wiser not even to say so."

The Holy Rocks stand on top of the promontory, there are two of them, both very weighty but they can be moved with just a single finger and serve to tell whether or not a young woman is a virgin, when she is called upon to pass over the rock, a phrase which also carries a different connotation.

"Confusing?"

"Well, perhaps slightly confusing."

The soul in torment of Lieutenant Jack Essex sings sentimental ballads and other songs in a tuneful voice in order to captivate the hearts of young widows or elderly spinsters, mulatto women offer less resistance and fewer excuses, Jack Essex served as navigation officer on board the *Captain*, the English warship which was wrecked on the Centulo, though nowadays nobody remembers it, his melodious voice from beyond the grave can still be heard on a solid-state radio or in a seashell sluiced with rosemary alcohol then smeared with wasp honey from Castromiñán dipped in the waters of the spring of San Xes de Paderne, patron of the deaf, the Portuguese General Paiva Couceira, who resided in Spain, wished to overthrow the republic and restore the monarchy in his native land so he organized the battle of Chaves, he let it be known far and wide that he would invade Portugal and warned that he would attack through Chaves, just across from Verín, on the other side of the border, my grandfather and my Uncle Amaro the Limousin, who was a tailor in Puebla de Sanabria beyond the Marabón mountains, ordered some pork pasties and then set off with some friends and actresses to watch the battle and enjoy a day out in the country, they took along an Edison phonograph so as to dance a little during the interludes, Uncle Amaro was a tailor but then he turned thief—you won't find a stitcher who never snitches a pair of britches—when Fideliño the Pig shot himself in the mouth all the seabirds suddenly fell silent out of respect and so as not to offend the Holy Ghost with complicity or calumny, you have no reason to know or to remember how savagely the winter kills off the poor in spirit, short-sighted fishermen and black sailors, they all spit blood, nobody should wallow in their own misfortune, quietly delight in their own downfall, there are fourteen articles of faith: the first seven pertain to the deity and the other seven to holy humanity, men get along as best they can and enjoy a few drinks together or beat the living daylights out of one another, it all depends, this can be seen at romerías, Lucheni the anarchist turned into a cemetery snail after stabbing the empress Sisí, nobody would acknowledge his right to oblivion and even his most loyal companions withheld their greetings, then he thought that the moment of recounting his frustrations had come and he turned into a cemetery snail, in the Corme tunnel, as you are heading for the stone crosses commemorating fallen goose barnacle fishermen, there are also tasty, plump, white snails, men get along as best they can, Finisterre folk and people from Cee never got along well, Finisterre folks are fishermen while folks from Cee are high and mighty, and folks from Corcubión are caught between the two and have no crow to pluck with anybody, nowadays Cee and Corcubión are linked by the Drylands, a salt marsh which was developed in ultramodern style, between Inquieiro point and Cabanas cove, where the wives of fishermen would go down to prepare a hot fish stew upon their return from the sea, stand the Saurade stone and the Cercado rock wherein the spirit of a Redemptorist monk was heard playing the hurdy-gurdy with the chords of the breeze, also the Xuncal spring whose waters cure weariness as well as heartburn and sorrow, too, they say, the ballast of solitude is intelligence, along with independence and pride, I know what I wish to say and what I wish to hold my tongue about, when you notice that people are avoiding your gaze, sleep with your shotgun at hand, the traitor is easy to scare off, my cousin Vitiño clad the hut at Calboa point with pine logs on the outside and lined it with mud flaked with whitewash on the inside, now there is no fear of the wind sweeping it away or the rain swamping it, there are no drafty cracks and the fire is always burning in the hearth so it is snug and cosy, my cousin installed a zinc bathtub which has to be filled and emptied by hand but that is no big deal, though what it lacks is a toilet, once Doña Dosinda, Antucha la Garela, Carmelina de Claudia, Vitiño, Moncho Bergondo and I gathered there to spend the evening, we used to meet up each year at around carnival time, first the women would bathe us men with scented soap amid gales of laughter, then we ate the food they had prepared for us: octopus with potatoes, chopped pork with fried eggs, bacon and pancakes, and quaffed the copious quantities of drink they served us, wine first, then *aguardiente*, and then we took a roll in the hay to be loosen us up and relax, everyone with his proper partner for this was not a time for promiscuity of the flesh but rather for spiritual instruction, finally we listened to what Doña Dosinda had to say to us, the men in their underpants and berets and the women stark naked, they were no spring chicks but still goodlooking women with full, firm breasts and their hair hanging loose, Lord, what a mess we made! leftover food and bodily filth were thrown into the hearth where the flames consumed it all, what I am talking about now and what then occurred took quite some time for nobody was hurrying us along, Doña Dosinda announced that she was going to say a piece which she called the sermon of the three words and then held forth as follows:

"Word one: solitude. I have grown weary of so much crossing the desert, I have been crossing the desert alone for many years now and am ashamed to have to admit it, I would wish to share the same fears with someone but everybody shuns me as though I were an outcast, I want to leave this desert because solitude is not worth the effort, I declare that I would be willing to spoon-feed my man—or my two men, or my three men—breakfast in bed, until they die of old age."

On Corveiro beach, below the church of Santa María de las Arenas, lovers are in their element, Doña Dosinda continued with her speechifying:

"Word two: servitude. I know full well that woman is man's handmaid because God ordained it thus, I take the opposing view but nobody believes me, a man with an erect penis is as beautiful as an eagle in flight or a trotting horse, woman should have three men to serve: her husband, her lover and her reserve man, woman should entrust her soul to God when she has no man to serve, purgatory is full of the souls of women who would not serve anybody or anything."

The storm sank the fishing vessel *Baitín* off the Muros estuary, the sea swept four seafarers away, Doña Dosinda concluded her speech:

"Word three: will. Everyone should put their will at the service of their own interest even though it may seem capricious, and woman even more so than man, Moncho, for instance, lets some rip-roaring farts and Antucha chuckles at him but that is because it suits her, nobody is pushing her to do so and it is her will to please Moncho, you fart better and better, Moncho, with every passing day you are perfecting the art, you are a real champion, Moncho, it is great to hear you."

The Christ of Finisterre was washed up on Cabanas beach where the sea gently deposited him and when he is able to and is devoutly entreated he assists seafarers in their battle against the billows and other perils, Holy Christ of Finisterre, saint of the golden beard, help me to brave the Touriñana shoals, his golden beard is darker now, darkened by time, for time and misfortune blacken everything they touch, the Christ of Finisterre put manners on the Moors when they rose up against him and wished to offend him, in a raid they made hereabouts in the second half of the seventeenth century Berber pirates mocked the Christ of Finisterre, one of them wanted to strike him down with a slash of his scimitar but the Christ glared at him, and left him rooted to the spot like a statue with a humiliating, high-pitched voice, the Moors then repented of their attitude and Christ let them leave, according to tradition they converted to Christianity and were baptized in the town of Cee, the Finisterre Christ is renowned as a firebrand—though whether justly or unjustly isn't rightly known—who will take the odd potshot when the need arises, the Finisterre Christ carries a golden gun, it may be that Doña Onofre indulges in sin like everybody else, sins of the flesh, that is why God made the flesh sinful and the heart to grieve and the intention to mend your ways, etc., God invented both sin and forgiveness for sin, the devil is but a servant of God's and may be struck down all of a sudden, even where sinning is concerned you have to watch your step and keep up appearances, Doña Onofre has nothing to do with Doña Dosinda, Antucha la Garela, Carmelina de Claudia nor, indeed, with anyone, the fact that they may have gone to bed with the same man, either wittingly or unwittingly, is not sufficient reason for not even fidelity is a must when needs are pressing, neither character nor good breeding are passed on like a dose of the clap, nor has good breeding any connection with lust, neither for nor against, that is not what is intended, lust unites will, reveals inclinations and lays bare temperament but is not on an equal footing with principle, the long-line fishing vessel *Velasco II* foundered as a result of the rough sea and her eleven crewmen went missing, pasties—just like omelettes and croquettes—can be made with anything at all and always taste delicious when cooked just right, on the Bofetóns and Xan de Palleiros rock, which lie at the foot of San Guillén mountain below the crag of the crows and Corveiro beach as you coast in from the open sea towards Finisterre harbor, you can catch delicious, tasty octopus, cooking them requires mysterious knowledge and they are said to improve when taken inland from the coast, the Melide octopus sellers are renowned, they set up their huge tin cooking vats along the highway, the Rumanian cargo vessel *Topolovani* sank in a sudden squall off Corunna, half of her twenty-eight crew perished, that was on Christmas Day ten years ago, when Xan from Labaña the Chainsmoker hollered to Fideliño the Pig to bury him on hallowed ground a shiver ran through all the maggots of death counting off the hours of grief and misfortune one by one, it is a pity that there are no storm clocks, as there are hourglasses and sundials, it would be a complicated operation though a highly curious mechanism and the course followed by the rorqual whales would indicate both air and sea temperature, wind speed, atmospheric pressure and the dance of the three last henchmen of runaway death, or death about to be unleashed, women believe that life and happiness or misfortune are governed only by man with his wiles and they strive to destroy the mask of conformity, the mask of patience, at Bardullas point, within a stone's throw of Finisterre harbor, Brother Ceferino de Tanantíns, an Amazonian bishop garbed in white vestments, went down to gaze out over the sea and say a Hail Mary when the wind swept him away like a Breton friar, men from the fishing smack *Boliche* picked up his lifeless body as they returned from the fishing grounds, the Norwegian oil tanker *Polycomander* struck Cabalo point, on the North island, or Monte Agudo, in the Cie archipelago and spilled over fifty thousand tons of crude oil into the sea, that black tide killed off seabirds, fish, shellfish and seaweed throughout the area and sowed solitude and death, in San Carlos castle in Finisterre the Moor Salem ben Tarhit was held captive for over three hundred years, his skeleton slumbers its eternal rest in an airless dungeon and at times his ghost still appears, harmless, good-natured, and runs errands for summer visitors, but the point is not to recount the tale of the Moor because everything that is said of him is more than likely untrue, El Porto is a little cove north of San Carlos castle between Bardullas point and Figueira cove, "pesco" refers to fisherman and fishmonger, netsman, fish-salter and shipwright, any man who fishes or earns his living from fishing, as well as to the language spoken by the coast dwellers of Finisterre and Muxía, although I don't think it goes quite as far as a dialect, the fishing vessel *La Xana* ran on the Moador shoals, at the entrance to Muxía, four crewmen perished, one went missing and three were saved when a sudden squall drove them onshore, a sudden jolt and she split in two like the gourds adorning the morgue where autopsies are carried out, seafarers sometimes sail with the wind and are driven inshore or offshore by wind and wave, towards life or towards death, eastward with its angler fish, or westward with its cachalot whales and seven sea serpents, on the beach in Figuera Cove there was once washed ashore the uncorrupted body of a beautiful young mermaid said to be called Mafalda, her lips and eyes were made up and a beguiling smile played on her lips, skipper Camilo de Androve placed her upon his dining room dresser and kept her there until she grew moth-eaten, then the skipper burned her body in the hearth because he did not know whether to bury the body or cast it into the sea, airborne as a puff of smoke the mermaid was closer to the Apostle St. James, between Bardullas point and Langosteira, or Lagosteira beach, the hamlet of Finisterre nestles south of Porcallón point, Riveira beach lies within the village itself while Cabalo and Raposo beaches lie below the Cruz de Baixar cliff, you can eat well and cheaply everywhere in Finisterre, Manuel from the Cape Finisterre restaurant dishes up delicious food prepared with great care, now they have opened new premises where they barbecue food to perfection, this stretch of coastline is rugged and confusing and off it lies Conserva point and the Porcallón weedbank, halfway up the hill the village of Insua can be seen on the slopes of the mountain facing east and west, with its ancient houses, patches of maize, fields of cabbage and potatoes, dun cows and sturdy, fleecy sheep, and were it not for the emerald and gold lizards you would think you were in New Zealand, Langosteira bay stretches from Finisterre to Sardiñeiro point, the beach is over one mile long and runs as far as Canto de Area point, the shoreline is clear except for an outcropping of the Pardas reef which dries at low water, the river Blanquiño joins the sea on Langosteira beach, after flowing through the villages of San Martín and Duio, though this is not the Nerian capital which was swept away by the wind and buried beneath the sea but a different village, a little farther on the river Grande meets the sea, flowing from Escaselas and from the two Hermedesuxo villages, collecting water from the Mallo and Vigo rivers, some folks call this spot Llangosteira in memory of the Catalans who set up the first canning factories here, Father Sarmiento states that even in ancient documents that spacious sea shell sweep which tapers into Corcubión was known as "mare locustarum", its vast dunes are still known today as the sands of Langosteiras or Lagosteiras—with or without "n", singular or plural as you wish—in the summer of 1943 a U.S. fighter plane which had been in a skirmish with a German plane over the Finisterre peninsula crashed into San Roque point, one of the airmen died and some courageous, resolute young lasses buried him, sisters who faced squarely up to life, which is how circumstances should be faced and what the seven gods, one for each sea serpent, see fit to order us without as much as a by-your-leave, in Finisterre it is customary to call the graveyard the Homestead, Finisterre folk returning from Buenos Aires brought that name back, the Finisterre woman has great character and presence of mind, she is agile, valiant, serene and level-headed, indeed she has little choice, the Finisterre woman eats apart, the surviving airmen were taken into the sisters' house, one of them had begun to swallow his documentation when Palmira, the eldest of the sisters, told him that he could burn them in the hearth, the U.S. vice consul in Vigo, Mr. Cowles, wrote a letter thanking her, the list of shipwrecks never ends, it is a never-ending tale, like the phases of the moon and the ebb and flow of the tides, naval charts marked at twenty-nine meters the spindle of rock which the oil tanker *Urquiola* struck, she started to list and the one hundred thousand tons of crude which she was carrying poured into the water, that black tide left the fishing fleet tied up in harbor for three full months, the Italian freighter *Marina di Acqua* sank north of Corunna, her thirty crewmen went missing, and another Italian merchantman, the *Tita Campanella*, was also wrecked within sight of Corunna, the twenty-four men on board went missing, sometimes the sea rages and buffets blindly, the Corunna fishing vessel *Aldebarán* went missing with forty men on board and the Singapore-flagged merchantman *Anna Leonard* foundered north of Estaca de Bares taking her fifteen crewmen down with her, there are four of the aforementioned sisters, well, there were four but now they have passed on, Palmira was the eldest, then came María, who wrote poetry and could cook a decent meal, when I was awarded the Nobel Prize they made an unforgettable stew for me and I've kept a bone from it as a memento, the smell of food lingered on the bone for perhaps six or seven years, Celia was the first woman in Spain to acquire a heavy goods vehicle license, she got it on April 19, 1932, her father rebuilt a truck which had been dumped as scrap after an accident, converting it into a passenger bus, and his daughters started to work with it, in 1936, at the outbreak of the Civil War, the army requisitioned the bus and Celia and María, in order to keep an eye on the vehicle and to look after it, volunteered to drive it to the Oviedo front twice weekly, in exchange they had access to the bus on the remaining days, when the war was over they returned with the bus fitted with new tires, neither María nor Celia ever wore trousers, when a lunatic has been locked away for a century in the madhouse he no longer knows why the nuns spit upon him nor why the asylum attendants tether him to the bed, at the outset he thought it was in order to poke fun at him and gradually train him in but ten or twelve years down the road he realizes that this was not so, that it isn't like this even though it may appear so, blackbirds trill with gay abandon and do not roost in the madhouse trees, madhouse lindens, madhouse willows, madhouse monkey-puzzles, except when they want to, nobody can make them roost here or there, it is the same with nightingales and robin redbreasts, only canaries, decoy partridges and some goldfinches roost behind bars, nor can seabirds bear imprisonment, the fourth sister was Julita and she was in the same call-up as me, on St. John's Eve 1987, in honor of some relatives, Julita prepared an unforgettable sardine feast for us, sardines, bread and wine for the Feast of St. John, Diego Bernal from the Agency, Cristovo Herbosa from the pari-mutuel, Evaristo Artigas from the funeral parlor, my cousin Vitiño and I each downed thirty rather large sardines that had been netted at dawn, it was too much for me, and when I reached number eighteen I had to throw up, no doubt it was the diverticulitis creeping up on me, but I was right as rain in a trice, we started at one o'clock by the sun and continued into the wee small hours, myself not so much, of course, but the others had a whale of a time and spent the entire evening singing, eating, drinking and letting off solemn, cracking great farts, my English cousins were rather taken aback but in the end they came to their senses, the traveling laborer Liduvino Villadavil, the blind balladeer, never let off such rip-roaring farts, Langosteira beach ends at Canto de Area point, behind this Julita owns a summer house where I spent some time seeking the key to the area, they have now erected a ceramic plaque which states: in this house on Langosteira beach in Finisterre, the writer Camilo José Cela spent the summers from 1984 until 1989—I think it was until 1988 but I may be mistaken—from the beach to the main road runs the Don Camilo pathway which starts at the viewing point dedicated to me adorned with a bust by Miguel Angel Calleja, the sculptor to whom the Madrid municipal council entrusts the repair of damage caused by vandalism: the hand of a Visigoth king, the tail of a general's horse, the crown in the Cibeles or Neptune monuments, Calleja is highly skilled and always does a good job, before this he worked outdoors in what is now the Barrio Blanco between Arturo Soria highway and the M-30 but Madrid is spreading rapidly and open-air art is on the way out, that viewing point bears a sentence of mine:

Finis Terrae is the final smirk of the chaos of man facing into the infinite, which is all very fine, my cousin Irene, a committed poet, helped me to compose it, as well as an inscription which reads: on Monday, eighth of June nineteen eighty-eight, Feast of St. Sallustian, Don Ernesto Insua Olveira, Mayor of Finisterre, unveiled this monument in honor of Camilo José Cela, the first Galician to be awarded the Novel (sic) Prize, in memory of his lengthy sojourns at this end of the earth, in that shady pine grove along the track and in the mountains beyond the highway there live squirrels and mink descended from the ones which escaped from fur farms, country folk hunt them down relentlessly because they damage crops, are prolific breeders and devour everything in sight, the life of left-handed Doña Onofre, nicknamed the Lefthander, because she is utterly left-handed, as left-handed as they come, was neither fun nor exciting, it was monotonous though bearable, the lure of a love affair with a canon soon wears thin, and being left-handed is little better than having a squint or a stammer, Doña Onofre always grew very bored, reading devotional literature is insufficient comfort, and adultery provides a welcome distraction only at the outset, the merchantman *Diana María* was carrying two tons of scrap iron from the United Kingdom to Ferrol when she ran aground in Corunna bay, her entire crew was rescued, in the lobby of the Atlantic Hotel Doña Onofre encountered someone from the *Diana María*, they had just met for the first time but matters moved apace and they spent the whole afternoon in bed, you should not take your eye off the ball nor let opportunity pass, because within each breast may smoulder a sort of spark-box of love, it is not possible that these quick-start love affairs are envisaged in the Book of Designs, one day Doña Onofre enquired of Don Sebastian but he merely smiled and remained silent, Don't you go getting into deep waters and just take things as they are or as they come, which is one and the same thing, if Doña Onofre had had an education she might have distinguished herself, the fishing vessel *Cabo Noval* went down in the Muros estuary without loss of life, you shouldn't brag, Xesusa's Manueliño used to boast that his daughter was a decent lass, there's not a man will lay my Xonxa, then when Xonxa turned up pregnant Xesusa's Manueliño declared it wasn't the boyfriend that had laid her, she got laid because she wanted to, so you can never brag, the fishing vessel *Segundo Costa* went down on the Lobeira islands off Corcubión, helicopter winching gear and cables do not always work, besides the two sailors from the *Rey Alvarez II* killed in similar circumstances a crewman perished from the German yacht *Baltic Mile* wrecked west of Corunna, he plummeted into the sea while being winched through the air, on Canto de Area point you can swim undisturbed because it is secluded by rocks, but when there is a sea running it is best not even to venture near it but, once the swell abates, it is a delight to take a dip in your birthday suit, humungous crabs breed on Pombeira point and in the cove, luck was not with me on Talón beach for I found it littered with condoms, the brothers Juan and Amado Gómez went missing while fishing at Sardiñeiro point a mere stone's throw away, just beyond Gaboteira point and the Muiña stream, the other two fishermen from the boat were rescued, both Julita and her sister María are accomplished cooks, Julita goes in more for fish, as well as grilled sardines she dishes up sea bass with onions, baked turbot, cod with peppers and hake, of course, what she does not cook is lamprey, hereabouts there is no lamprey, nor are Finisterre folk overly fond of it, lamprey is a food fit for the gods but it gets a bad name because it is a scavenger, María goes in more for meat, she is a champion cook: brisket of beef, belly of pork, pig's head—"brawn" I always heard my aunt Gerarda call it—ham, marrowbone, chorizo sausage, chickpeas, turnip tops and potatoes, María is also a dab hand at salt pork with turnip tops and chorizo sausage, tripe with chickpeas Galician style: a handful of corn meal, a calf's foot, sausage, onion, garlic, paprika, cumin seeds and lard, a kilo of tripe makes enough for four or five servings, and chopped pork with fried eggs and twice as much paprika as chili pepper, this can be served with boiled potatoes or potatoes fried separately, though you shouldn't eat more than five because they may be a little hard on the digestion, in the olden times, when it was time to take someone up the mountain to die, *old nags and worn-out hags, off to the mountain crags!* but nowadays these customs have fallen into disuse, they would be served three fried eggs with chopped pork to comfort them, *my old wife she's through with life, up the mountain high, leave her there to die*, then the ghost of the Fungairiño priest stopped short and muttered hoarsely :

"I've been hearing the contrary for some time now, I'm fed up, to my mind people don't know what to think. Don't you think this is too neat and tidy?"

"No, to my mind it is only slightly neat and tidy."

"Like life itself?"

"Indeed, though I try not to say so in order to avoid insolence and misfortune, life is very vengeful and begrudging."

Right here in Finisterre, the fishing boat *Virxe de Pastoriza* sank after ramming some drifting timber balks, her four crewmen were rescued, Respiciño delivers telegrams by bicycle and has a great eye for measuring corpses and getting the size of the coffin right from the word go, Respiciño's way with women was to hypnotize them, there wasn't one who could resist his charms, he also hypnotized hens so that they never laid eggs again, the vapors are the undoing of mothers, Viruquiña paid for this hypnotism with her life, Celso Manselle was a man who never knew the meaning of restraint, the judge sentenced him to hard labor and was within a hairsbreadth of sentencing him to death, there was once a condemned man who requested walnut cream as dessert with his last meal, not only did nobody pay a blind bit of heed to him but they split their sides laughing, so then he requested plain custard and downed four helpings at the expense of His Honor the judge who wished to salve his conscience, leftover food can be chucked into the sea because it provides food for fish and spider crabs, what you cannot throw into the sea is oilcloth, plastic or aluminum foil because they either kill off living things or leave them in a half-dead state, which is even worse, the fishing vessel *Teté* capsized off Muxía and two men—father and son—went missing, Sardiñeiro bay is square, well-balanced and regular in shape, the cove measures one mile along each of its four sides, and runs from Sardiñeiro point, in the west, to Mosgenta point, in the east, or to the Corno shoal or Cabalo rock depending on how you wish to look at it, both stretches of coastline are steep, sheer and run almost parallel, the inner coast, with the hamlet and beaches of Sardiñeiro and Estordí, is divided by Arnela and Restelos points, here in Sardiñeiro bay is where the retired municipal guard from Corcubión, Casto Verdines, alias the Chocolate Maker, tried out his submarine, the submarine dived satisfactorily but one day did not return to the surface and her two crewmen, Casto and his assistant Alfonsito, died from suffocation, when the submarine was finally refloated their bodies were found locked in one another's arms, nobody has ever seen a house with boxwood beams, boxwood generally has other more customary purposes, besides, nature does not allow for quirks, nature is pernickety and not given to straying from the beaten track, it is not unusual for a man to sin with a nanny goat or a woman with a dog, it may even be customary, or a man with a hen or a woman with a highly-strung, head-butting ram, but indeed it is unusual for a man or a woman to have carnal dealings with a grouper or an eel for they are slippery and cold and die when taken from from the water, cats do not countenance it and wild animals do not count, a little beyond Sardiñeiro bay lies da Vella cove which is like a sea bass farm where it is a delight to watch the fish leaping, this was where the young lady Trinidad Besada, the notary's girl, took her own life, she swallowed an entire tube of sleeping pills and let herself be carried away by the current, first she undressed, folded her clothes neatly and placed a stone on top of them so that they would not blow away, the only garment she did not remove was her bra, her body was washed up two days later on the Furadiño shoreline, just before you reach the Sedeira factory, it was no easy task to prise away the goose barnacles which had latched on to her eyes, almost all the rocks in this sea have stood here for many years, for thousands of years, inhabited by clams, winkles, scallops and cockles, but the sound of the sea is always the same, sometimes it sounds like the skirl of Anxo Canido's bagpipes, not that he can play the pipes, or like Chinto Sevil's harmonica, not that he can play the harmonica either, the sea surges above Floro Cedeira's whistling and below the divinations of Telmo Tembura, that fellow lamed at Demon's rock, he who doesn't ask doesn't get and you, Cam, you will not wind up building a house with boxwood beams, for you lack merit and you know you will never be anything but a poor man, for you know full well that poverty can wreak havoc upon virtue, in the Pomariños narrows a young seminary student drowned, they say that he separated from the group to have a wank, he felt a sudden surge of lust, that is the temptation of the devil, sometimes it passes, he slipped, struck his head upon a rock, tumbled into the tide and drowned, folks die when their time comes and it doesn't take either cold steel or firearms, why, not even germs, here nobody is either forewarned or fooled, in these waters of Langosteira bay, the best anchorage after Corcubión in northwesterly to northeasterly winds, they shoot sweep nets, in order to avoid mishaps they have placed marker buoys indicating exclusion zones, west of Porcallón point there stands a five-meter-high stone pyramid painted white and on the eastern facade of the Vitro factory there is a letter J the same height painted in black, on Sardiñeiro point—that is on the other side—stands a six-meter-high stone pyramid painted white and another one four meters high lies just south of it, these markers should be treated with respect, Tobiño Méndez got a hammering for being lame, he crossed the path of Xácome das Mortes who was a braggart with a criminal record, Xácome glared at him and said: "Get out of my sight! No devil is going to hobble past me!" and then beat the daylights out of him so that he wound up in the hospital, nobody was expecting it, Tobiño took some time to recover but get over it he did, Sardiñeiro folks are outgoing and willing to talk to strangers, you can savor a varied selection of shellfish in Sardiñeiro and dance there in summer at dusk, Sardiñeiro girls are known as good-ookers, love cannot be measured nor weighed though indeed beauty can, here in this village there died a well-known English poet called Oliver Lovell who had served in the Navy during the First World War, Oliver played the pipes and at times would climb a rock on Arnela point or Restelos point, depending on the direction he was walking in, and would recite verses by Richard Brathwaite, I saw a puritan hang his cat which on Sunday killed a rat, coffee-colored goats graze on the rocky slopes of

Carballeira, bearded, long-horned, lonely looking goats, the billy in the flock has a somber, menacing air about him, you can see that he is in his element and looks contented, the cliff at Corno point closes the little cove of Abeleira where the Portuguese coastal cutter *Cristinhade* ended her days, without loss of life, shortly before this she had struck the Corno shoal and sprang a leak, the Muiños and Anguieira narrows are tricky to navigate, a sandbar stretches south from Cape Nasa to Cee head, across from the Lesser Carrumeiro island, and should not be approached in a southerly wind because the sea breaks violently there, a journalist wrote in the local paper that in Grallas cove, between Pia point and Piñeiro point, some German naturists were camping and Manuel Rubén, the young lad from Corcubión, also known as Moncha's Manueliño, along with a few pals, burned their clothing, then the naturists were arrested by the Civil Guard for walking around in the buff and the following day they left without a word, nor did they have any other clothing, the consul took charge of them, but this is untrue because hereabouts there never were any German naturists, a few years ago there were some Dutch naturists but truth to tell they were not much of a nuisance, fifteen crewmen were rescued unharmed from the Guipuzcoan fishing vessel *Ezequiel* wrecked on Estaca de Bares, in the extreme north of the kingdom of Galicia, farther north lies nothing but England, Tina Coribio lived in Ceuta for several years and returned to Spain with a small fortune, when she was quizzed as to how she had made her money she quickly changed the topic of conversation for she owed nobody any explanation, folks gossip and are not to be trusted, they often say more than their prayers and are given to lying and slandering, Tina Coribio had been a fine-looking woman and some of her eye-catching allure still lingered, some women weather the years with great dignity, while others go to seed early on, pile on the pounds and turn into gossips and do-gooders, Tina Coribio is held in low esteem by some, though not many, but she knows it, and it is preferable to being glazed in flattery, the flatterer feeds upon carrion and is like a hyena or maggot gnawing at the pestilent, while the person flattered is like a consenting cuckold who thus gives rise to infamy, prudence is not sufficient to ward off evil and grinding poverty is the converse of beauty, smoking fag ends of filthy weed is not the same as puffing hand-rolled Havana cigars, everybody has to make do with what they have for time marches on for all of us and the barometer which foretells of joy and misfortune has yet to be invented, the Alicante-registered merchantman *Benitachell*, with her cargo of dates, went down off Diñeiro point, some folks call it Salto point, west of it lies the narrow entrance to Porto Mariña, and all hands were lost, a wretched southerly gale was blowing and her entire crew perished, rocky slopes run down to Vaca point, across from Baleira rock, the enemy is always a stranger and nobody with whom you could end up coming to blows or getting in a knife fight should ever be greeted, Cee head closes the Corcubión estuary to the west, it is rugged, steep and strewn with inshore rocks as far as the Outer shoals, Saramuxa point lies a little farther west, this is where the French-flagged steamer *Salingres* sank with her cargo of bri-quettes, five crewmen perished along with the skipper's mulatta girl who was just thirteen years of age, they could be seen from the coast, buffeted by high seas but help could not reach them, when seawater tastes of horse piss and takes on a yellowish saffron hue it is a sure sign that the devil is on the rampage sowing misery among the off-spring of seafarers, before evil was seen Christ was born, may evil perish and long live Christ! the mouth of the Corcubión estuary is nine cables wide and ends in Galera point to the east, where a few days ago the Cypriot-flagged merchantman *Frihav* ran aground, whilst making for the Brens dock in Cee to load ferromanganese, her crew—all of them Polish—were rescued alive but the vessel could not be refloated despite the efforts of the *Ría de Vigo* tugboat, here-abouts many vessels break up and much mention has been made of their wrecks, others are less widely spoken of, that always happens, the Italian barque *Margarita*, which was making from Cardiff to Trieste with a cargo of coal, was riding out the storm on the port tack when she sprang a leak, rock is harder than steel and always gains the upper hand, the vessel ran on to the Pardas reef in Langosteira bay but Finisterre folk were vigilant and managed to rescue her entire crew, one of them remained in this area until he died and was the founder of that line of Mouchos justly renowned for their fireworks and skill at dominoes, they are also fine rabbit hunters, the English merchantman *John Tenat* lost her rudder and her skipper ran her on to the Cabanas rocks, the Finisterre Christ was washed up on Cabanas beach, her undersides were badly damaged so the vessel could not be refloated, the merchantman *Makaria*, also English-registered, sought refuge in Langosteira within hours of the *Idelfonso Fierro* business because her cargo had come unstowed and she developed a perilous list, Doña Dosinda is highly discerning and has been trying to explain to my cousin Vitiño for at least two years now that you should never suggest to the devil swapping what you have for what you would wish to have for you might wind up with nothing at all, the devil is highly astute and difficult to deceive and at times ambition is but a phantom shrouded in frustrated dreams, when the shipping agent for the *John Tenat* saw that the hull could not be salvaged he attempted to save the cargo from pilfering which he did not fully achieve because the devil—and hereabouts it's always the devil, Lucifer is on the loose more than anybody else—is schooled in the skills of stealth, sly patience is mightier than brazen force and perseverance yields results, everybody knows that, but holding out is the key to success because perfection is the byword of constancy and the luck of the valiant lies in learning in time that love does not flourish in timorous souls, Respiciño would have liked to join the masons but he did not know where to sign up, afterwards, when the Civil War broke out, he never spoke of this again, prudence always pays, Salustiano, the fellow from the gas company, turned to good account the size of his prick which he put down to solid nourishment, the most suitable for these purposes is perhaps tuna baked with ham and chorizo, there is nothing better for winning the hearts of women, making them flush with fever and setting their pulses racing, Doña Onofre was luckier than Viruquiña, Don Celso Camilo used to read Galdós and Valle-Inclán but was never noted as a bright spark, nothing repels the virgin Locaia a Balagota but habit has tamed her bit by bit and now she is resigned and acquiescent, the Singapore-flagged vessel *Charles Lewis* caught fire off Pombeira point, the fire broke out in the engine room and could not be quenched, the sea was rough and her entire crew drowned when they leaped overboard so as not to be scorched to cinders, the *Charles Lewis* was making for Southampton with a cargo of delicate jewels from the Philippines, each item wrapped in a little bag woven from Manila hemp, the jewelry sank to the seabed, the pearls were surely the first to tarnish, elegant ladies have a liking for black pearls, St. Xoán is clued into the ways of this world, St. Xoán and Magdalena were quite a pair of peaches, and underneath the peach tree they each lost their britches, Xoán de Outel grows cinnamon to cure rabies and is carrying on a love affair with Magdalena Dominguez, Saturio the blacksmith's lass, Xoán de Outel also heard the voice of the Fungairiño priest's soul in torment, growing hoarse and doleful.

"For the sake of all the souls in purgatory I beg of you to swear to me that all this is too neat and tidy, have no fear that I would harm you in any way and just tell me the truth, remember that saving his skin can lure a man from the road to victory, I beg of you, for the sake of every single soul in purgatory, can you swear to me that this is all too neat and tidy?"

"No, I don't think so."

"Can you tell me that you are answering in all conscience, that implement which can churn out cowards and cheats?"

"To your first query, I do not, for I never respond in conscience, and as for your second question, no, I do not, for cowards do not crawl forth from the conscience but spring from the earth."

"Like buttercup and burdock?"

"Yes, surely everybody knows that."

"Wild thyme, which cures the hex, also sprouts from the earth, did you know that?"

"Of course I did."

On Talón beach strewn with condoms, the Liberian-flagged merchantman *Demetrius* was wrecked, two crewmen drowned while the rest escaped on board the English containership *Barnaby*, or so they say, which sailed out of Corcubión the following day, Don Celso

Camilo would like to have written *The Lady of the Camelias*, now that is no sissy book, though it might appear so at first glance, instructing the spirit is what matters to me, it is not my fault that my spirit is not so cultured, I had neither good health nor indulgence to cultivate the spirit as I would have wished, my wife has a greater predisposition for these matters than I have, across from where the river Blanquiño flows into the sea the coastal cutter *Barileza* from Camariñas ran aground, she had ignored all the marker buoys and was tacking to windward close-hauled when her skipper made a blunder and when he attempted to correct his course it was too late, one crewman perished but the rest were rescued, the *Sunrise* ran aground on the Duio shoals, Finisterre folk rescued the shipwrecked sailors one by one, so scared out of their wits were they that they did not even want *aguardiente*, the *Sunrise* sank violently, the French cargo vessel *Lionne* was wrecked on the Centulo like the English vessel *Rousseul*, both without loss of life, whereas ten men from the *Bitten* were killed when she ran on to Cape Finisterre after hitting the Outer Paxariño shoal, the German collier *Forstect* ran aground on the Bimbio shoal beyond the Porcallón weedbank, the sea was calm but the fog was dense when the vessel, which was traveling at full tilt, struck the shoal so hard that she veered off course and sprang a leak, her crew were rescued but the hull stayed afloat for only a short time and then sank, in Toad's Mouth Cove, between Subiante point and Seixo point within the Corcubión estuary, Ruddy Margarida, the wisewoman, and Bastián Severiñón, the excise officer who used an exercise bicycle, drowned while bathing, Ruddy Margarida used to warn pregnant women to eat neither rabbit nor hare lest their child should be born with a harelip, this stretch of coastline looms higher than the other side of the bay but both shores run parallel, about halfway along lies Cardinal point with its eerie ruined castle haunted by the ghost of pirate skipper Andresiño Bocanegra, with six fingers on each hand and fleshy cauliflower ears, who was killed by Cardinal Luciano Donociello, a Sardinian who became famous because he could see through solid objects: that pot is full of doubloons, behind that wall there are three Moorish muskets, that chest

contains a wolf snare and a sack of gold cutlery, the cardinal killed
the pirate with a hunting knife which he poisoned with turpentine
then smeared with the dung from a consumptive cow, but that is a
murky tale which nobody wants to talk about, the cardinal could
find treasure simply by studying the marks he made when he pissed
upon the ground, the wisewoman and the exciseman were bathing
nude and God wanted to teach them a lesson and chastised them for
their indecency and lack of consideration, some folks even alter the
names of the characters in the drama of the castle so as not to fall
under a curse or be avenged, the memory of souls has its obligations
which should neither be despised nor belittled, I often heard it said
though to me it never rang true, the worst thing, Cam, and I've heard
it said over a hundred times, is to die far from where you were born,
never forget that, it is a worthy thing to burn at the same time as the
beams of your own house, nobody ever built a house with boxwood
beams, you could have had one but you lacked the courage, your
strength was sapped by letting women love you and by reciting Poe
in Galician, the English-flagged merchant man *Hedwig* ran aground
on Cardinal Point transporting a cargo of machinery, they say that
she was also smuggling tobacco and whisky, though no drugs, and
that she had transshipped from the barge *Margot Perth* on the high
seas, the entire crew from the *Hedwig* drowned along with two
Portuguese passengers, father and son, coming from Liverpool and
heading for Leixoes, between compass points south and north of
Quenxe lies the beach of the same name with its marine industry
buildings and former coalyard, here on Quenxe beach those of us who
worked in the postal service would meet up every year for a sardine
feast, our boss was called Don Cándido, on the stony ground at the
Castle and in Ollo de Cuiro squirrels skip while at Cabalo point
goose barnacles disport themselves and octopus cling to the rocks,
my pal Pepita Lestón, Pepita the Secretary's girl, R.I.P., was a well-
built, generous woman with a fine spirit and courteous manners who
would at times invite me to sample scallops in her bar at the
Hydrangeas campsite beside the cemetery with an attractive, spacious terrace overlooking the sea, Corcubión is known as the town of

the hydrangeas, Macías de Lourenza's kiosk where my son Paulo
worked went down the tubes hot on the heels of the marriage of his
boss and friend to Lucila, Don Eudaldo's granddaughter, it is unwise
for largish vessels to try to pass over the Sartaña reef of rocks which
lies just off this point within a cable and a half offshore since they
might touch bottom, Corcubión nestles at the foot of Estordi mountain the spurs of which stretch down to Prison point, a stone's throw
from the sea, where the road switches inland, this is the start of the
district of Cee with its helicopter rental company and the Hotel
Galicia on the other side, the owner allowed me to use the telephone
and did not charge me for my coffee, I could even have a second cup
or as many as I wished, Corcubión is sizeable and wealthy with all
modern conveniences: notary public, land registry, magistrate's
court, post and telegraph administration, harbor office, etc., while
industry and commerce thrive in Cee, on Brens beach a huge emer-
ald-green sea serpent called Leopodina appears from time to time, she
is at least eleven or twelve meters long and as plump as a pampered
child, the serpent does not bother anybody and nobody troubles her,
they say that she sleeps where the river Ameixenda flows into the sea
just south of Pion point where a type of blind crab breeds, with no
eyes and a soft shell which tastes delicious, the brigantine *Fornelos*
foundered on Pion point and her six crewmen drowned, her masts
can still be seen, the lass Miliña Valcarce has the deepest, most beautiful eyes in the world, they are violet in color, the most curvaceous
and discreetly mysterious boobs and the finest, most shapely legs in
all of Western Europe, hardly anybody knows this for she seldom
leaves Fadibón, Miliña works as a laundress and cleaner and she is
also well-versed in dressmaking as well as opening oysters, cooking
goose barnacles and spider crabs, nowadays in New York black
women with giraffe-like necks are all the rage, Miliña would be better suited to Baden-Baden with its parasols, wide-brimmed hats and
rhododendrons, between Berroxe and Raso the Civil Guards discovered a brothel where three mulatto women from the Dominican
Republican were being held against their will, their passports had
been burned so that they could not run away, their pimp was a beam-

ing Peruvian by the name of Nestor, who used to beat them and gave them only raw fish and potatoes, not even corn bread, to eat, at times they got the odd piece of fruit, in Ameixenda vocations for the priesthood and domino players flourish, it is justly renowned for its plump, fearless gulls as well as the wind, all the saints face out over the sea, but Ameixenda glares into the teeth of the northwesterly gale, in the late '40's Ameixenda castle belonged to the Press Association, Madrid, the orphaned offspring of journalists from the College of St. Isidro would come to spend the summer months in the castle, they did gymnastics and classes were given in religious instruction and national spirit, the director was a canon from Madrid who one day organized a day-trip to the Lobeira island which lies some three miles offshore and set off with half the children in a open punt which was hard to handle, he tried to return to shore to pick up the remainder of the children but the wind blew up from the northeast and the current began to sweep the boat out to sea, a boat was sent out from Corcubión and by the time they were found they were already drifting far offshore too tired to row, one of the day-trippers was journalist Carlos Luis Alvarez, Cándido, it was fortunate that darkness did not descend upon them for when the northeasterly wind blows this stretch of sea becomes tricky for rowers, James E. Allen no longer plays rugby or tennis, the calendar may be deceptive but time pardons no one, least of all those who do not even make it to runner-up, Doña Onofre is left-handed but she never gave rise to any scandal, her husband departed for the other world yet nobody could call him a cuckold, that business with Father Sebastian the canon never became public knowledge, Purita Margariños was the very heart and soul of discretion, Doña Onofre tried her luck at target shooting, three shots for a quarter, steadying the rifle on her left shoulder, she also shot the Aunt Sally with her left hand, she had a surefire aim and when she hit a doll fair and square she would let out a guffaw, Doña Onofre was fun-loving, she adored puppet show marionettes: Pierrot, Harlequin, Punch and Judy, if a man does as he is told and forgoes forbidden skills it is a sign that he is ready to die at any moment for nothing really matters to him any more, this business of abolishing the death penalty is all very well though not for heathens, Johnny Jorick was castrated for a bet, it is shameful but funny too, Johnny Jorick was in hospital with viral pleurisy, or maybe it was peritonitis for they would not tell me for sure, hospitals are tight-lipped, mysterious places, it is not permitted to castrate anyone much less for a bet, indeed, it is against the law, the Italian tenor Guido Valtelini concluded the aria from *Nabucco*, Act One, at the bottom of the sea, it seemed a worthy and decorous attitude to us all, in Testón del Castillo there lives an eagle owl which serenely flits forth by night hooting gravely, the Portuguese merchant vessel *Castro Laboreiro* went down on the Aguillones de Sagrelo on her return trip from Ferranchín, five of her six crewmen perished, the sole survivor was washed up, neither alive nor dead, on the Cagadora rock south of Galera point and the Petón de Trigo in the mouth of Caneliñas bay, where the whaling station is, it is easier to swim than to walk to these parts, harpoonists flourished three quarters of a century ago, after that it was downhill all the way, the Gulf stream flows at a rate of three knots and spans one hundred miles at its widest point, thousands and thousands of whales always swim against the current, this may appear exaggerated though it is not, Caneliñas never posed a serious threat to their survival, Cósmede the deaf-mute came from the hamlet of Cospindo when his parents passed on, he trudged day and night like clockwork and did not stop at all along the way, this business of being used to losing gives great strength, Cósmede lives on Gures beach with his wolf and his bear, he always keeps a fire lit so it is warm and cosy inside the shack, one day a dying knife grinder who could scarcely speak was washed up on the shore: "May I kick the bucket in this neck of the woods?" although Cósmede could not hear, he understood and nodded to him that he could, the wolf and the bear sniffed and licked the knife grinder but did not bite him, misery and charity fight with the same weapons throughout the world and do not generally use their teeth to attack, such challenges count for nothing among those who go through life with their engines falling to pieces, remember that there are fearful folk who implore the heavens for what lies within their grasp, the seven last

traíñas sank in seven treacheries of the sea, in seven curses of the
devil, in seven wearinesses, blacks smell heavy and sweet like marzi-
pan and in summer the scent of black women grows stronger, *traíñas*
are generally named after women, the *Rita* was wrecked at Robaleira
point, her seventeen crewmen drowned while the two support vessels were unable to rescue them, the swell was not followed by wind
nor is it always, at spring tides the ways of the sea change and the
rorquals swim deeper, the telltale signs of the northwesterly gale can
be felt one or two days beforehand but the wind does not always follow, a pent-up sea thunders when the southwest wind buffets the
cliffs, seafarers strive to keep the sound at bay by playing the accordion for misery seeks out strange complicities, the Chinese smell of
raw fish, the *Neniña Vicenta* went down at La Carraca, northwest of
the Centulo, three sailors drowned and another three went missing,
everyone makes landfall wherever they can, vessels coming from the
north of Europe, from St. George's Channel and the English Channel,
put into Finisterre and Cape Vilán, preferably Cape Vilán, and then
enter the estuaries, the Indo-Chinese and Filipinos smell of old horse,
it is not known what happened to the *Miña Maruxa* because the sea
swept her away at the Turdeiro rock, Lourenciño Reira, the lad who
eked a living scraping for goose barnacles on the Roncudo, was
pecked by a hen in the privates and since then has been going around
clucking and laying eggs, nobody believes him but he swears blind
that it is true, it would be worse if he thought he was a werewolf and
had to be killed with wolf-shot, that is if the shotgun was not
bewitched and could actually fire, it is also a bad thing to turn into a
sheep and to go around butting at doors, or into a lizard which says
the Credo while keeping time with its tail, off Finisterre a French
yacht was found drifting, her only occupant was a babe in arms perished of cold whose parents had been washed overboard, fame sweeps
away loneliness but also feeds it, Lourenciño Reira will not give up
cackling and laying eggs until the demon is expelled from his body,
it is a rule of thumb that you should take advantage of a falling tide
which is when the syzygy helps put to windward, Indians smell of
cinnamon and chickens, the *Hilaria II* went farther afield to perish,

her hulk hit Porto de Baixo on the Great Lobeira island, half a mile from Deseada point lies the hull of the English merchant vessel *Clovelly* which the sea covers at flood tide, redskins smell of minerals, the *Gloria Pita* struck the headland at Boca da Sapo cove, her crewmen escaped with their lives, Dominguiño the Sprat was left limping but alive nevertheless, better a live rat than a dead lion, the soul of life, that mysterious essence which can smile and weep, makes clock time soar higher than eagles, we whites smell of the dead, the fishing boat *Nuevo Marqués de Pola* was wrecked beyond Corunna, one fisherman died while three more went missing, the hermitage of San Andrés de Teixido can be seen from the southern part of the Gabeira islands, this does not mean that we men cannot turn into animals, lizards, bats, toads or whatever, the *Lauriña y Margarida* was wrecked at Xoramelo point at the foot of Caldebarcos mountain, there is tremendous variety in this business of smell, tastes do not always match smell or color, skin color may be masked by the scent of mercy and taste of spittle, the following morning the knife grinder was dead, and started to stink as quick as a flash, Cósmede kept the seven thousand pesetas which the dead man had on him, never before had he seen so much money, he also kept his wheel and grindstone, but he had to spend the money in dribs and drabs so as not to arouse suspicion, he burned the clothing and left the body on the waterline for the crabs and gulls to devour until it would eventually be carried away by the current, all this makes you very cold, it is like watching a starving child in the throes of death, and Cósmede crouched over the fire in order to warm himself, nothing further was ever heard of the dead man, God orders the angels to hasten away from the daily round of the dead, the guardian angels flee mixed up with the very life of the person they protect because they are frightened, they do not linger even for a single minute, more than likely the sea smashed that dead man against the rocks of the Lobeira islands, the balance sheet of the living and the dead is never quite as God ordains, A Caralleira head, across from the Cardallosa shoals, covers and shows, the Greek steamer *Maria L.* is still aground on the Raposo rock, the *traíña* is a vessel which now sails only in the

sea of memory, the seven last *traíñas* sank in seven slips on the part
of the Virgin of Carmen, on Malva point there lurks an ownerless
parrot, Cósmede wanted to help it to survive but the parrot would
not let him for it was too frightened, Cósmede will try his hand once
more when the cold strengthens, the vixen who comes marauding
pullets from the villages also roams as far as Malva point, in el
Covadoiro and the whole of Ezaro bay and along its beaches delicately flavoured, lusty sea bass breed, Cósmede catches them whenever
he can, and broils them over a tin which he sprinkles with partly
evaporated sea water to strengthen the salt, on each of the two masts
of the lugger *Chirlateiro*, which wolf-woman Susiña Taboadela inherited from her uncle Colás Fernández, there keeps watch an ungainly
dusty-blue-colored fowl with a yellow bill and a green and white tuft
in its crest which is rare in these waters, Ceferino Erbosa the fellow
from the fitted kitchen factory, who is knowledgeable about mysterious marine birds, does not know what it is, it may be a shearwater,
a bird which has well-nigh disappeared, but it turns out to be a type
of slightly meaner looking merlin, at times it can be seen perched on
the rock known as the Meixón de Penouxel across from Atalaya
mountain in Malpica, perhaps this shearwater is not a bird of flesh
and bone but a figment of the imagination, an illusion, nobody can
swear that animals have ghosts, some say they do while others hold
that they don't, ghosts come from the soul and when a soul sets the
ghost flits away in terror, priests generally claim that animals have
no souls, maybe they are mistaken, Claudina Xeda, the holy woman
of Ancordoiro, claim that not only animals, but also trees, plants and
some rocks, particularly if crystallised, have souls, birch trees ward
off misfortune, newlyweds plant a birch tree by the door of their
house in order to protect themselves against adversity, witches'
broomsticks are whittled from birchwood, it would be more noble
and luxurious if it were boxwood but it is birchwood, Claudina has a
cousin, a priest, Father Xiao o Merengueiro, who says that in his final
struggle with the devil who comes to steal his soul, man is always
hemmed in by a legion of sorrows and pains of body and spirit, the
final five minutes of the lost may be troublesome and bewildering,

lugger hulls are clinker-built, their planking overlaps like slate shingles on a roof, nowadays there are hardly any of these boats left, this is a vessel which now sails only upon the sea of memory, the shipwrecked sailors from the Cypriot merchant vessel *Miriam* which sprang a leak off Corunna were rescued by various naval personnel, breaking seas forewarn of rocks and sandbars and prevent the whole operation from running aground and lying at the mercy of the tide, deception should leave no room for doubt, wise folk say that it is preferable to be utterly deceived rather than only sort of confused because cowardice springs from the conscience and lurks like a lizard beneath the heart, on Sartaxens beach a portly German woman who talks to nobody does calisthenics every morning, she lives in Porto do Pindo and, whatever the weather, she does her exercises and then hides away until the following day, they say that she lives on beer, velvet swimming crabs and roast chestnuts, one morning there was washed up on Sartaxens sands the body of Marcos Samil Carril, skipper of the fishing vessel *Gran Solero* wrecked off Cape Touriñán, he had sailed dead for many miles without anybody seeing him, the Portuguese merchantman *Portamieiro* ran aground on the Tarracidos shoals, on the reefs lying off the Gabeira islands, as she was heading for Liverpool laden with walnuts and oranges, also carrying three Belgian passengers and six Maltese terriers each in its little cage and complete with documentation, it all went like clockwork and everything was saved: passengers, crew, animals and cargo, the vessel was refloated and continued on her way, she was towed off by the tugboat *Hercules IV* summoned from Ferrol, in Mesones do Reino a man returned home early one morning and found the door lying wide open and a wolf warming himself by the fire, the man crossed himself, drew his knife and slashed the wolf on the cheek, you do not generally graze a werewolf let alone injure him but sometimes it happens, it is better for him to be wounded by a stranger though this is not a hard and fast rule, then the hairy almost jetblack pelt tumbled from the wolf, and feeling the blood trickle down his cheek, he began to weep, the wolf was a son cursed by his father to wander in the wilderness, Mesones do Reino lies a long way off from Porto do

Pindo, but no matter, for distance is nothing to the devil, at the mouth of the river Xallas on the Covadoiro side, some nights there fishes the soul of Simeón Siguelos, Bellows, the lighthouse keeper who died a couple of years ago after an anisette drinking spree, since he cannot take his catch with him he throws the fish back into the sea, what does he want with it anyway? bringing foodstuffs into purgatory is forbidden, Siguelos the lighthouse keeper must only have a few years left to do for he frequently slips away from the Holy Company and wanders alone, once Siguelos met a beggar who said to him: you cannot contemplate happiness through the eyes of others, try to look avidly upon both life and death and the suffering will be more bearable, Siguelos the lighthouse keeper was known as "Bellows" because when he got drunk on half and half sweet and dry anisette he would bellow like a bullock, Siguelos the lighthouse keeper was one-eyed, his brother-in-law Moisés gouged an eye from him with a lash of his belt, he clipped him with the buckle which burst the eyeball, Siguelos the lighthouse keeper did not harbor any grudge against him since restraint shines brighter than any torch and he got by just fine with his one remaining eye, Siguelos the lighthouse keeper was prone to vice, when he was alive he would wank nearly always twice every night, blackbirds do not venture too close to the sea, they do not generally flit beyond the last trees, blackbirds have a tuneful trill but do not like to be distracted, in that respect they are like Cistercian monks or a drug dealer skulking in a shady alley, Bellows always said that happiness was a privilege which could not be bought or sold like a punnet of dried figs.

"Do you know whether hope is as bitter as gall?"

"Just as bitter, or even more so, depending on how you look at it, but at times resignation, the poor man's remedy for misfortune, may be even bitterer."

Siguelos the lighthouse keeper had a fondness for doughnuts and anisette, that's true, also for pumpkin fritters laced with herb-flavored *aguardiente* or pancakes with gin from the keg, Judas Iscariot hanged himself from the Judas tree which bears beautiful, stubby blossoms, treachery bears a high price and whoever sells their friend

down the river will wind up burning in hell forever and nobody will
be able to redeem them because masses run off the souls of base trai-
tors like water from a duck's back, the German woman who does calisthenics sleeps with Cósmede the odd night and makes a beetroot
borscht with winkles for him, or sometimes she stews a rabbit with
chestnuts, he catches the rabbit while she supplies the rest: chestnuts, brandy, garlic, onions, saffron stamens, Cósmede and the
German woman meet and sleep together but they do not talk,
Cósmede is a deaf-mute and besides they have nothing to say to one
another, we Galicians had to throw the Moors out of our land twice,
they have very different ways and superstitious customs, the first
time we were assisted by the Apostle St. James, Slayer of Moors,
mounted upon a dapple-gray steed and later by Charlemagne, the
king of the Moors was Admiral Balán, some history books state
where the Moors buried their belongings, some folks swear that the
Moors still live beneath the earth which opens and closes to them
when they utter the magic words, Respiciño, the hypnotist of
women, gave Doña Onofre a gift of a copy of the Cipranillo penned
with a quill dipped in the blood of a carrier pigeon, Doña Onofre
keeps the manuscript wrapped in silver paper so that the strength is
not sapped from it, the original is kept under lock and key in Santiago
Cathedral so that nobody can read it, Respiciño shows proper respect
and knows how to keep his distance, on the Turcos rock the
Pontevedran coastal cutter *Jeremías* sank, she had all sails furled but
could not drop anchor nor put out to sea, the wind drove her on to a
leeshore and her five crewmen perished, the sea gave up the bodies
the following day, Salustiano the fellow from the gas company used
to say that losing a ship was the easiest thing in the world, just like
letting go a fart, on the Carallete rock which covers and shows,
another coastal cutter, the *Cedeira* from Arosa, foundered, her skipper perished but the crew were rescued, Cósmede believes that the
seabed is full of blind birds in eye-catching colors which rise to the
surface only on nights with a full moon, deaf-mutes live on their
imaginations and give great pleasure to German women, the bear and
the wolf sleep outside the shack when the German woman stays

over, Galicia was always rich in gold and precious metals, writers in antiquity speak of the alluvions and mines of Galicia which were the El Dorado of the Romans, in Mons Sacer there was so much gold that sheep would dig it up with their hooves, the plowshare would prise it from the earth but only the one who could draw lightning from the earth with the force of his spark was permitted to profit from it, the Irish also came in search of gold, the Moors hid their belongings before they fled, much of this treasure is enchanted and the spell is very difficult to break, the *Great Book* of St. Cyprian lists one hundred and forty-six items of treasure, the first at the Lobios crossroads and the last on the Valiña hillside, it also explains everything that must be done in order to break the spell cast upon the treasure, the wisewoman from Albán, in Rairiz de Veiga over la Limia way, says that the treasure of Morgadán Fort will not be discovered until the spell upon a lame, one-eyed Moorish woman who lives there is broken, she is at least five hundred years old and rattles on about Almanzor, Filomena the wisewoman from Torbeo says that the first thing to be done is to break the spell cast upon the serpent guarding the treasure, you have to find a priest who knows the magic scents for each day of the week and reliably performs exorcisms in dulcet tones, then root around until you find the serpent, once it has been found try to kiss it upon the head and, if you succeed, the spell will vanish, during the Civil War Filomena prophesied that the Reds would win and the military authorities dared not shoot her for fear of provoking the spirits of the Moors guarding the treasure but they forbade her to practise her trade, at Barra de Brens point the launch *Inés de Toxosoutos* was lost, Cosme Fernández the sailor was riven by a thole-pin in his side and could not free himself, but the rest escaped with their lives, Oh, St. Cosme of the mountain, hewn from birchwood, brother to my wooden clogs, rescue me from this tight corner! magic skill is found in both men and women because this does not go according to sex but compassion and indulgence, the one on top is the winner, that is, the one who calls the shots in bed, the sorceror must have a brazen desire to triumph and must not enter into pacts with evil powers, on pain of death, he must also govern energetical-

ly without great scruples and keep ready at all times the dozen imple-
ments, the Catoira coastal cutter *Rey Melchor* ran on to the smaller
of the two Aguillones de Sagrelo, which covers and shows, while
transporting mules for the 16th Light Artillery Regiment garrisoned
in Corunna, her crew, artillerymen and some mules were rescued but
the sergeant commanding the troops was drowned, he was very sea-
sick, Michael is the angelic power of Sunday, saffron, red sandalwood
and frankincense are its scents, the magic plants are heliotrope and
bay, old people still know by heart the adventures of Oliveros,
Fierabrás, and Guy de Borgoña, tales of princess Floripes and Galafre
the giant, young people feel less curiosity about cultivating the spirit, they have grown soft in their ways, the Portuguese merchant vessel *Montelavar* foundered on the Furrenchín rock which covers and
shows with a cargo of machinery and seven passengers on board: a
husband and wife, their three children and two servants, the storm
raged relentlessly and not a soul was saved, slowly, solemnly, stingi-
ly, the sea gave up her dead, the first implement is the sword with a
rounded ivory handle, the round globe of the world, ending in a knob
of magnetized steel, this is the strength of love, it is sprinkled with
moisture from the breath and three masses are said over it and it is
swathed in a white silk shirt, Gabriel is the angelic power of Monday,
white sandalwood, camphor and aloe are its scents, the magic plants
are the yellow buttercup and mugwort, between Lobeira and Cabalos
hill lies a mine of seven kingdoms, seven of gold, seven of silver,
seven of venom which can kill, at Caneliñas point, here it all gets
jumbled up, well, everywhere really, one night the crews of two
Cypriot vessels started firing potshots at one another, when dawn
broke they had already scarpered, some folks claim that they were
not Cypriot at all but Maltese, five naked bodies with no papers were
found floating, the sea caresses mystery and cradles it in her lap, the
second implement is the white-handled knife with a marble haft, it
is consecrated and stored like the sword, Raphael is the angelic
power of Tuesday, pitch and sulphur are its scents, the magical plants
are wormwood and rue, in Doña Onofre's notebook there are jumbled
lines blotted out with spittle, everybody knows that God shouts but

nobody dares to recall the impetus or rhythm of his word, nor could anybody do so because to imitate God is a very difficult task, for wishing to copy God, which is a way of mocking God, many dreamers who believed themselves sustained by good intentions have gone to hell, the third implement is a blued steel knife with an ebony haft, it is purified by sprinkling it with Holy Water and is used to kill a black cat the body of which is then burned in the flames of a bonfire of willow, cypress and holm oak, it is swathed in a black leather shirt, Amael is the angelic power of Wednesday, benjamin and storax are its scents, the magic plants are daffodil and sandalwood, in the river Ulla there is a deep well with an iron grating halfway down from which hangs a bell cast from cannon bronze, at the stroke of twelve midnight out comes a ghost and a snow-white hen with twelve golden chicks, this is a sign of riches and hidden treasure, at Limo point, halfway between Herbeira's lookout and Pedro Botero's cauldron, every summer there drowns a summer visitor from León called Matías Pereje Carracedelo, who spent a long time, over half his lifetime, prospecting for for gold in Castroquilame, below the Médulas, yet what nobody can account for is that it is always the same fellow, the fourth implement is the dagger which must be new, slender and well-honed with a ring through which you thread a red cord in which you tie seven knots while you repeat: I know my defense against mine enemies, you hang this dagger about your neck after consecrating it by stabbing it in a cemetery gate one Saturday night upon the first stroke of midnight, the prayer is a challenge to Lucifer, Sammael is the angelic power of Thursday, incense, amber and balsam apple are its scents, the magic plants are pomegranate, poplar and holm oak, holly wards off misfortune and adorns the caps of sparring lovers with its red berries, is it true that you have a lady friend in Portela de Caldelas?, no, not any longer, last week she left me in the lurch, the fifth implement is the lancet which is consecrated just like the sword and the white-handled knife and is used by the sorcerer to draw blood when required, Zachariel is the angelic power of Friday, musk is its scent, the magic plants are violet, rose, myrtle and olive, tales of pirates, as well as stories of smugglers of tobacco, whiskey and fountain pens, were beneficial for cleansing the soul, Red-Haired Peter harangued the navy, all aboard, lads!, Lauro Reinante, Forefinger, was thrown out of the seminary before he got to say mass, and although he was daring and strove hard he did not manage to disenchant treasure properly, south of Carnota bay offshore from the hamlet of Sasebe the Mexillueiras shoal shows which draws less than three fathoms and the La Paz bank which runs from Porto Cobelo and draws some five fathoms, on the Mexillueiras shoal the coastal cutter *Simeón García* split in two, without loss of life, she was laden with cod, the ship's terrier Chuchín was rescued along with her last seaman and on the La Paz bank another coastal cutter, the *Pilarín Sestelo*, foundered and all hands on board perished, she was also laden with cod, her terrier Twig drowned, at times death strikes swiftly, giving nobody time to escape, the sixth implement is the magic needle which there is no need to consecrate, just so long as it is new and clean, it is used to sew whatever is necessary, Orofiel is the angelic power of Saturday, copal and resin are its scents, the magic plants are ash and cypress, when I was passing the Santa Clara stream my ring fell into the water, and when I fished out the ring, I picked up a jewel with the Virgin in silver and a gold Christ on it, four miles southwest of Remedios point lie the Miñarzos rocks upon which the coastal cutter *Volvoreta* broke up as she was ferrying minerals to Gijón, all hands were saved, coastal cutters handle well in gusty conditions, their topsides are well-designed, even so the odd one does break up, this vessel was skippered by a woman, Etelvina the Wisp, who wore her hair tied back in a colored kerchief and carried a whip, which she seldom used but never let go of, on Pico Sagro there is an idol with thighs of gold, called the Zancarrón, which is worshipped by Mohammedans, though nowadays there are no Mohammedans left, on Castros mountain in Ponteareas there is a rock called Peneda da Fenda and inside it is a great palace filled with riches, Etelvina the Wisp hails from Gándara, a village on Larayo mountain which is clearly visible from the sea if you can spot it, Etelvina's father, skipper Salustio the Pitcher, was slain by the Civil Guard in a murky settling of old scores, a cousin of Etelvina's fled

into the mountains and finally managed to cross over the border into
France, Etelvina is knocking around forty or forty-two and is a widow
but very happy-go-lucky, her late husband was a Belgian pilgrim who
stayed on here, he was a good cook and knew a bit about accounting
and even mythology, I cannot recall what his name was, but life left
Etelvina unscathed and carefree and sailing was what she liked better than anything, Sunday and Thursday are the best days for invoking the forces of good, Tuesday and Saturday are the best for calling
up evil, infernal powers, Friday is for love and Wednesday is good for
delving into the area of mystery, treasure is myriad though difficult
to disenchant, fear usually gets the better of disenchanters, there is
as much buried as enchanted treasure and it is also difficult to get
hold of, on Salomba point the brigantine *Marechal Deodoro*
foundered as she was coming from Recife with her cargo of misery
and green and red parakeets, she was carrying great hunger and more
than two thousand parakeets on board, when he saw that his ship
was surely sinking, skipper Feliciano Itpetinga ordered the birds to be
freed and they flew away towards the mountain, away from wind and
sea, looking as though they were clad in fine silks, many birds flew
to the Muiños gully in search of shelter where they raised a great
rumpus though whether from fear or joy nobody could tell, Casto
Verruga, the Agrafoxo sorceror, died smothered in smegma, he looked
like a jar of sour cream which costs a pretty penny in the Latorre con-
fectioner's, Casto Verruga started to decay directly so they had to nail
down the lid in great haste lest the maggots escape, upon his
deathbed Casto Verruga told me that the other six weapons were a
magic wand, which should be left to soak for nine days in mother's
milk with a dash of cinnamon, a seven-knotted cord (from a
Franciscan friar if possible), a consecrated quill (if possible from the
right wing of a white hen weary of laying double-yolked eggs), a gob-
let, preferably silver, for libations, a small perfume burner to scent
the wine for offerings to the saints—St. John and St. Martin stopped
along the road to dine, St. John brought the bread while St. Martin
brought the wine—and lastly magic plaster crushed to a powder with
the bones of a bird of prey which died of old age, it is preferable not

to insist because the devil cannot swim but drowns, boy does he drown! he drowned the entire crew of the brigantine *Inés Bódalo* which sank off Chirlateira point in order to whisk them off to hell, they were in mortal sin, sins of pride and avarice, Doña Onofre passes the time by having masses said for her late husband, I remember, Don Celso Camilo de Cela Sotomayor, retired notarial official, he lived to a ripe old age, on the q.t. Doña Onofre cheated on her husband all his life, though not afterwards, of course, since fidelity does not apply to the dead, the saints give one another gifts and then at last it rains—St. Martin of Salcedo wears a ring upon his hand sent him as a gift by St. Andrew of Lourizán—the Libureiro rock stands clear and is not difficult to avoid, gulls are voracious, valiant birds that leave the sea only when death is at hand and things go out of kilter—Our Lady of Darbo has a fine mantilla sent as a gift by Our Lady of Guía—the Seixo rock also stands clear and is not difficult to avoid, if you keep cool, calm and collected you can see that it is not difficult to avoid either, all you need to do is concentrate on staring at it, octopuses nourish the poor and delight the rich, if you could crossbreed octopuses with mermaids you could have a fish farm raising bleached blonde whores, I did not find anybody who could say it clearly but St. Eulalia of Abdegondo has a votive offering which might be related to this, the battle of Chaves, across from Verín, was no laughing matter, General Paiva Couceiro's troops were crawling with crab lice and hardly knew their orders, nobody wins a battle like that, Father Saturnino Figueiro, the priest in Zacoteiras, used to say that Angustias Tomeiro's brothel in Xinzo de Limia was a hotbed for crab lice, General Paiva Couceiro's troops could not defeat the Portuguese republic and restore the monarchy, as soon as they had guzzled the pasties and quaffed both the wine and anisette, my grandfather's and my uncle's actresses began to dance with the officers, how brazen! Holy Mother, the groping and pawing that went on! in Galicia the belly of the planet is solid gold and moles die because it clogs up their windpipes, they say that gold skews the compass and it must be true because pirates, even when they are very wealthy, Dutch and some Englishmen, do not sport gold hooks except when they give up sailing for good, Area Maior beach separates the sea from the Louro lagoon whence the tide ebbs and flows nobody knows, in summer in the Louro lagoon there bathes a strange sea creature which looks like an eight-legged camel with a loud, shrill whistle, in winter it slumbers on the seabed and does not even breathe, if it were to breathe its lungs would fill up with slime, Suso Golpellás, the *Valdoviño* wisewoman, had a tame tawny owl which used to catch eels for her, the ones in the Forcadas dam are plump, juicy and fry up nicely, on the shoals of Ruña ridge the Portuguese merchant vessel *San Bento* ran aground with a cargo of cod, all her crewmen were saved but her skipper shot himself in the mouth, not all dead bodies can be used for playing buzkashi, some will not stand up to it, custom forbids playing buzkashi with human bodies, even those of enemies who speak a foreign tongue, the dead are like the billows upon the sea which are all different yet all worthy of respect, what remains of the dead is but foam scattered by a lively breeze, spirits can get used to navigating shadowy shoals, reefs in the murky depths, treacherous sandbanks and rocks which loom on an ebb tide, think what you will but this is all perfectly orderly, why, it is a very model of order, like the clankety-clank of the Holy Company, Camouco islet is a knoll covered with vegetation which lies a short distance offshore and should be approached only by small boats, some folks call it the Warren because it is swarming with rabbits and also Blight island, you never know but in general it is better to repeat things than forget them, the Roncadoira reef covers and shows, the Ardeleiro reef covers and shows, and the Baixa Cativa reef covers and shows and so on and so forth until the end of the world, a fortnight beforehand Maruxa Mórdemo foretold the catastrophe of the steamer *Numide* which struck a German mine drifting off Cape Tiñoso and caught fire and sank on the Frei Pérez shoals and not a soul was saved, the *Numide* was carrying a cargo of fireworks, folks who were there said it was a sight to behold to see it shoot through the air so cleanly, Maruxa Mórdemo had had a love affair with Don Arturo Catasol—they were a pair of pigs—the cargo skipper who gave her the slip and was later spotted in Montevideo, spruced up in a bow tie and Panama hat, like all hunchbacks Vincent suffers from urinary tract problems, more than likely he left on board the *Noirmoutier* with his gold coins, Annelie's jewels and the stamp collection, Vincent was also sighted in Montevideo, this business of running off to Montevideo is becoming a habit, Florinda Carreira pays men with silver *duros*, it is a delight to hear them clink on the marble of the kitchen table, Florinda never runs out of silver *duros*, for wealth begets wealth and renders placid and profitable the rich man's slumber, the belly of these horizons is gold, everybody knows it, it does not envelop gold, gold wolves, gold bears, gold serpents, but is enveloped by gold leaving no room for the wolves, bears and serpents, through Cornwall, Brittany and Galicia there wends a way strewn with crosses and nuggets of gold.

IV

THE KEYS OF CIBOLA
(WHEN WE GIVE UP CRICKET FOR GOOD)

THE PROUSO LOURO half-wit started to howl like a wolf pup before he reached the age of fifteen, his mother abandoned him on the beach as a newborn babe for the gulls and crabs to devour but he was rescued by a mermaid from the Shetland Isles known as Dumfries Whalsay who sighed tenderly over him, my cousin Vitiño does not trouble himself about the tricks of love and falling out of love, jealousy and greed, he delights in more immediate and delicate events, the trilling of a tame blackbird, the breasts of a woman newly delivered of a child, sea bass in the Lires estuary and so on, he had to kill the blackbird Chirlirenciño because he used to whistle the Republican anthem and would not fly away from the elder bush by the north door, blackbirds and song thrushes root for earthworms among the ferns, they feed on earthworms, seven or eight cables southeast of the Chungo rock looms rugged Cela point followed by the tiny bay with the same name which is wretchedly confusing to navigate, here the Moor Xiliño Terzón came to prise goose barnacles from the rocks until he was swept away by the sea, at times he would gaze up at San Cristovo mountain—follow the Moor with your eyes, that is where the treasure lies—Xiliño the Moor had a wisp of a moustache, on the Feast of St. Xil trim the oil lamp to keep vigil, not to slumber.

"Can you understand the vicious preoccupations of your cousin Vitiño?"

"Not really, what about you?"

Jeremías Arceiro stared into his interlocutor's almost lashless eyes, reddened and smarting from conjunctivitis.

"Calm yourself and listen carefully to what I am about to tell you, this business of I understand them or I can't understand them is something which doesn't matter a bit. Do you think that your cousin Vitiño and Doña Dosinda know this better than I do?"

"I could swear by all that is sacred that not even they themselves could answer your question."

Carmeliña Barbén, daughter of the beggar from San Bieito da Cova do Lobo—to holy St. Bieito my daughter I bring, ailing she comes, pray restore her again!—likes to sunbathe nude on the hull of the English steamer *Clovelly* which foundered off Fornos beach, the hulk shows at low tide and when the sun is not shining Carmeliño windbathes which is even healthier and does not harm the skin, Celso Tembura does not dare to stuff weasels for they shed their pelts, the weasel is a proud little creature that needs to be cajoled: pretty little weasel, stout little stoat, whereas it cannot abide insults: musty, dusty, mousy little ferret, then it turns venomous and you have to wait for seven donkey stallions to bray and for seven knells of the churchyard bell to toll before it calms down, a wild weasel is a dangerous beast, the toughest sailing along this coastline is from south to north in northeasterly winds in summer and in years of northerly winds, sailing vessels riding out a gale have to be careful not to overreach for they would not be able to make up the way to windward lost, it is a sin to kill a ladybird for they belong to St. Anthony, ladybird, ladybird, fly away home, your house is on fire, your children are gone, Dumfries the mermaid was one-eyed, her other eye was gouged out by a dolphin at play, dolphins weep when they are caught in nets and sense that they can no longer frolic freely, the Prouso Louro innocent is not flesh and blood but newspaper and sawdust, his hair is glued on with gum arabic, Charles E. Allen, brother of James, gave up cricket for good and returned to India in search of his bygone days as a lieutenant with the Bengali Lancers and a reader of Kipling, he was shot in the chest in the Tezpur pass, he had the bullet encased in gold and presented it to his grandmother, he was always very fond of her, he spent his entire childhood at his grandmother's house, Charles E. Allen never set foot in Spain but did indeed visit Portugal, he went to Figueira da Foz and Carnaxide, the imagination is an overly docile mistress, poverty-stricken poets have only imagination and are skilled at binding their verses between velvet covers and inscribing the titles in copperplate, some use red ink for the headings, doubts about Pilarín Zamboanga Gonsales made her worthy of the judge's clemency and the hangman's obtuse queries, thus she was spared death on the gallows, Pilarín was Charles' unruffled Philippine lover, I've heard it said that she wet the bed but this should be taken with a pinch of salt for we should be wary of scandalmongers, a rumormonger should be taught a lesson by cutting his tongue out and ramming it up his backside, the vast majority become enraged and huff and puff like wild boars, some cricket matches last for several days, when the old hands at the Marylebone Cricket Club proffer advice, none endeavor to console cricketers by encouraging them to take up croquet, when we give up cricket for good we do not have the consolation of playing croquet, they are entirely different matters, hope is the viaticum of the poverty-stricken and the defeated, the burst condom of the loser, that wretch who in the end does not even save his soul, a newly purchased pig should be rubbed down with garlic and placed backwards in the sty, pig bile cures carbuncles, while the broth in which the trotters have been simmered soothes toothache, pork lard with mulled wine cures a cold, in soups with corn bread it cures the trots and in a wormwood poultice it gets rid of worms, the sea area of Bueu stretches from the island of San Clemente to Morcellos point including the islands of Ons and Onza, a floating torpedo should be towed by catching hold of the eyebolt on the head, a reddened sky foretells a storm, the prudent response is to shorten sail and stand offshore, a blue flare lighting up the night sky gives warning of a vessel aground requesting assistance, if the flare is red, it means a fire or a leak on board, Cristinita Sanlouzáns had a love affair with a footballer from the Celta de Vigo team called Isidoro Celeiros who later went off on missions to convert the blacks to Christianity, Isidoro was the nephew of the Tomeza Bellwether who learned the healer's art from his neighbour Xanciño the Dwarf, a cranky cuss who used to run errands for the Cosoirado Scaredy Cat, these mysterious escapades of witch doctors and *pastequeiros** pertain to Pontevedra, Scaredy-Cat lives in the hamlet of Santa María de Pombal, in the parish of San Pedro de Tomeza, peace be with you, stand still till I drape the stole about you and make the sign of the cross, stand still till I bless you and scare off the evil owl which senses death, if you labor under an evil spell, free me O Lord! if you are afflicted by the evil eye, free me O Lord, if you are spirited off by Satan requiem en pax, now let us eat the bread and drink the wine, part of witchcraft is for souls in purgatory, first you have to urinate on the bramble patch trying not to piss on the glowworms, whooping cough can be cured with owl broth, you have to simmer it all night long without plucking the feathers off, if you eat owl droppings you will be filled with wisdom, he who makes the pilgrimage to Santa Comba and not to San Cibrán journeys in vain, you should go to both places in order to avoid squabbles and spite, the Tomeza Bellwether is always half smashed and has a rowdy, quarrelsome nature, the Tomeza Bellwether journeys only to San Cibrán and not to Santa Comba, everyone believes what they want to believe since faith obligates only the believer, with this bread and with this wine I stem the scourge of the dead and the scourge of the living, the Polish steamer Ustka, with general cargo on board, struck the Estaquín rock and swiftly sank, her entire crew perished, the hull of the vessel was swept by the sea towards the blackish, towering peak of the isle of Siguelo which appears to be full of sluggish eyeless bats, Hilario Ascasubi divined the city where the tree they call the ironwood languishes in the Sonora desert beyond the three great kingdoms of Marata, Acus and Totonteac situated in the country of the seven famous cities, the Indians know where they are but they lie through their teeth and deliberately lead the traveler astray so that he either starves to death or is parched from thirst, the city of Cíbola was engulfed by desert sands, it was swept away by the wind and buried beyond Pexatlán, entombed deep beneath the earth because it has never been seen since, tradition has it that Indian

---

* *pastequeiro*: a traditional healer who starts his cure with the words *pax tecum*—peace be with you

witches fashioned the magic key to the city of Cíbola from gold and honey and left it to dry in the sunshine of the North Pole, under orders from Burillón Tapoc, the god of wealth and war, they sewed it to the skin of a whale which they then clubbed to death on the return journey so that it could not tell anyone, the city of Dugium Duio was also swept away and submerged beneath the sea between the Mañoto rock and the Centulo, Don Damian Taboada, shipping agent, chandler, canned and dried provisions, telegraph and telephone service, claims that life is an adventure which can end only in the foreseeable calamity of death, according to this rule the wisest thing is to selfishly kick the bucket as soon as possible, purgatory does not budge and, according to Luther, lies somewhere between Denmark and Schleswig-Holstein, limbo is rather more difficult to locate, it is said to lie on the border of Anatolia, hell lies within the center of the Earth, fueling the flames of volcanoes while heaven lies beyond the planets and the Milky Way, since life is hurtling towards doom and gloom, why then don't we speed things up and put a bullet in our heads? wonders Don Damian, with a pea-shooter the devil shot a centipede into Don Damian's mouth which was lolling open as he lay sleeping, he hit his target fair and square and Don Damian swallowed the bug, Father Xerardiño Aldemunde believes that the devil swims at Seiside beach where the Prouso Louro half-wit was abandoned by his mother to be devoured by dumb beasts who cannot tell good from evil, the devil does not swim in his birthday suit but sports a nightshirt and beret, in hell only the souls of those who declare war upon the devil and lose are burned, these battles are almost invariably lost because the devil is strong and cunning, a fighter by nature, heathens have no respect for the virgin Locaia a Balagota, they shamed her by gilding her most intimate recesses with gold leaf, the death penalty will have to be brought back for heathens, terrorists and rapists, but especially for heathens, death on the gallows with schoolchildren swinging from the ankles of the hanged man, Johnny Jorick had no luck, for a body to be castrated for a bet at a *romería* is not a sign of luck, if souls in purgatory could learn the crafts of the Camariñas lacemakers all the houses throughout

Galicia, as well as in Portugal and León, would be adorned with handmade lace, everybody knows that mermaids were the first lace-makers, but of the souls from the Holy Company and their skill in this regard not a word was ever spoken, you should be cautious with your suppositions for you cannot trifle with anybody's good name, mind your p's and q's with fools so that they don't preen themselves like peacocks, insincerity is not a habit of fair, respectful men, the wings of angels are always white but custom permits their streamers to be bright like flags, it is not healthy for the soul to pursue solitude, the worst thing about avidly pursuing solitude is to end up finding it empty while your fellow men forgo it and live, love, hate and amuse themselves, nor does the pursuit of good suffice, that rorqual who swims against the current, you have to plunge the harpoon into him, off Castro da Moura point lies the broad shoal known as Monterón de Terra, the rocks show at low tide, the most perilous is the Xoana shoal, my uncle Knut Skien sings the verses of Poe in Galician to the accompaniment of the accordion, you have to let sports die of their own accord, they all wither under their own weight, the same thing happens to them as with friendships and most chronic hatreds, while the rest fester, my uncle Knut Skien took James E. Allen off to hunt Marco Polo sheep and left me in Caneliñas staring out over the sea, in those days I did not yet dream of building a house with boxwood beams, that was an illusion as contagious as mumps though not so ignoble, apart from saving your soul the only noble illusion which is left for a countryman is hunting a bear with a knife and nowadays there are no bears left, the last one to roam around these parts was slain by Cirís from Fadibón before his escapade with the devil on Cabernalde hill, Cósmede the deaf-mute's bear does not count because it is tame, wild bears feed on currants and bilberries though not on dead crabs or cod, in my family we have not been able to raise a house with boxwood beams and now we are ashamed and blame it on our lack of roots, that is just an excuse even though we may not know it, my uncle Knut invited me to have a glass of red vermouth with him, I started to tremble like a leaf, and he told me: our bones will be scattered hither and thither and what good will it do us to

have devoted our entire lives to hunting rorqual whales?, that is
something which cannot be swept aside by a few wretches, a handful
of half-starved vegetarians and pacifists, the stage is now set and all
we have to do is learn our parts by heart, the prompters cannot be
relied upon for they are generally drunk, my uncle Knut and I speak
English, Galician, or Castilian, depending on the moment, I don't
speak Norwegian, a confused cherubim may fall into sin and soil his
wings with greasy soot from the chimney of the soul, let nobody forget that Niceto the Hired Assassin is capable of the most abject obe-
dience in return for a few coppers, the hard thing is to prevent families scattering and men going off to die far from where they entered
this world, a pregnant woman should not eat goose barnacles, sole,
ray or strawberries lest her child be born with birthmarks, the stench
of mercy may confuse anyone who journeys aimlessly, on Gures
beach one morning there appeared an oak coffin with bronze fasten-
ings filled with brand new smoking pipes each individually wrapped
in silver paper packed inside a plastic bag, the pipes were hewn from
heather and roseroot, Cósmede stored the goods in his shack and
gave away three of them as gifts: one to the harbor master in
Corcubión who juggled masterfully, making filigrees, with his false
teeth, one to the priest in Carnota who intoned mass while keeping
time with his foot and one to Don Marcelo the fellow with the peg
leg from the grocery store, the remainder he kept, he had three dozen
long-stemmed ones left, he used the coffin as a bench and sometimes
as a bed, the wolf also liked to sleep in the coffin, my maternal great
grandfather squandered a fortune on vice and when he found himself
without a bean he allowed himself to be invited for drinks and
smokes without the slightest embarrassment, even by the poor? even
by the very beggars at *romerías*, the lame, one-armed, blind, lepers
and deaf-mutes like lumps of quartz, Cósmede was also a deaf-mute,
it is not enough to scrimp and save all your life for a good funeral and
a preferential seat at the right hand of Our Father, life is as dear as
death and vice versa and in the Holy Company there are in the end
only orphan souls devoid of the help of charity, my great grandfather
Cam used to tell stories to little children: once upon a time many

years ago there was a young girl from Abeleiroas who went out for a
stroll in the woods to sample the strawberries, smell the violets and
caress camellias, her name was Maruxiña Cerdedo the
Consumptive's daughter and she wore her hair in a long braid down
to her waist—Maruxiña, Maruxiña, come give me a kiss and I'll give
you a shilling! to kiss men who reek of tobacco Maruxiña is not willing—Maruxiña knew the cherry tree wherein the goldfinch sang and
the sedges where the tuneful, lovesick nightingale hid, one morning
Maruxiña met a fox lapping water from a brook and it spoke to her
in Latin: Maruxiña, have no fear for I mean a young damsel no harm,
here between my eyes is wedged a large-headed pin mounted with a
sea-green emerald, if you will pluck it out and stick it in the highest
quince upon the quince tree of the Apostle St. James the spell will be
broken and the Virgin Mary will whisper a verse so I will regain my
true form, my silver armor, my golden shield embossed with snow-
white fleurs-de-lys and my dappled colt with its flowing mane
groomed by the dwarf Mafalda the Stubborn, for I am Prince
Xacobiño de Lebouzán and I shall entreat my father King Moses of
Mesopotamia to request your hand in marriage, but my great grandfather Cam never finished recounting the utterances of the fox in precise detail, for he would fall asleep first so nobody ever knew for certain whether Maruxiña the Consumptive's daughter ever plucked out
the pin and whether or not she became a princess, my great grandfather Cam died from cold and boredom, from syphilis, too, they say,
in a corner of the whaling station, nobody was there to close his eyes,
truth to tell the family was already sick and tired of him, he was
amusing but useless, and when you become useless the family dis-
cards you unfeelingly, some folks do not even get a burial, across
from the saltworks right on Gures beach the coastal cutter *Serrapio
Pequeño* caught fire, all her crew members and their belongings were
saved since the sea was fairly calm, Cósmede allowed the sailors to
dry themselves by the fire in his hovel and in return they gave him a
gift of dried figs and a bottle of rum, as well as a set of oilskins and
two flannel shirts, Cósmede slung a strip of canvas over the wolf and
the bear so they lay quiet and obedient, newborn baby boys should be

given plain chocolate and a spoonful of full-bodied wine, what goes down well with girls is a drop of cocoa and a spoonful of sweet anisette, this advice upon the feeding of babies is only for those born along the seashore and does not apply to babies born inland, boxwood is slow to burn, like iron, but when it catches fire it consumes everything before it, like the storm itself, high and mighty folks don't like their daughters to marry before the age of sixteen because they believe they are not mature, any trade will do—tinker, tailor, soldier, sailor—any trade will do for sons-in-law, the main thing is that they become hardworking men rather than sippers of soft drinks, to build a house with boxwood beams you need both time and roots, nobody ever tires of saying so, nobody recalls ever seeing the souls in the Holy Company happy, they do not dance jigs, play the tambourine, smooch, stroke one another's bodies in search of delightful consolation, that is because spirits have no flesh, against sins of the flesh the best thing is to see how the soul escapes while the body is devoured by feverish maggots which do not even breathe, the city of Cíbola contained every treasure that man could imagine, the cobblestones in the streets were made of gold and sparkling wine flowed from the fountains, the key to the city of Cíbola, some call it New Canaan or the Chalice of the Truncated Cross, was hidden by the billy goat Cifontes at the foot of a maranta grove protected by a band of rattlesnakes ruled by a second-rank demon, nobody could tell me his name, some seafarers call the Galluda shoals the Farelo, this was where the steamer *Gumersindo Junquera* foundered, she split in two and is inhabited by witless octopuses and giant galoots of jellyfish, in the Gran Sol huge, witless jellyfish breed and in leap years they swim down to the Gulf of Cadiz to put the wind up the Moors and Portuguese, some seek shelter in the Peñón, the Holy Ghost told me the other night that the stage is now set and that all we have to do is ponder the words of self-sacrificing demands, in a manner of speaking, Isidoro Celeiro played center forward, he was strong in both legs, could shoot energetically with accurate aim and headed the ball well, in the parish of San Pedro they still recall the kick in the pants he gave Xanciño the dwarf and sent him flying through the air while the

witches were splitting their sides with laughter and all the glowworms went out at once with the fright, on the Carallete only
Frenchwomen in their forties swim and they are generally brazen
sluts, kneel down so I can kiss your forehead, stand still and close
your eyes so I can well-nigh bless you with scorn, there's no use pre-
tending and trying to distract me for Beelzebub will never forgive
you, within the gaze of Bieito Montemarelo the owl is concealed the
exact spot where the key to the city of Cíbola is buried, or maybe it
is a whole bunch of keys, Father Tristán Diz the priest, alias Tapioca,
who was a greedy-guts and a show-off though fair-minded, used to
feed the owl so that his tongue would not tattle and all be lost,
secrets cannot be shared with just anybody, let alone with summer
visitors, we are all sloughing our skins along the path, little by little
we are all rusting from tedium and monotony, that stubborness, we
are all being blotted from everyone's memory, memory is like a barnacle clinging to the hull of a vessel, folks forget that in order to go
on living comfortably it is not enough to feign reason, you must pos-
sess, devour, even digest it, nearly ten croquet lawns would fit within a cricket pitch, sometimes a boar stands up to a wolf and is not
always the loser in the battle, the boar is a ferocious fighter, steadfast
and strong, he has stamina and presses forward without looking to
either side, in San Mamede they levy a fine of thirty ducats for each
pig caught chomping chestnuts, in the words of the adage: chestnuts
lying in the street they are not for you to eat, nowadays they don't
use ducats, that is a coin which has long since disappeared, half the
fine goes towards Holy Sacrament oil while the remainder covers the
court costs, the owner of the pig serves eight days in prison on bread
and water, he may have homemade food taken to him: chorizo,
bacon, black pudding, corn bread, butchering the pig is a barefaced
cold-blooded crime, a joyous, unwholesome murder in the stable
which titivates the crotch and yields comfort to both palate and
stomach, when men stick pigs and women wring the necks of chickens, grasping them between their thighs, it is like young lads and
lasses taking a roll in the hay, there is not a judge in this world capable of ruling upon so much subtle confusion, all interlinked and jum-

bled up together, my piggy-wiggy, my porker, we'll have three fine feasts from you, first the butchering, second the quartering, third the feasting, everyone as happy as a clam bar the pig, it is a real pity to see that nowadays instead of flaming torches, welding irons are used to singe the bristles from the skin of the pig, butchers have even less respect for the pig than harpoonists do for the rorqual whale, familiarity breeds contempt, perhaps they do respect them just the same but in some muddled, mysterious way, in hell they have a special egg-shaped, green-painted cauldron for drying the water from shipwrecked mariners' lungs of the soul which is the final, most resistent and elusive part, there is no point in burning the bodies because souls do not burn unless bedaubed with phosphorus and sulphur paste breathed through the nostrils of the devil, you have to watch your step for give them an inch and they'll take a mile, from Outeiriño Gordo hill which looms above Ostreira point, the coastline falls steeply away and curves eastwards into Avilleira beach where hundreds of cans of condensed milk were washed up by the sea, Cósmede took loads of them and buried them in the sand so he could later fetch them one by one, on the Cubierto de Bolteiro reef clusters of tame goose barnacles grow, they are tricky to catch and are said to be the cleverest on the entire coastline and should be cooked over a fire of wild seawrack, kelp is even better, here the river Bornalle, where eels breed which can be eaten fried or raw, flows into the sea, the two Carracas cover and show and the Foradiña, the Pedra das Moscas and the Galiñeceiro shoal too, all perilous to navigate, on Shrove Tuesday last year a cloud of mauve butterflies almost blotted out the sun on Sorrego da Braña point, it must have been the devil disguised as a shark some fishermen saw cut through the water around the Petón dos Turcos rock, because the hour was not yet ripe, the butterflies formed the hammer and sickle in the heavens, they were communists you see, and then fluttered slowly away, the shark swims in curves when he is sad and hungry and in zigzags when well-fed and in fine fettle, in The Compass Rose, Farruquiño Sticky Wicket's tavern, they make cocoa, brew coffee and serve not only wine and *aguardiente* but soft drinks, beer, vermouth, gin, brandy and other spirits as well, Sticky Wicket wants to make a go of things and scrape a bit of money together and keeps his eye firmly on the main chance, Noah Rebouta the Warbler, Chelipiño Pérez Wolf Rump, Doada Orbellido the Rasher, his brother Froitoso Wooden Face, Lucas Abuín the Piddler, Martiño Villartide the Whiner and Renato Fabeiro the Comedian, who never learned their lesson but went on thumbing their noses at the sermon and being disrespectful to priests, from time to time they sally forth from purgatory and teach butterflies to form revolutionary insignia in the heavens, and then return, as though nothing had happened, to burn once more, Farruquiño set off for Santiago to purchase an Italian coffeemaker but he lost his money on bingo, why, he could not even go to the red-light district to find a Portuguese whore, they come in three types: melancholy, greedy or singing girls, since Farruquiño is a skinflint he opts for melancholy girls, Farruquiño had to return to his village as sick as a parrot, he confided in nobody lest they should laugh at him, the Montalvo de Fóra rock lies less than one meter below the surface at low water, Montalvo de Terra and the Chanote rocks lie deeper but are treacherous nevertheless, a southeasterly wind drove the steamer *Mourelos* with general cargo on board on to these rocks after her rudder snapped, the skipper and three sailors drowned but the rest were rescued, the housekeeper to Father Socorro the priest in Morquintiáns told me on the Feast of St. Barnabas, when the sun is at its zenith in the heavens, that most saints are related and meet up at family gatherings to combat the devil and prevent him wreaking evil upon faithful Christians, María Flores rules the roost from her wicker rocking chair and makes jam and *aguardiente* from bilberries, strawberries and redcurrants, she makes a supply which lasts the whole year long, she also knits scarves and gloves and passes the time playing solitaire, there is time enough for everything, even saving your soul and helping your neighbour to save his too, my uncle Knut Skien has one eye one color and the other another, that sometimes happens, it was the same with my late sweetheart Xertrudiñas and Agostiño Taborda the puppeteer, the Dodge belonging to Micaela's Carlos bears memories of many a sin which the rain is slowly sluicing away, the wind also sweeps them away, but sins of the flesh are wiped out only by fire, it wipes them out but does not teach a lesson, purgatory is not to teach anybody a lesson but to set straight the story of the dead, the story is always of the dead who will only be miraculously resurrected upon the Day of Judgement when the last trump sounds, I declare that I have saved up some money and that I am going to build a house with boxwood beams, I don't know where, with boxwood floors and stairs, on the seashore, for sure, I don't wish even to contemplate a fire, in the end even stones and sheet iron and steel from the hull of a ship will burn, an echo does not repeat the snoring of a soul nor do mirrors reflect the soul's face, it is useful to carry a box of matches in your pocket at all times in order to scare off the mountain wolf, bear in mind that the sea does not forgive but then neither does the earth, they are two flesh-eating animals, two bloodthirsty beasts, water burns like fire and the wind flees in terror from the other elements, Florinda Carreira looked like Joan of Arc's older sister, but history is written with ups and downs and muddled toing and froing yet, even so, it is still understood, I could spend my whole life eating sardine pasty because it is such a well-balanced food containing everything: vitamins, proteins, starches, carbohydrates, now that is real learning, the art of sousing partridge and quail, tuna and sardines lends merit to women even though it may lead to patricide and espionage, this is far from clear, from Remedios point to Louro mountain the Meixidos, Ximiela, Mean, Carballosas shoals and the Os Bruios rocks show, in the Meixidos channel which runs between Figueiroa Head and the Insua Light the young lass Rosalia the Lintel, who dances and swims better than anybody, goes swimming, a strong healthy young lass is a blessing from God and a gift from the heavens, if I were King of Spain I would surround myself with lasses as strong as oak trees and healthy as hydrangeas to infect me with happiness and make me fair and beneficent, it seems to me that this should be the natural state of man although it is as plain as a pikestaff that it is not so, Rosalía the Lintel arm-wrestles all the clerks, shopkeepers and almost all the fishermen and seafarers, she laughs heartily and accepts invitations to drink chocolate with buns to dunk in it but nobody gets farther than that unless she so desires: it's my life so I call the shots and tangle with whomsoever I please, memories which I do not wish to hang on to I simply wipe out and that's that, God smote the laborer Liduvino for lacking respect during the Our Father and now he wanders around *romerías* singing ballads about pirate brigantines and criminals hanged on the gallows, outsiders all of them, Castilians, Leonese, Portuguese, the blind are given the perfect voice to sing with real feeling, Liduvino came within a hairsbreadth of drowning in the Braña Rubia lagoon, between Rodeiro and Salgueiras, he missed his footing, slipped and lost his balance but he was saved by the Holy Spirit and his acolyte St. Bieito of Cova da Lobo—St. James sends the bread, St. Bieito sends the wine, St. Eneón sends the acorns and St. Bieito brings the bacon—the blind have little to fall back on, when *Chubby Manteiga* landed in limbo Our Lord realized that the wolf and the bear had been left forsaken so he sent him back to Gures beach once more, and since time does not count with Our Lord nobody noticed either his coming or going, the wolf and the bear were heartily glad but never knew why, intuition is not governed by the same law as will and understanding, the journeys wrought by the divinity are magical and cannot be measured by the clock or the calendar, sharks do not swim in these seas, rorqual whales—though not sharks—swim in these seas, Liduvino offends nobody for he begs for alms for the love of God in a deferential blind man's voice, the blind are more courteous and circumspect than the deaf and blaspheme less, here there is neither stealing nor deceiving and Our Lord's will is humbly observed, in Bosenxo, on the road to Arzúa, there lived an old woman who played Wagner on the accordion, *Twilight of the Gods, Tannhäuser, Parsifal,* the devil used to appear to the old woman every Tuesday, he did not enter her body or her soul but merely appeared to her and conversed venomously, he was a young goodlooking demon although he stank, of course, but he washed his armpits and groin in all the springs and sprinkled himself with essence of lavender, the woman was called Polipia, nobody knows who St. Polipia was, maybe she was a martyr from Antioch who, after suffering great insult in the name of the

Redeemer, attained the triumph of the ancient serpent, the neighbours claimed that Polipia who played the accordion was a sort of
witch and wanted to burn her at the stake, the Civil Guard had to
intervene and whisk her off to sleep in a cell in the barracks every
night in order to save her skin, Father Xerardiño tried to scare off the
demon, although he only sort of succeeded, by invoking St.
Euphemia of Arteixo, protectress of the possessed, matters were sorted somewhat though not entirely, Polipia was freed from the presence of the demon with skills recommended by Madame Kurachi,
hairdresser to the Countess of Festro, that is by bathing her in the
milk of a Maltese goat and drying her with a Manila shawl, her house
had to be aired for seven days and seven nights and then sprinkled
with rosewater, damask roses are the most effective, the Civil Guard
and Father Xerardiño convinced the country folk that the demon had
departed for Castromil de Santiago, he was not hard to recognise for
he was wearing a commercial traveler's apron, peaked cap and bow
tie, not that Polipia was ever actually possessed by the demon, as I
have said, so purging her with jallop and smoking her with gold,
frankincense and myrrh proved unnecessary, but it came within a
whisker, some folk are more resistant than others to invasion by the
devil with his tolerance and knavish tricks, consumptives are more
susceptible, there was a great turnout at Belarmino Bugallo's funeral,
people came thronging from far and wide, they polished off all the
bacon and drank up all the wine in the house, the dead man was the
brother of Father Xiao, priest in Escravitú, who was renowned for
being highly respectful of Divine Providence, Belarmino was a master at parcheesi and dominoes, nobody could hold a candle to him, in
parcheesi he rolled the dice to great effect, and in dominoes he could
memorize all the combinations played and could guess the tiles in
each player's hand, he could read them reflected in their eyes and was
seldom wide of the mark, Pepiño, Belarmino's other brother, believed
that in purgatory you could play parcheesi and dominoes, that is no
sin and, besides, Our Lord God is compassionate and charitable,
among those who wind up burning in purgatory some heal well and
the scars and sores fade quickly from their skins but there are also

those who are forever oozing pus, feverish and trembling, they are a hideous sight, Alfonso González Puentes, bootblack, suffers from chilblains in winter, the poverty-stricken get chilblains on their ears and fingers which sting and itch even worse when scratched, Alfonso González Puentes is also called Dámaso Alborache Monsagre, lottery ticket seller, suffering from piles and an itchy ass, rather, his name is not what has just been stated though he might well have been called Dámaso Avellar Muñoz, gasman, Russian sailors from the Vladivostock burned in the Cove of the Scorched Corpses, their souls still flit over the sea but do not join the Holy Company because they cannot understand one another, the whores in Santiago are most submissive and obliging, especially the girls from Orense and Portugal, some will even do up the undone buttons of your fly, nowadays nobody wears a button-up fly, my aunt Adela calls a fly a placket, Dámaso has a slight stammer and patiently puts up with half-cured clap, he might also be Antonio López Correa, cross-eyed grocer's assistant, brazenly scratching the crab lice he cannot get rid of even with Crabesol or lavender oil, or Ceferino Cendejas Domingo, gravedigger, suffering from gout, or Salustio Beleña Escalantes, sacristan, suffering from wasp stings, or Camilo Reboleiro Fervenzas, luggage and goods clerk, who has had intestinal worms since childhood, or Angel Soutullo Martiñán, netsman, who fathered a string of good-for-nothing bums one after the next, Alfonso was a clean sort of fellow who healed well and his scars faded on their own, Alfonso was born in Vigo, his mother was a deaf-mute and his father sold candy, gum and peanuts in the street and at the school gates.

"Have you heard it said that the Centulo rock laments like a mistreated beast?"

"Yes, and whistles, too, at times, the Centulo has great life and envelops much mystery, it was from here the mermaid whom Farruquiño, oarsman from the *Xibardo*, would not forgive for her indifference or scatterbrained bad behavior—what difference does it make anyway?—left weeping for he was green with jealousy."

Alfonso grew up in the street, it was also in the street that he learned the knack of scraping by like the sparrows and the bluebottles crawling on the windowpane who have no escape, living from moment to moment like sewer rats and wild rabbits, God protects innocence even more than wisdom, his father put him in the orphanage, a barrack of a building inhabited by ghosts disguised as bats, the dormitory was a long hall with two rows of narrow cots and half the windowpanes broken, in the center stood a pail for your number one, for number two everyone had to go down in the morning to a yard behind the building, it was bitterly cold and if you were taken short during the night you did your business in a newspaper and then threw the parcel out the window, the warden always walked around stick in hand whacking the living daylights out of the inmates, Dámaso, or rather Alfonso, was a skinny thirteen-year-old with a silver *duro* and a two *peseta* coin, also silver, which they never discovered for he tied them around his balls with a ribbon, winger James E. Allen gave up rugby for good because he felt himself growing old, there are seven old ages or seven stages of old age and each one comes all of a sudden without warning, in order to hunt Marco Polo sheep you must be rich, age matters less, nor should you play tennis, or cricket, if your old ticker is tiring, in the Surrey Cricket Club they do not want players who bowl with their mouths open, croquet is well nigh a parlor pursuit, *cíbolo* is what the Indians call the bison but where the city of Cíbola lies there are no bison for the earth is too parched for grazing, one fine day Alfonso escaped from the ophanage by leaping from the third floor and almost killing himself in the process, he plummeted to the ground and every bone in his body groaned, while the hollows of his body—his lungs, stomach and belly—rang out, his brains sang within his skull, his teeth rattled inside his mouth, his chin dug into his chest, his feet turned black and blue and his joints were jolted out of kilter, once he was able to catch his breath, Alfonso managed to make his way to the station and scramble aboard the buffer of a freight car on a train which was about to pull out.

"You know as well as I do that preoccupation with order is unhealthy; this is all too orderly but it's not up to me to explain it, be off with you! I contradict nobody for I have already learned my lesson."

Recesinde, the priest, Father Antonio Recesinde, who was parish priest in Rabuceiras, but nowadays there is no parish priest in Rabuceiras, for there are fewer and fewer priests and more parishes are closing down, I don't know where all this will end at all, Recesinde the priest was always deeply concerned with sins of the flesh and would rail relentlessly against lechery and everything human and divine once he got on to his second glass of coffee liqueur, Mariquiña Gandarelo de Muñoz had an operation on her womb in Santiago and they told her that she could not have any more children, she had three under her belt already, three little girls: Chucha aged seven, Uxía five and Modesta two, Maruquiña had not yet borne a son and would have liked to have nine children like her mother before her—nine is a good round number—but when Maruquiña was discharged from the hospital Recesinde the priest told her that it was a mortal sin to sleep with her husband because the purpose of matrimony was none other than the perpetuation of the species, as you know there are seven old ages and also seven deaths, which are not the same nor is there any particular reason why they should coincide, my brother-in-law Estanis Candíns was a basketball player but when he died for the first time he was reincarnated as a schoolmaster, this is misleading because in reality these are not reincarnations strictly speaking but invocations or guardianships of Our Lord who lets us go on living though with altered feelings, the freight car upon which Alfonso was traveling was uncoupled in Redondela, the lad alighted from the buffer taking care not to get crushed and fashioned himself a pair of crutches from a couple of sticks so that he could stand upright, kelp is a wholesome seaweed for it contains metals and trace elements which are beneficial for the health, when Alfonso was about to leave the station he was stopped by a railway guard who then handed him over to the Civil Guards, Alfonso told them that his name was Antonio López Correa, an assumed name, but he did not succeed in fooling them and they marched him off to the Redondela barracks, but there was a fair in town that day and the spectacle of an injured boy, handcuffed between two guards, unleashed the ire of the

fairgoers who hurled insults at the guards and rushed to the aid of the
boy and he arrived at the pokey armed with two loaves of bread, a
cheese, half a dozen sausages and his pockets bulging with money,
the post commander called him a liar, for the lad's escape had already
been reported so his real identity was known, but he also told him
that they did not want to see his face ever again in the orphanage so
he could go wherever the hell he liked, in order for him to leave and
endure the pain they bound his body with a rope, tin cough lozenge
boxes from La Cubana factory, manufactured by the Widow and Sons
of Serafín Miró, Reus (Tarragona), Spain, are useful for storing pic-
tures of the Virgin, dried flowers, silver coins from abroad, condoms,
stamps from Bosnia-Herzegovina, First Communion photos of a
deceased cousin and expired identity cards, Alfonso had a La Cubana
cough lozenge box but he had to leave it behind in the orphanage,
since he did not wish to return to his parents he set off for his grandmother's house in Corunna and got there by hook or by crook, in the
village of Panches, above the Costa de Cabra and Pedra Rubia point,
where the collier *Salvador* foundered, three sailors perished while
another three went missing, the holy woman Micaela Cerdido was
alive until recently, she was killed by a bolt of lightning which came
tumbling down her chimney, Micaela could work cures for love and
loss of love, as you move south there are fewer shipwrecks, though
they still do occur, unfortunately, but they are fewer and farther
between, in order to bind a man with the snare of love you must take
three yards of white ribbon, tie seven knots in it and then tie it about
a rag doll named after the beloved, if you wish to undo this step you
sever the knots and repeat: I now release Roquiño (or whomever)
from the spell wrought upon him by the knots and thus destroy the
spell thereby formed, Charlemagne put the wicked inhabitants of the
city of Valverde to the sword, he was helped by the Apostle St. James
who demolished the walls of the city harboring such abominable sin
with the hooves of his horse, Valentín Noriega was unworthy of the
love of Magdalena Lemon Face so, in order to rid herself of him, she
seized her opportunity one Monday with a waning moon, when the
cock would later ward off midnight demons with his crowing, head-

ed for the river Eume, beyond Filgueiro and, by permission of the souls, dipped her bare feet thrice into the water and each time plucked a honeysuckle flower, said three Hail Marys and repeated a phrase which must not be written down but learnt by heart, Celso Tembura the sacristan knows it and will pass it on to anyone who wishes to learn it, Magdalena Lemon Face returned home before the cock crowed again and placed the three flowers in a vase of water with half a spoonful of vinegar, she placed this on her windowsill for three nights at dusk under the influence of the heavenly bodies and meanwhile observed a rigorous fast, abstained from carnal contact, lewd thoughts, drinking alcohol and wearing the colors green or red, on the thirteenth day she added to the vase three spoonfuls of honey harvested in fall, with her eyes tight shut at daybreak, she poured in a large tumbler of water in which the flowers were standing and upon the stroke of midday, on a fasting stomach, she drank the entire tumblerful holding her breath as long as possible, said another three Hail Marys, repeated the phrase which must not be written down and that was that, she then sought out Valentín Noriega and, without looking at him or touching him, spat upon the ground and sent him packing while he meekly stood aside, perhaps somewhat shamefaced, maybe he was suffering from qualms of conscience, this remedy is also good for obesity or apoplexy, though not against earache or chicken pox as some folks claim, Alfonso enlisted in the Galician Legion at the age of seventeen, though he claimed to be nineteen, and served in Ceuta, in the 2nd Duke of Alba infantry regiment, 4th Batallion, 1st Company, his musket went off in a guardhouse and scorched his face, he had been fiddling about with his weapon and was lucky for he might have been shot in the mouth, Bienvenido Tomás, a commissioned second lieutenant, had already shown him how a shot can be fired from the stock of a gun, and in order to remind him of this, always booted him on the behind, kicking so hard and with such force that Alfonso fell flat on his face, three years later Alfonso returned to Vigo and worked as a builder's builder, such work is not hard to come by, in '57 he took up the brushes and began to get to grips with boot polish but it was not until '66 that he devoted himself full-time to the trade of bootblack which is more secure and you spend less time out in the cold, then he married, fathered seven children, six of them still alive and kicking, and took to reading novels with gusto, Alfonso is a dedicated reader, with sound judgment and a sharp memory, he knows whole books off by heart, *The Hive*, for instance, Alfonso works as a bootblack at Labacolla airport in Santiago, and when he is in good form he suprises his customers by reciting entire paragraphs of some well-known novel or other, the entrance to the Muros and Noya estuary opens up between Louro mountain and Castro point, or rather, between Castro point and the Leixoes islets which lie off Louro mountain, hereabouts there went fishing a young lad who in the course of time was to become Nuncio to His Holiness in a Central American republic, they would not tell me which country it was nor the name of the person who became a high dignitary of the Church so the story cannot be recorded, the coastal cutter *Eloisa Trabancos* with general cargo on board ran aground on the Ximiela, one sailor drowned and all the rest were saved including the two dogs which were on board, Tim and Tom, two smooth-haired fox terriers, smart, fearless, like the ones on the His Master's Voice label, upon making landfall after the wreck the terriers attached themselves to Paquito the cabin boy who was the skipper's nephew and followed him home to Reboredo, over beyond O Grove, close to where the deaf and dumb school is, Paquito's mother is a goodlooking woman by the name of Ermitas and some years back she won the Miss Pontevedra contest, Ermitas did not want the dogs sleeping indoors because they clambered up on the sofa, during the daytime they behaved themselves better and were less of a nuisance, so Paquito built them a kennel where they could shelter from the wind and rain, the cold hereabouts is fairly bearable, the Muros estuary lies at the foot of thirteen mountains of which Albino Nogueira never tires of talking, viewed from the sea the Muros estuary has a whole array of mountains as a backdrop, thirteen mysterious mountains wherein slumber so many other dreams, both reverend and solitary, upon which people turn their backs, Ezaro mountain where the wrath of God raged in the guise of a nest of rabid

vipers capable of rupturing the skin of the planet, the earth's crust
and rocks of the planet, the sea pike which breed in its shadow are
the fiercest known to man, Remedios point at the foot of which a
vessel with her seafarers is wrecked every eleven months, Galera
mountain with its gorse bushes which are used for curing leprosy,
Oroso mountain, home to weasels which hunt greenfinches in flight,
the Tremuzo where a poverty-stricken demon lives on alms from pilgrims, his name is Abafalliño and he lives on the roots of plants,
Louro mountain whence the lighthouse beams forth, in order to
enter the Muros estuary by night it is best to stick close to Louro
mountain, avoiding the southern shore and sailing within the shadow of the Reburdiño lighthouse until you cross the Castromonte
Louro line, next there looms the Xarpal crag full of half buried
Frenchmen, with the arms and legs of some of the dead sticking out
of the earth, San Lois mountain where a half-blind hermit called Friar
Fame lives, surviving on the charity of summer visitors, during the
summer he hoards dried figs, sides of dried cod and corvina as well as
cans of condensed milk and then ekes them out throughout the
entire year, Iroite or La Franqueira mountain where until recently
there lived a type of lizard which has now died out, Enxa mountain
where daytrippers go on picnics and stroll hand in hand, Curota peak
where rays rebound, the Curotiña with its wandering turtledoves and
the Castro indicating the sea where the lad who came to be Nuncio
used to fish for octopus, Albino Nogueira knows many a tale of land
and sea, though he does not write them down because he does not
dare to, Albino says that Erundiña, the spinster whale, has not come
here for two years now, Albino does not like to tell sad stories, or
even to contemplate them, he prefers to believe that Erundiña is still
alive and well, playful and carefree, lame Telmo Tembura does not
greet drinkers of herbal teas, strawberry flavoured soft drinks nor
lemonade, everyone has their own principles and obligations, Ofelita
Garellas is for ever giving birth, she hands her children over to the
foundling home for she has no means of supporting them, the sign
above the entrance reads: Abandoned by Your Parents, Rescued by
Charity, Ofelita is a half-wit and spreads her legs for the asking,

Ofelita sleeps by charity in Micaela Piñeiro's henhouse in Berducido and keeps the vermin at bay, for a time Ofelita lived in the cemetery of San Xurxo of the Seven Dead Foxes, Telmo Tembura allowed her to sleep in the little building where the autopsies are carried out, will-o'-the-wisps and shades of the Holy Company, too, were like old friends but from the accursed tolling of the bells you have to run like blazes because they warn of the presence of Beelzebub, Ofelita fled one night when she heard the bells of Valverde ring out, the city inhabited by sodomites and submerged by the chastisement of God and the Apostle St. James, Telmo Temburo enjoys his trade as gravedigger because it yields great serenity to the character, the Barbanza mountains lie south of the Muros estuary, besides the port of Muros there are other tricky, treacherous bays: O Son, Portosín and O Freixo, Ofelita washes herself and rinses her clothing in streams though not in the sea, the entrance to the Muros estuary is tough, however the width of the entrance and the distance the rocks and shoals lie offshore leave sea room to enter with care, Petronilo was the favorite of Paxaro Bori II el Frontaleiro, King of the Xusteos, who, desirous that the physical perfections of Queen Benigna Coeck could be admired by his favorite, arranged for Petronilo to see her in her underclothes, Queen Benigna was outraged by her husband's decision and lying naked in the arms of Petronilo, who had left off playing his flute the better to attend to her, threatened him with a horrible death in the dungeons of the castle if he did not murder King Paxaro Bori, after the king was killed by an arrow when hunting, Petronilo married the Queen and was crowned king under the name Gavilán Bori I the Sleepyhead, Ofelita Garellas takes fright at these old tales and mutters the Lord's Prayer, approaching from the north by night on a relatively calm sea you rely upon the beams from the lighthouses of Finisterre, Insua point and Corrubedo, after passing the Meixido shoals you approach the estuary until you come within the beam from Monte Louro lighthouse, steering clear of the Ximiela and Carballosa shoals and Bruio islets you can enter after passing one mile beyond the lighthouse, in Segundo the Murcian's inn, I mean Segundo Alporchones Malvariche, born in San Ginés de la Jara,

province of Murcia, who was once a Civil Guard and prison warder,
in Segundo the Murcian's inn an Irish seaman who gave nobody a
chance to find out what his name was, nor was he carrying documentation, stubbed out his cigarette in the face of lame Telmo
Tembura who immediately took umbrage, caught hold of him by the
throat, squeezed hard and throttled him, it was a swift, clean death
and nobody stepped forth in defense of the Irishman since, after all,
he was in the wrong, this business of being in the wrong carries a
high price while the matter of stubbing out a cigarette in someone's
face can unleash dire consequences, they waited until darkness fell
and then threw the Irishman's body into the sea, when approaching
from the south you have to sail within the red occulting sector off
Insua point, O Rocín, O Guincheriro, A Roncadoira, O Bustaxán and
A Baia, when you see the beam from the Reburdiños lighthouse you
head towards it, Segundo the Murcian had been living in the area for
over twenty years, his wife, Virucha Cotiño, red-haired and freckled,
was the owner of the inn which she had inherited from her father,
Segundo and Virucha met at the dentist's in Santiago, in Segundo's
inn folks minded their p's and q's, Virucha used to prepare octopus
better than anybody, she also fried little Herbón peppers to a T, cutting the stalks off so they did not taste bitter, Delfín Pousa
Cuspedriños, castrator of pigs, for devilment known as the Dolt, who
hailed from Cartimil in the Trasdeza valley, had a violent rowdy temper, had more than has, that is true, but in Segundo's inn he minded
his p's and q's so as not to provoke either the owner or the customers
for they would not put up with it for a minute, Segundo does not like
his customers to raise a racket, he throws out drunks and sits them
on the ground, if it is raining he leaves them in the outhouse by the
stable so they are not drenched to the skin, Celso was Telmo's brother, Celso Tembura the sacristan knows four prayers for four spiritual
and bodily necessities, to intercede with God on behalf of good souls,
coastal vessels considerably shorten their course for entering Muros
by putting inside the Basoñas and the Baia shoals when coming up
past the Corrubedo shoals, you need a calm sea and light wind, the
second prayer he knows is to ward off evil spirits, after passing

between A Marosa and Corrubedo or between A Marosa and O Rinchador you continue on the same course and when you approach Louro mountain continue straight ahead until you pass the Teilán de Fora, sailing outside the Basoña Grande, then set a course with Castro point off your starboard bow in order to pass between the Nuevo and Tremalleira shallows, leaving the Basoña on your port beam as stated, you continue until Larayo mountain dips behind Louro mountain and you set a course leaving Reburdiña point to port, the third prayer is for healing ailments which occur naturally or as a result of meddling by the devil or by witchcraft, makes no difference, the only Chinese crewman from the *Good Lion*—her entire crew were saved from the wreck—reached Muros and got himself a job first in the fish market and later in the Good Value Food restaurant, Segundo the Murcian tells me that this should not have been so because he did not fit in, the Chinaman was called Pablito and folks were fond of him, as time went by he was able to sort out his papers and set up a laundry, the fourth necessity Winkle the sacristan deals with is to ensure that evil spirits cannot reenter the body and that this escape hatch is closed to them for ever and ever, amen, folks do not show proper respect to the virgin Locaia a Balagota, the times they are a-changin' and foreign ways are being copied, folks learn them from the television, Dubliner Johnny Jorick still takes a posy of wild flowers to the virgin Locaia a Balagota, fresh colored flowers: yellow, purple, white and blue, it was a mighty trick they played on Johnny Jorick, his voice did not turn high-pitched but his desire for living ebbed away, or rather, was deflected, outside the Basoñas and Baia shoals you can enter Muros at your leisure, after the Corrubedo shoals you continue towards Louro mountain outside the Basoña Grande, steer for Remedios point, keep clear of la Guincheira which lies to the west of the Basoña shoals and do not head towards Louro mountain until you have lined up Curotiña mountain with the Basoña Grande, then head for Louro mountain and continue until you reach Cabeiro hill, then set a course for Reburdiño point and Bob's your uncle! before Feliberto Urdilde was killed by the blow from a bottle widows slumbered more peacefully and had less sinful dreams, indeed he arm-wrestled my cousin Vitiño, that's true, but Vitiño is still alive and kicking, nothing beats craft and sheer dogged-ness for survival, Knut Skien took my cousin James E. Allen off to hunt Marco Polo sheep, life has no plot, when we believe that we are going to one place to perform certain heroic deeds the compass wavers wildly and carries us helter-skelter wherever it wishes: to the school yard, the brothel, the clink, or directly to the graveyard, also death begins to weave its disorienting, bewildering dance, the bag-pipe drones with a hoarse sound, why in my family have we not been able to build a house with boxwood beams? nobody knows the rea-son why, nor do I, ignorance does not decrease as it is doled out, this business of it being several generations since we have been buried together is but an excuse and superstition, the Catholic dead meet and gather together in purgatory, greet one another with respect and utmost affection, and others too although they don't say so, that is the farce of the dead, if you take proper precautions to steer clear of the Leixoes and O Son shoals you can set a course for Reburdiño point, not dropping anchor until you line up the Town Hall clock with the Chapel of St. Joseph, Delfín Pousa skilfully, cheerfully cas-trates pigs, they don't have time to know what hit them, baked sea bream is what the Dolt enjoys more than anything, some Sundays he drops by the Murcian's inn so that Virucha can cook this dish for him, it would be highly dramatic if a house with boxwood beams were to burn with one of us inside, someone who was outside but slipped indoors to save a few letters, a snapshot or a scabby old dog, also to burn to death, that is like purging the heart and feelings, Father Anselmo Prieto Montero, author of *The Diving Bell*, explains to one of his cronies in the Café Galicia this business of exposition, crux and dénouement, which are the three elements which have to be present, the model is taken from Emile Zola or Emilia Pardo Bazán, nowadays it is not like the old times, nowadays folks have dis-covered that the novel is a reflection of life and life has no more dénouement than death, that ever-changing pirouette, first of all the scene must be set and drawn with great accuracy, no license is per-mitted because the characters could run away if they do not feel at

ease, my great uncle Dick's three brothers—that is Cam, Shem and
Japheth, I am descended from Cam—used to hunt whales but were
always at daggers drawn, quareling over everything and the share-out
of the catch was akin to blasphemy, that was their way, some men
have a way of thinking ill and being mistrustful, they cannot find
happiness but console themselves with the thought that neither can
anyone else, Vincent liked to plays bowls, indeed, nothing further
was ever heard of Vincent, it is as though the earth swallowed him
up, hunchbacks are elusive but Vincent even more so than most,
lagoons are generally treacherous and their fish are poisonous and
taste of slime, the Dolt claims that eels from stagnant waters spread
disease, everybody knows that he is right although some deny it, in
order to reach O Freixo from Muros you point towards Cabeiro point
and line up the Xarpal crag with the middle of Quebra island until
you see Aguieiro beach outside the Cabeiro, then steer for Cabalo
Baixo point leaving Quebra island clear to port, you avoid the gravel
spit running southeast, then head for Carreiroa point, at the eastern-
most point of Broña bay, you can make out the Louro lighthouse over
the Carreiro, then set a course for Corbeiro point and follow this
until you line up the Atalaya del Son with Larga point, continue with
these points lined up taking care to pass at least half a cable off
Corbeiro point and shortly afterwards you can steer to close on the
port side in search of an anchorage, it is funny, indeed illuminating,
to see how a Portuguese pilot boat laden with brightly garbed actors
can sink, when they realize that all is lost they get drunk and burst
into heartfelt *fados*, it is comforting, ill-intentioned and straightfor-
ward to see how they save their lives and can make it to dry land dog-
paddling like lapdogs, Tim and Tom, the two terriers from the coastal
cutter *Eloisa Trabancos*, were the same breed as the ratters in the
Caneliñas factory, it is not wholesome to round off carnal relations
with the devil by drinking coffee, it serves no purpose and merely
adds to confusion and upset and increases bewilderment, nor to have
protracted love affairs with fat women with high-pitched voices,
light Italian sopranos, the ones from the Milanesado are the clearest
and showiest, Betanzos fishwives who yell like blazes when they are

at it, destroying the eardrums of spectators with their yelling, the Quindimil brothers cheat at cards, Vincent was right, Doña Dosinda gave a gift of a new radio to my cousin Vitiño Leis, he keeps this under his hat but everybody knows about it, Vincent who has vanished would have liked to play tennis, it is just that he was not in a state to do so, hunchbacks cannot play tennis because the ball veers sideways on them, swinging on its axis like a spinning top, you can leave O Freixo at half water on a rising tide, the last anchor to be weighed is the southern one, steer for the Misela until you see the Atalaya del Son outside Larga Point and the southern side of Quebra island then turn to starboard and head for the point, steering just short of the Coviña, then turn to port making for Portosín and continue until Louro mountain heaves in sight, here you can steer with Cabeiro point to port and set your course depending upon where you are headed, in the seventeenth century Saracen pirates put the inhabitants of Muxía to the sword, they swept around the Pedra dos Cadrís rock and came in to sack Muxía, the memory still lingers of the cruelty of Solomon Bimbón, the captain commanding the three Moorish schooners, some nicknames last a lifetime while others are soon forgotten, perhaps through weariness, and lose their purpose and freshness, hardly anybody called the deceased Annelie Fonseca Dombate, R.I.P., "the lass from Mosquetín", San Francisco bay lies between Bouxa point and Outeiriño point, a little inland lies the village of Louro, Micaela's Carlos managed to repair the horn on his Dodge and he hoots it from time to time, the wild animals scuttle off in terror when they hear it, scurrying under the bracken and rocks, while others crouch motionless close to the ground, their stillness feigning death, Micaela's Carlos chortles aloud frightening the wild beasts, when the sea took on an orange hue after the sinking of the Moroccan vessel the *Banora*, Micaela's Carlos had not yet repaired the horn on his Dodge, Father Anselmo Prieto Montero was well versed in literary theory, his cronies would listen astounded, dumbfounded even, although, indeed, with all due respect, life and, let us say, consciousness, changes every seven years and turns in on itself ever uncertain and fluctuating, if you could pinpoint that precise

moment you could measure the duration of life and the coming of
death, the Dutch steamer *Kafwijk* with a cargo of metal office furni-
ture and Remington typewriters foundered on the Ximiela shoal,
three sailors perished, the police uncover only one murder in every
five, the Asturian collier *Luz de Ribadesella* ran aground on the
Meixido shoal, perhaps her cargo was poorly stowed, she sprang a
leak and sank, another three sailors perished, husbands find out
about only one infidelity in five, the Muros coastal cutter *Sixto de
Abelleira*, sailing close-hauled, was driven to leeward and could not
tack as she should have and was driven on to the Baia shoal, one man
drowned, doctors do not discover any cancer in time and only
attempt to console one patient in five, the Jack of Spades shows an
impudent woman of licentious ways, the sea gives up her dead belly,
some drift ashore of their own accord, it could be the homing
instinct, that way of animals in the throes of death, while others
have to be fished out deftly so they do not disintegrate as they are
hoisted on board, from the paradise of drowned seafarers, from the
drowned rod fishermen's corner, Arthur Hicks would softly sing the
ballad of one thousand surprises: it was when you told me that you
loved me and I started to laugh which only madmen understand gazing into the mirror of their consciousness, the king and the queen of
spades denote a man from the legal profession: a judge, a notary, a
lawyer, the safest anchorage for larger vessels in the Muros estuary is
in the center of the bay, the town nestles on the slopes of Costiña
mountain, at the mouth of the Baldexeira the coastline rises sheer,
San Antón mountain, San Antón point and San Antón island close
the bay to the north, across from the island this rampart of coastline
is indented and continues thus to Treito do Salto point, the seaward
side is known as Pedra Carniceira which covers and shows with the
tides, ballads generally comprise two parts, many years ago I prom-
ised you that everything you loved so tenderly would turn into wolf
howls and now that you are about to die you have hardly the strength
to scare off the specter of oblivion, Nocencio Estévez, galley hand on
board the packet *Saint Malo*, drowned off Cagada Point, not off the
Aforcamento rock, when the vessel was wrecked he could not escape

from the galley, follow suit, the ace affirms whatever, black or white makes no difference, truth and falsehood, fish and flesh, the two and the three sow confusion and, in the words of the old saw, the fish died for its belly yet nobody wound up on the gallows for singing dumb, the four denotes the bed in which you are born and die, the five foretells sickness of the body, the six is the recruiting office for indifference while the seven sings the passion or ills of the soul, a crewman from the fishing vessel *Julita* was dragged overboard by a purse seine and got entangled in the net, the art of reading the cards often fails because it is neither ancient, accurate nor scientific, it insists upon your poetic, barren agonies, you wished to be reflected in your beloved object and turned yourself into a stone on the road, the god of clemency chastises those who wish to transform the world along lines learned by heart, from Treito do Salto and Santa Catalina island Bornalle bay opens five or six cables wide, the father of Antonio Maroñas, owner of the cargo vessel *Vicente Maroñas* wrecked on the Espiritiño rock, died of old age, there was a big turn-out at his funeral and those who did not attend made their proper excuses, the boat was named after the owner's father who could neither read nor write but smoked a clay pipe and listened to the radio, for the television made his eyes smart, the Jack of Diamonds is the woman who reads the cards while the king and queen represent the man seeking for truth or the person about whom you wish to find out something, between Salto and Ostreira points is a small creek where you can land in calm weather, the rumor is rife that Father Xerardiño, the priest in San Xurxo, has been dead for several years now, but this does not bother a soul for Father Xerardiño is still walking around on his own two feet cooking up Galician fish stews, my brother-in-law Estanis is very tall and also claims that Father Xerardiño is not dead but simply smells of death, that has got nothing to do with it, my brother-in-law's stature lends him great prestige but does not diminish his fear of sins of the flesh and its attendant spiritual and bodily perils, Gumersinde the cyclist was killed in the Civil War, the war dead still have a lot of life left in them, the source of their health was not tainted or withered and the soul smiled within them like a heifer in a spring meadow, birds also smile as they flit through the air joyful at death unknown, birds are killed in a volley of shots in peacetime, there is no point in wanting to gird love with the white ribbon of indifference, with a white ribbon you also fish for octopus, nobody would like to be shut in a cellar with one thousand dragonflies flitting about, the water in the tumbler of death tastes of onion and the suicide who is about to plunge from the balcony is comforted and bitterly smiling, Outeiro Gordo is a mound of rock which rises north of Ostreira point, inland fly the crows which scavenge from the trash cans for summer visitors, the bags are never properly sealed, life has neither beginning nor end for when some folks die others are born and life continues always the same, I can hear the seven sirens foretelling the distant passing of the rorqual whales, Noya is not far off but warnings should be heeded, perhaps this is the sign that the brambles are whistling the end of this particular journey of the soul, you could be talking of the sea time and time again, Celso Tembura tells me to hush before we reach Noya, one of the most beautiful towns in the West, I would have liked to take a trip into Padrón at high tide and moor the boat to the Apostle stone, after sailing past Santa Uxía, Santa Euxenia or Santa Oxea, depending on what you call it, now this is all very muddled and capricious, and Palmeira and Puebla del Caramiñal and Rianxo, what I mean to say is the Corunna side of the Arosa estuary, but I must take my orders from Celso Tembura the sacristan, known as Winkle to his friends, while others call him Barnacle and he takes it all in good part, Celso Tembura has always been very generous to me, whenever he sees me he invites me to eat fried songbirds, everyone knows it but I will never tire of repeating it: the underbelly of all these horizons is gold, it does not envelop gold, gold foxes, gold rorquals, gold gulls, but is enveloped by gold leaving no room for the foxes, rorquals or gulls, through Cornwall, Brittany and Galicia there wends a way strewn with crosses and nuggets of gold which leads to the heaven of those seafarers perished at sea.

THE END
Madrid, Feast of St. Epaphroditus MCMXCIX